MW01205433

Diary

Based On A True Story

Shane Layman

authorHOUSE™

1663 LIBERTY DRIVE, SUITE 200
BLOOMINGTON, INDIANA 47403
(800) 839-8640
WWW.AUTHORHOUSE.COM

First published by AuthorHouse 09/26/05

ISBN: 1-4208-5933-1 (sc)

Printed in the United States of America
Bloomington, Indiana

This book is printed on acid-free paper.

For Mom and Dad – Who never gave up on me.

FORWARD

By Dean Starking

Supernatural encounters. The words produce immediate fear and doubt. Doubt, the precursor to fear, is experienced first. The questions that pop up in your imagination are extreme and mind-boggling. Are there such things as ghosts? Aliens? Poltergeists? However, doubt is a fleeting thought; gone as fast as it is forgotten. Doubt breathes life to fear. Doubt stokes the fire and acts as kindling for the conflagration that burns deep in the minds and hearts of us all. Fear *is* the eternal pyre. Fear causes hesitation. During that hesitation, there is a quiet recognition that we all share or experience, an unsettling, disturbing moment when the line between fantasy and reality is not merely erased, but shattered completely.

The moment of interaction is preceded by a dull cone of silence. A knot in the pit of your stomach churns and twirls, making you nauseated. You have no idea that the moment is at hand, you simply know there is something wicked lurching forward at you from the darkness. Your glands secrete sweat and fear trickles down your body in little droplets of pearl-sized water. Your senses are ultra-alert. The little hairs on the back of your neck begin to tingle and goose bumps ripple up and down your spine and appendages.

All the while, you are oblivious to what is in store for you.

Your palms begin to sweat and the oily residue makes your hands feel clammy. The knot in your stomach makes a quick trip to the back of your throat. The lump hardens and you feel the pain surge down the back of your throat as you try hard to swallow. You begin to feel disoriented and dizzy. You stumble forwards, backwards, maybe even sideways as your vestibular senses race around your inner ear playing games with your equilibrium. Your auditory senses dull slightly, momentarily, and a complete lapse of time and rational, cognitive ability is imminent.

You have become exhausted already and you have not yet had a chance to question what is going on. What feels like an eternity has passed, but in unfortunate reality, only mere seconds have passed.

Just a few seconds, ten at best. You lose all motor functioning ability and experience a complete collapse of rational thought. All in the time it takes to snap your fingers.

Finally, the moment is upon you. Like a monster jumping out of the bushes, the attack is quick and painless. The monster is upon you before you even have a chance to react. A cold chill of arctic air blows past you sending goose bumps, once again, up and down your appendages. You try to swallow, but the sudden, paralyzing fear has caused your body's voluntary systems to shut down; you are too terrified to produce saliva. The dry ache in the back of your throat is painful and uncomfortable, but you cannot concern yourself with that. Right now, your undivided attention is focused strictly on the cool air blowing by, or that ice, clammy hand grabbing at your neck from behind, or perhaps, the muffled cry for help from a lonely soul which has been long since dead and buried.

The attack is over as suddenly as it began. You have no idea how or why you know, you simply know. The goose bumps, like a mighty glacier, have retreated. The knot in your throat is slowly dissolving. Your sweat glands have closed. Your hands no longer feel clammy. It's over. You know it's over. Everything has returned to normal.

Until the next time you pass this way again and begin to feel those same familiar, uncomfortable feelings. You have been changed. Your life has been altered. Even if the changes are minute and unrecognizable to passers by: things will never be quite the same, and you know it. You begin to worry that you will feel those familiar feelings elsewhere. You worry it will happen more often. You worry that no one will believe you . . . you worry.

ABOUT THE EDITOR

I had my first supernatural experience when I was young. To this day, I cannot provide an accurate explanation for what happened. Everything happened so quickly and I was so scared that my mind did not have adequate time to rationalize what *was* happening. However, from that day, and for the rest of my life, whether there is a rational answer or not, what happened to me on that day was my first supernatural experience.

I was in my favorite rocking chair in the den of my parent's house. I was eight years old; yet I remember every detail so vividly. I had coerced my parents into allowing me to stay up past my usual bedtime to watch an episode of *Cheers*.

Sitting alone in the den, I saw a shadow pass by the entryway and into the kitchen. Thinking my mother had gone into the kitchen for a late-night snack, I went into the kitchen too, to try to persuade her into allowing me to have a late-night snack as well.

I stepped across the threshold of the kitchen, like I had thousands of times before, and for the first time, felt an air of uncomfortable dread. Not only had my mother *not* gone into the kitchen, but *nobody* had gone into the kitchen. I walked to the living room to see if my mother was still there. And there she sat, cross-legged in her rocking chair with a pillow in her lap, watching television.

"Did you just go in the kitchen?"

"No."

Just my imagination then, right? Walking back to the den, uncomfortable and unnerved, I sat back down with my legs crossed, hunching into the chair thinking perhaps the more of me that was invisible would be less visible to some *other* thing invisible.

A short amount of time passed without incident. Still hunched uncomfortably in the chair, legs crumpled against my chest, a cold sweat forming on my brow, I waited for the Bogeyman to jump, inevitably, out of the closet; his dark fur matted and mangy with sweat and rife with the fear of young children; eyes blazing red lightening bolt dread and razor-sharp teeth calling me home.

But nothing happened.

Turning the television off, I stood up to leave the room when the lights flickered and burned out. Petrified into a state of immobility, my mind could not rationalize an adequate strategy.

So I just stood there. Frozen.

Looking out of the den, I could see that the lights were still on in the kitchen; the lights had not failed through the entire house, just in this particular room; the same room I just happened to be in.

I tried to move my legs but couldn't. They had become dead weight, two giant logs that were not going to budge even the slightest bit. I yelled for help but nothing came out of my mouth.

From behind me, a cold chill brushed by, sending goose bumps up and down my spine. I began to shiver from the cold and felt an icy, clammy hand grab the back of my neck.

At that point, the lights flickered back to existence and I collapsed to the floor and passed out; unable to speak or even move. I had just been engaged by an ethereal spirit and all I wanted to do was cry out in terror.

But I couldn't. I was too exhausted. It hurt to just lie there, but there I stayed.

When I regained complete motor functioning and the ability to speak, I looked at the clock; only fifteen minutes had elapsed since my encounter with the paranormal and when I regained consciousness. Nobody had come to check on me thinking I was still watching television. Nobody had witnessed what I had witnessed. That moment was one set aside just for me. I've never spoken of it. Until now, that is. I feel it is necessary to share this moment, as well as the few others I will share, to prepare you for the contents held within this book. While my encounters are nowhere near as exciting as those detailed in the following pages, they are still encounters, they are paranormal, and they are mine to do with as I see fit. You could probably rationalize the light bulb surged and blew momentarily, that the cold air was a draft and the clammy hand was the over-exaggerated imagination of impressionable and over-zealous youth, but they weren't. Not to me.

During my seventh-grade year, I had another encounter with the paranormal. I was house sitting for my neighbors while they were away on vacation. This particular house had been the topic of many tall tales and late night stories outside in the dark. The rumor was that the lady who originally live in the house had committed suicide by drowning herself in the river down behind our houses. Allegedly, her spirit made the journey back to the house but, tortured, tormented and lamented, must walk the halls of the house for eternity suffering the consequences of her actions.

Horseshit, you say? I know; I felt the same way. However, I witnessed some eerie undertakings during my adventures in house sitting that made me change my mind. The family had been gone for a few days already and nothing had happened that would lead me to believe the house was haunted. The owners of the home had told me that if I wanted to use the house to get away for a while that I should feel free to do so. I was a little uncomfortable making their house my house so I never stayed there long. However, one day as I was getting ready to leave, I was struck with an insatiable urge to defecate. Stupid, I know, but humorous at the same time. Hey, shit happens, right?

I figured, what could it hurt to use their bathroom. So I ascended the staircase to the second floor. Immediately, as I stepped into the hallway, a blast of arctic air swept passed me chilling me to the bone and I heard a voice ask, "Are you all right, Shane?" I'm surprised I didn't defecate in my pants right there. I don't even remember descending the staircase or running through the kitchen. What I do remember is hunching on the ground, beneath the window encased in the door, trying to lock the door and thinking, "if I have the only key to this house, then who is in there asking me if I'm all right?"

I ran home to tell my parents what had happened and they were just as spooked as I was. I kept telling them that I distinctly heard a woman's voice asking me if I felt all right and that the clarity of the sound was as pure as water. At first, they too tried to rationalize but came up empty-handed.

What was I going to do? I was in quite a pickle because I was to feed the cat for another four days before the family returned from their vacation. Returning hesitantly the next day, I crept up to the house, eased the key into the lock and quietly opened the door. I stood on the threshold for a long time before I actually braved stepping into the house. Countless seconds passed by like hours.

An eternity passed before I mustered the courage to step in and cross the kitchen.

So far, so good. No bumps. No ooooohs. No ahhhhhhs. No chains. No sheets. No voices. Maybe it was all in my imagination. I darted down the stairs to the cellar to feed the cat.

I had gained a new sense of confidence by this point. I walked back up the stairs not nearly as scared as I had been, a new found sense of courage billowed out of me, radiating like heat. I left the cellar door open a crack so the cat could get in and out to eat. As I turned to leave, the faucet in the upstairs bathroom turned on.

I froze. *What was going on?* Did someone else have a key?

I walked through the kitchen, down the hall to the foot of the stairs and hollered up, "Who's there?"

I received no reply.

Again, I yelled, "Who's there?"

With the water still running, I heard footsteps walk from the bathroom to the top of the stairs. "Who's there?" I asked one more time. The footsteps stopped before they reached the top of the stairs, before I could see who or what was up there, walked back into the bathroom and turned the water off.

"Who the hell's there?" I was more frightened than assertive. My voice was cracking and my knees were shaking, barely able to support the weight of my own body. The click of footsteps cascaded in echoes down the staircase as whatever was up there was about to breach my line of sight. At this point in time, my rational mind kicked into high gear and I thought if the person who is up there was supposed to be up there, they would have answered me by now. This left me with two options: 1.) a really clean robber was robbing the place, got sweaty in the process and decided to clean up, or 2.) I was about to encounter the supernatural for the second time in as many days. Either way, I didn't appreciate my options. So, I did the same damned thing every logical, fully reasonable young man would have done had he found himself in the same eerie predicament I find myself in; I turned tail and ran like a crying pansy.

For the next three days, I made my mother come with me every time I had to feed the cat.

What the hell does any of this have to do with *anything*? That's the question you are asking yourself right now, I bet. Well, I'll tell you: I graduated from the University of Maine in Orono with a bachelor's degree in English with a concentration in creative writing so I could write books. Now, as you may or may not know, writing a book is no easy chore. It takes hard work and dedication. I'm up for the task but I was having a little trouble coming up with something to write about to make my first million, so to speak.

In November 1996, my friend, John Savage, approached me with a diary he had found in his attic. It wasn't your typical Hello Kitty diary with the plastic cover and the rubber, spiral binding. It was leather with leather binding. I opened the cover and read the name on the inside leaf: Hayden Walker.

"So?" I asked.

"Read this," John said to me. "I think you'll like it."

I took it home and read it that night. The diary consisted of handwritten accounts of Hayden Walker's encounters with the supernatural. I was enthralled. I had found what I wanted to write about. At first, I had entertained the idea of writing a novel about a fictitious paranormal investigator but when I researched further, I found so much more than I bargained for. Hayden Walker *was* a paranormal investigator. He traveled all over the world investigating paranormal activity and doing what he could to help. His story was so intriguing that I started a web page dedicated to Walker and his achievements, I wanted to find out everything I could about Walker. I encouraged anyone who knew or know of Walker to e-mail me with any information they had. I got much more than I ever could have imagined. We found four more diaries and a whole slew of people who knew Walker personally.

So, instead of making something up off the top of my head, I am able to deliver to you the actual first-hand accounts of a paranormal investigator. Whether or not you believe what is written in the following pages, I leave to you. What I hope to do, in putting together this book, is to help answer questions we have been pondering for countless decades.

I thought it would be terribly difficult to write my first book. Now I find my first book will actually be written by Walker. The blueprints have already been drawn out in his diaries. All I have to do is cut, paste and edit what I think is relative and pertinent. I hope you find the details in this book as fascinating and important as I do. I hope questions will be answered, doubts extinguished and folklore explored and ultimately reinvented.

Most Sincerely Yours,

Shane Layman

ABOUT THE AUTHOR

In May of 1958, Carl and Norma Walker gave birth to the third of their eight children; a boy named Hayden Walker. The family lived on a small piece of land in Newport, Maine, thirty miles south of Bangor. Hayden's father, Carl Walker, worked as a security guard for a pulp and paper company in Brewer while his mother taught eighth grade English at the local junior high school.

Hayden's father, a strict disciplinarian, taught Hayden early the rewards and benefits for being a responsible child and the punishments and disciplines for those without responsibility. Hayden's mother, who retired from teaching before Hayden reached the eighth grade, instilled in Hayden the importance of education and the influence of power held by those people who were willing to excel at academics and take responsibility for their lives.

Being the third of eight children, Hayden quickly learned the meaning of sharing and caring for others. For many years, Hayden helped raise the family. While Carl worked evenings and into the early morning hours, and Norma worked into the evening, Hayden stayed home and watched over his sister, Marcy. James and Steven, Hayden's older brothers, worked during the day to raise money to help support the family. While most boys his age were engaging in deviant behavior after school, Hayden stayed at home to watch over Marcy and made sure the house was clean and in order for his mother and older brothers when they returned home.

When Norma retired from teaching, Hayden was just starting the eighth grade. "He always said he didn't want me teaching him, anyway. He said he'd feel weird calling me Mrs. Walker instead of 'Mom'."[1]

---

[1] Extracted from an interview in *The Undead*, 1988. The title story was *What's Super About the Supernatural?* The article interviewed Norma Walker and detailed the chronicles of Hayden Walker's experiences. For further reference, see the article in its entirety.

When Hayden started High School, he chose to go to Bangor High School. He made many friends and started concerning himself less with his family and more with his friends. Now thirteen years old, the emotional and hormonal changes that afflict every teenager had not missed Walker. Many nights he would come in late and tell his mother he was out with friends. "I've got to give him credit, though," his mother quoted in another interview, "he stuck with schooling. He never gave up on his education. Education came before even his best friends and I was always proud of him for that."[2] Pulling mostly A's in school, Walker never lost focus of his academics and he never forgot the lessons ingrained in him from his mother and father.

In his senior year, Walker would take a class that would change his life forever. He signed up for Introduction to Psychology with Mr. Eugene Carter. Mr. Carter would have a huge impact on Walker's life. "I remember Hayden Walker being an exceptional student. He received the only 100% grade I ever gave out in that class. And he earned it."[3]

Walker found an increased interest in psychology and his grades reflected this. Although Walker was receiving low A's in almost every class, he excelled in psychology. He received no grade lower than a 99% for the entire year and actually started tutoring other students at the high school.

Walker graduated second in his class for grades and missed being the school valedictorian by two-tenths of a point. However, Walker never concerned himself with trivial matters like school valedictorian and graduating second in his class. What *was* important to him was the fact that he was enjoying the fruits of his labor and applying them to his goals and achievements.

Walker's choice to attend the University of Maine in Orono was a simple one, joining the Psychology program in the fall of 1976. Determined to help those with special needs, Walker emphasized abnormal psychology in his degree program. Walker's transcripts show that he attended PSY 138 Understanding the Human Brain, PSY 232 Abnormal Psychology and PSY 242 Social Deviance

---

2   For further reference, see the complete interview with Norma Walker.
3   Sampled from an interview conducted with Carter in 1998. For more details, see the full interview in the back of this book.

during his second semester. He received a 3.9 GPA in his first year of college. During his sophomore year, he attended several more psychology classes and did as well in those classes as he had in his previous classes.

During his senior year, Walker wrote his thesis on a young man with Multiple Personality Disorder, a very rare and dangerous disorder. The young man had been in and out of prisons and mental institutes since he was young, but had never been properly diagnosed. Walker spent two weeks with the man and diagnosed him as having MPD, or Dissociative Identity Disorder, in which two or more personalities are present inside one individual. The young man had been misdiagnosed by thirteen doctors before Walker, still an undergraduate, determined the cause of the young man's problems. After several years of counseling and the right medication, the man was deinstitutionalized and sent back into the world to live a normal life. He never saw the inside of a prison or mental institute again.

Walker's teachers and supervisors, obviously impressed by the young man's ability to diagnose and determine proper ailments offered him a job with the department at the University diagnosing patients with psychological problems. Walker had other plans. In 1980, Walker graduated Magna Cum Laude from the University of Maine and decided to get his Masters in Abnormal Psychology. He was accepted, without difficulty, to Stanford where he would meet another incredibly influential man. Dean Starking, was the head of a cutting edge field of psychology at Stanford: paranormal psychology. This program was revolutionized two years earlier by Starking himself; funding most of the department out of his own wallet; he also received funding from agencies and businesses in the area which were interested in this dynamic field of psychology. In 1980, Starking approached Walker with the idea of joining his staff of undergraduates for one class, just to see if he would like it. "That boy's eyes lit up like a cat on fire. He was so intrigued by the idea of another level of existence . . . he came up to me after the class and said, 'Mr. Starking, I believe I just might be interested in your class. Do you have room for one more?'"[4] Walker was hooked. Paranormal psychology became his life's work.

---

[4]   Sampled from an interview with Dean Starking in 1998.

In 1982, on one of his routine investigations, Walker met a girl named Jennifer McPherson. She had called the Department of Paranormal Psychology using the number on the leaflets the department handed out weekly and tacked to cork boards and telephone poles wherever they could. She called to see if they could help her with a recurring "ghost." Of course, eager to face the possibilities of contacting the other side, Walker and his crew hurried over to her apartment. The crew found no consistent evidence to suggest that there was telekinetic or paranormal activity occurring anywhere in the apartment and dismissed the claim as a hoax. However, there was something about the girl Walker could not resist. He called her back that night, under the guise that he was just doing some follow-up questions, routine of course. They hit it off. Walker asked her to dinner that Friday and just over a year later, in July of 1983, Mr. and Mrs. Hayden Walker walked down the aisle for the first time as husband and wife.

The year prior, the business of paranormal investigation increased by tenfold. Walker found himself working around the clock. He was spending less and less time with his girlfriend who tried her best to be sympathetic to his dilemma. Walker would go weeks without returning home. Spending five minutes a night with Jen on a pay phone in some cheesy, run-down motel was all the time Walker could afford her on some nights.

He hated it. He wanted to spend more time with Jen. The year of their marriage, Walker took a year sabbatical from the business to re-root his relationship. Their first and only son, Steven, was born eleven months later in 1984. During this period of time, strange turns of events were happening in Walker's life. Nobody really knew what was happening. Things seemed to be going well for Walker: a wife and a new son on the way, a family to call his own and one day he just vanished. "He got a call from Dean saying he needed him for one job. 'One job is all I need you for, buddy. You'll be back home in four days.' He disappeared for four weeks. Things were never the

---

5   Sampled from an interview conducted with Jenny Wilkens, Hayden's estranged wife. For further detail, see the entire interview in the back of this book.

same after he returned. He was distant. He wasn't the Hay I knew and he definitely wasn't the Hay I fell in love with."[5]

Nobody could quite figure out what was going on. Family and friends tried to rationalize why the man they knew and loved would turn his back to them and ultimately cut them off. In the fall of 1987, two and a half years after Walker disappeared, Jen filed for divorce. Everything had fallen to pieces and nobody knew quite why. There were those who speculated and those who started rumors of torrid love scandals and a beaten wife. None of them were true, of course. The truth was, nobody knew the truth.

Until now.

In finding these diaries, we have uncovered the truth about a man who sacrificed everything by devoting himself to the one thing he could not control: his life. The diaries you are about to read have never been seen by the public. There are many who would probably prefer that you not see them, and in seeing them discover the truth. The truth can exist only after the lies have been exhausted and expunged. The truth can exist only after we accept it as fact.

So, dear reader, I urge you to read and discover the truth, to exhaust the lies, expunge the deceit and find out for yourselves what happened to Hayden Walker, an educated man from Newport, Maine, who clawed his way up the academic ladder and found the truth high above everything else.

ABOUT THE BOOK

This book would not be possible without the combined efforts of several very interesting, and very intelligent people. First, and foremost, without John Savage, perhaps the world would have never known about Hayden Walker. It was John who approached me with the first diary back in 1996. Without having read that diary, I would never have had the idea of chronicling the life and times of Hayden Walker.

I would also like to thank Professors Jonathon Ashton and Professor Keith Trembly for helping me better understand the details involved with paranormal psychology. Without their expert knowledge in the field of paranormal anomalies, this book would never have been written. I wish to thank Jason Craft, a long-time friend and one hell of a private investigator. Jason helped me excavate one massive bag of bones. Without his assistance and dedication, the facts about Walker's life would still be myths. I am indebted to all of these men for their fine work and dedication to this project.

This book consists of two parts: 1.) Walker's diaries. For the first time ever, you will be able to read about Walker's paranormal encounters, and 2.) interviews with Walker's friends and family members.

Back in 1996, when I first created the web page dedicated to Walker, I was amazed by the onslaught of information that was sent to me. I was actually overwhelmed by it. The very first e-mail I received was from a man named Carl Stevens. He claimed to be a longtime friend of Walker and insisted that he had details about Walker that would be imperative to this project. At first, I dismissed his claim as a hoax, much like most sceptics will dismiss this book; however, two weeks later, I received a large box in the mail. It was postmarked in Cleveland, Ohio and the return address was labeled to Carl Stevens. The box contained a manila envelope and a letter. The letter was very brief and to the point:

Dear Shane,

I feel I made no impression on you with my e-mail. I really hope the contents of this box will convince you otherwise. I implore you to believe me. I knew Hayden Walker when he worked for the Agency. The contents within are very confidential but they are very real. Please, handle it with care and do not lose it. I am quite certain these documents are very few and far between, indeed.

Most Sincerely Yours

Carl J. Stevens

The content of the envelope was a small, leather-bound book. The design of the book was one I was very familiar with; the cover of the book was hard, brown leather. The front was blank, very plain. A flap folded halfway down the front cover. Attached to the flap was a long, thin strip of leather which was wound around the diary several times and tied in a knot halfway down the front of the journal. I could smell the glue from the binding as I opened the front cover and read the name stenciled on the inside leaf. The penmanship was very familiar to me. I had seen the signature many times before: Hayden Walker. My knees went weak. I could barely stand up as I stumbled over to a chair to collect my bearings.

Was it possible? A second diary?

I quickly flipped through the pages. The dates began in 1983 and ended in 1984. The first diary I received from John Savage back in 1996 was dated from 1981-1982 and documented the beginning of Walker's career as a paranormal investigator at Stanford University and his growing frustration with the lack of convincing evidence to support the paranormal psychology department. The diary I received from Carl Stevens documented a very controversial and critical period of Walker's life, a period of turmoil and a point of confusion for many of Walker's friends and family members. This diary dealt with the period in which Walker disappeared for the first time. Many questions were answered and many truths found, many lies discredited and many myths resolved.

A few months later, I received another manila envelope in the mail. This envelope was postmarked Sacramento, California, but there was no return address. Inside, another simple letter:

Dear Shane

For personal and professional reasons, I cannot disclose my name to you. I can say that I knew Hayden Walker when he worked for the Agency. Walker and I were very close and during a point in his life, when things were looking quite bleak, he gave me this book and told me to hold on to it. It appears to be a diary. I have not read it nor do I have any inclination to do so. Perhaps you will find more use for it than I will. Perhaps this will help you to discover the truth you so desperately seek.

Most Sincerely Yours

J.

No name was signed; just the J. To this day, I have no idea who sent the diary to me but it was most helpful and if you, unnamed hero, read this book, I am forever indebted to you for your courage in delivering this important parcel to me. Thank you.

The diary inside the envelope documented many of Walker's encounters during his tenure in the Agency. The pages documented from 1984 to 1985. Many fascinating stories were found in those pages. I enjoyed countless hours of intriguing reading.

All told, I received five diaries from all over the United States. I am most appreciative to those people who were willing to give up their own possessions to help the world better understand the legend behind Hayden Walker. I am also very thankful to those individuals who helped me put this book together.

It is important to mention that some of the diary entries are incomplete. For whatever reason, many of the entries have pages missing. What I have done, with the help of Jonathon Ashton, Keith Trembley and Jason Craft, is tried to recreate the events that went on during those periods that are missing. I believe we have accurately depicted, through years of research and countless hours in small quarters hypothesizing what could have happened, what actually did happen during those time frames. However, we realize our efforts are not perfect by any stretch of the imagination. I am not convinced that everything we hypothesized is accurate. I am convinced, however that what we hypothesized is, to the best of our knowledge and expertise, what *most likely* happened.

Do not let this fact discourage you. What lies in the following pages are the actual accounts of Hayden Walker, a paranormal investigator who became a federal agent and what daunting effects his career had on his life. What lies beyond is a heart-wrenching story of failing love intertwined with an intriguing story of the paranormal and the supernatural. Combined, the two offer you, kind reader, a compelling true story about the life and times of a man whose life was shrouded in mystery and confusion.

Diary 1

September 18, 3:00 am[6]

Another restless night without sleep. The uniform construction of this tiny motel room irritates me to the point of insanity. Outside, the glaring neon sign of the Mobile gas station across the street penetrates through the Venetian blinds turning the darkness of night into day. If I have to spend even one more night in this worthless, drab piece of hell, I believe I will have to consider suicide to be a healthy alternative.

September 18, 10:30 am

I was jerked from sleep this morning by the incessant ringing of the telephone. I slowly came to consciousness, not realizing the noise I was hearing was the phone. How many times had it rang before I realized. Half a dozen? Who's counting?

I picked up the receiver and tried hard to talk. "Hello?" It was barely a whisper and my throat ached due to the lack of saliva.

"Hello?" A voice asked.

I cleared my throat and again swallowed hard. "Hello?"

"Hayden?"

"Yeah."

"How are you holding out in that pit?"

"Plans are currently in effect to purge this run-down, ramshackled shack you call a motel from my existence. I hate this place. Please tell me you have something for me. Tell me there's a reason you're calling me at . . . what the hell time is it, anyway?"

"7:00."

---

[6] This diary, the first of five received, was given to me by John Savage. We are very fortunate that Hayden Walker kept very extensively detailed diaries of the events that took place in his life. We have no idea how many diaries Walker completed in his life. We are also uncertain of how many diaries came prior to this one. We do not believe that this is the first diary in the series due to the fact that the entries start up on a random day with no explanation as to why the diary is even being written. Of course, this is all speculation, we may never know if this is the first diary or if there are more diaries preceding this one. This may not be the first diary in the series but it is the first diary in our series.

"Liar." The alarm clock screwed into the night stand indicated that it was only 6:45. "Tell me you have a damn good reason for calling me at this God-awful hour. Tell me you have a reason for waking me up not four hours after I finally fell asleep."

"I just might."

"Really?"

September 18, 1:30 pm

Lunch with Dean.[7] As usual, he was sitting at the back table of the Broche Café.[8] He had already ordered his coffee and was sipping gently, steam puffing up into his face.

"Dean."

"How are you doing?" He stood up and shook my hand.

"I'll be better when you get me out of that hole I've been calling home for the past week and a half. What have you got?"

"This could be what we've been looking for, Hay. A full-torso apparition was spotted on the third floor of an apartment building on Maple St. The old lady, Ms ... uh ... Ms. Himmelstein was just waking up this morning when she saw the apparition floating above her bed. She called the police first. Of course, they couldn't do anything. What are they going to do, shoot it? So, she remembered reading our brochure we sent out in the mail last month and gave us a call. This could be it, Hay. This could be our first legitimate encounter. I sent Jay[9] and the crew down with cameras and all the equipment. Get your ass down there and prove to the department we are well worth the funding involved. Proving they're wrong is proving we're right."

---

7   Dean Starking, head of the paranormal psychology department at Stanford from 1978-1991. Walker worked with Starking at the University heading up many of the investigations conducted by the team of undergraduates and graduates from 1981-1983.

8   The Broche Café was a little coffee shop just around the corner from the university. It was closed due to competition in 1988. The owner, Lewis Harris, said that Hayden and his friend frequented the cafe many times between 1981 and 1983.

9   Jay Munson, third year undergrad at Stanford in 1981. Worked with Hayden from 1981 until his untimely demise in 1982.

September 18, 5:30 pm

I arrived at the apartment of Ms. Himmelstein. As Dean had assured, Jay and the crew were all ready to conduct the investigation. Jay and Carla[10] had the cameras set up in the apartment and the tape recorders ready to record. The two of them were sitting in tattered chairs and an old, decrepit lady sat on a couch covered with plastic. She looked so tiny sitting there, engulfed by the couch.

"Ms. Himmelstein, I presume." I walked over to the couch and shook her hand. "I'm Hayden Walker. I'm with the research team for the Paranormal Psychology division at the University. I understand you may have something of interest to share with us."

"I do." Her voice was weak but shrill; it cracked and croaked. "I was so scared. I saw a lady standing over my bed."

"Did she have arms or legs?"

"She had arms but no legs. She was just hovering over my bed."

"Uh huh, and did she try to touch you or speak to you?"

"No. I screamed loudly and she disappeared."

"Have you ever seen this apparition before?"

"No. Never."

"Have you ever heard any of the other tenants complain about ghosts?"

"No."

"These next few questions are a bit personal and you don't have to answer them if you don't feel comfortable, okay?"

She nodded.

"Ms. Himmelstein . . .?"

"Call me Alice." She smiled.

"Okay, Alice, do you have a history of mental illness?"

"No."

"Has anyone in your immediate family ever been diagnosed with schizophrenia, multiple personality disorder or mental retardation?"

---

[10] Carla LaVeque, second year undergrad, worked the stop-flash cameras and in the blackroom developing photographs taken by the crew during investigations.

"Not that I'm aware of. Good Heavens, no."

"Alice, are you currently taking any prescription drugs?"

"I take aspirin for my back pain and Insulin for my diabetes."

"Nothing else?"

"No."

"Alice, we're going to conduct a little investigation to see if we can find anything, okay?"

We left the living room and went into the bedroom where Alice said she had seen the apparition.

"Jay, are we ready now?"

"Yes sir, Mr. Walker. The cameras are ready and the recorders are set to go."

"What about the PDC and the TIS? Are they ready?"

"Yes, sir."

"All right, Carla, you may begin taking pictures anytime."

Carla began filming. I covered every square inch of the room with the PDC100X and the TIS50C. Jay put the headset on and began recording audio.

Ten minutes later, we were on our way back to the University.

In the van, doubts were high and hopes were low.

"Jay, did you get anything on the sound recorder?" Jay shook his head.

"What about you, Carla?"

"I won't know until the pictures develop."

"What did you get?" Jay asked.

"I didn't find a thing. The PDC didn't pick up any density change and the TIS determined the same results." I sighed. "I just hope those pictures come back affirmative."

September 18, 8:45 pm

I am anxiously awaiting the results of the investigation we conducted at the apartment of Alice Himmelstein, an 81-year-old widow and mother of two. I have serious doubts to whether or not what she saw was indeed a ghost, or a subconscious joyride of the waking mind. So many clues and leads only lead to other clues or dead ends. This waiting is so damned frustrating.

September 19, 9:10 am

On the phone again.

"Mr. Walker?"

"Yeah."

"It's Carla."

"Carla, tell me you have something for me."

"I wish I could."

"Nothing?"

"Not one thing."

"Dammit! I was really hoping this time, you know? I was counting on this one."

"Well, look at the bright side," she said.

"There's a bright side?"

"We developed some really nice shots of the interior workings of a building that should have been condemned decades ago." She laughed trying to ease my mind. "She was so certain, though, you know?"

"I know."

"How can you be so certain about nothing?"

"Have you ever had a dream that was so real you could actually smell the air around you or feel the hairs on the back of your neck stand out? Have you ever been so certain that what happened in a dream was so real that you wake up believing it?"

"Yeah, I guess."

"When I was a child, I had to help raise my younger siblings. There would be nights I would fall asleep and dream that I had fed them and that chore would be behind me. I would wake up and my mother would tell me to feed them and I would tell her that I had already done that. She would just give me the strangest looks. I hadn't actually fed them. I had fed them in my dreams but it seemed so real. I could feel the tension of trying to pull the spoon away from their mouths after they took a bite. I could smell the funky vitamin-enhanced smell of 'all natural' baby food. I could smell the pungent odor of regurgitated bananas as I wiped it off their faces with their bibs . . .and none of it happened. The unconscious mind and the sleeping mind have it out for us. Things just work out that way."

"I just get so damned frustrated with all these false leads."

"I know. Me too."

September 19, 10:30 pm   ·

Why can't we get the one break we need? These false leads are becoming increasingly frustrating for the crew. Tensions are brewing and emotions are high. For too long we have come up empty handed. I wish I had someone I could share this frustration with. I'm a victim of terminal loneliness; it's my lot in life, I guess. Everything I do revolves around the struggle to maintain a certain validity to the department heads that we are not frauds and charlatans. We have a solid argument with absolutely no evidence to support it. The department is getting short on patience and so am I. We need something. Anything. Why can't we find it?

September 29, 8:45 am[11]

Breakfast with Dean.
"The department wants to revoke our grant."
"What? Dean, they can't do that."
"Unless . . ."
"Unless what?"
"Unless we can provide adequate and irrefutable evidence that there is paranormal activity on at least one of our investigations."
"We can't catch a break."
"Listen, Hay, we can do this. It's just going to take more patience and more man-hours. We set up in shifts and work 24 hours a day. I know how much you'd like to be at every investigation, but we need to come up with a new approach. We have to prove we're right."
"How do we do that?"
"We increase the number of leads we decide to investigate. We take every call from the little old ladies who are blind but swear

---

[11] It is important to note that any noticeably extended period of time between entries is, in most cases, my editing choice. Walker wrote in his diaries everyday but what I have tried to do is cut and paste the most important pieces for you. I will not withhold any worthwhile information unless it is information Walker's family has specifically asked me to leave out. Any gap between entries, unless otherwise specified, is intentional to keep the rhythm and pace of the story.

they saw a ghost to every always-stoned, stupid teenager who's experienced deja vu. I mean we take them all. No exceptions."

"That's a heavy load, Dean. Last week alone we took more than seventy calls. We turned down forty of them and we were still exhausted. There's no way we can pull those kind of man-hours. What you're talking about is work-assisted suicide. We can't possibly take every call."

"We can and we must. We're out of options, here. If we do not accumulate significant data to prove that what we are doing, these experiments we're conducting, carry even the slightest inkling of merit, they will revoke our grants and the idea of obtaining any other grants in the immediate future will be futile. We don't have a choice here, Hay."

"So who's going to head up the investigations?"

"We're splitting you, Jay and Carla for now."

"Whoa. Wait a minute. We're the best three investigators you've got."

"I know and that is why I am making this decision. I have a lot of my own money riding on this little project. You are the best we have and what we must do insists that we do nothing less than the best to assume responsibilities not otherwise employed by us. We have to do it this way. No exceptions."

October 30, 8:45 am

I haven't slept in three days. I'm exhausted. We still have no hardcore evidence to prove that paranormal activity is evident. I'm beginning to wonder what the hell we're fighting for. I know, in my heart, that the realm of the paranormal exists. I know that spirits walk the earth: there are no plausible explanations at this point as to why they walk the earth but I know they do. I can feel that what we are doing is important. I feel a sense of fulfillment. I feel that what we are doing is going to help so many people. But I also feel an extreme sense of urgency. I know that what we are doing cannot be rushed but if we do not succeed in providing the needed data in the next two months all of these inner-struggles and endless days without sleep will be for nothing. I wish I didn't feel so depressed about my job but I do and the self-loathing, bitter, angry attitude I have developed over the last few months is killing me. Why does it have to be this way? Why does humility have so many faces? Why does struggle carry with it such a heavy burden? Why can't success ever come as easily as failure?

November 2, 11:15 pm

We conducted an investigation at the house of Mr. and Mrs. Peter Starling.[12] We arrived just after noon. I headed up the investigation while Mike[13] ran the camera equipment. I had Jennifer[14] taking pictures.

Peter and Sherry seemed very excited to see us. They expressed their emotions about the "entity" that was residing in an unwelcome manner in their home and told us they hoped we could help.

I began making a sweep of the first floor while Mike and Jennifer worked the next two floors. I went to the truck to grab the PDC100x and the TIS50c. Sherry met me at the door.

"Would you like something to drink?"

"No thank you, ma'am."

"What's all this equipment?"

"These are instruments we use to measure different levels of air density and temperature. When spirits are present, the density and temperature in the immediate area change."

"What's that one?"

"That's what we call a PDC100x."

"Sounds expensive." She laughed.

"It is but it's very reliable."

---

[12] Peter Starling and his wife, Sherry, had, for years, insisted that their house was haunted. Their story was smeared all over the local headlines and even graced the covers of many prestigious newspapers including *The Globe, The National Examiner, The Sun,* and *The Weekly World News.*

[13] Mike Jensen, first-year undergraduate, ran the recording equipment for Walker when Jay was unable to do so or when Jay was heading up his own investigations.

[14] Jennifer Beales, third-year undergrad; in charge of photography when Carla was not present or when she was heading up her own investigations.

"What exactly does it do?"

"This device is used to detect any significant change in air density. You see the numbers go from 0 to 1.0?"

She nodded.

"Zero means absolutely no paranormal activity. If the needle spikes, we have extreme paranormal activity. Anytime the needle rises up past 0.5, we can almost always assume there is paranormal activity. There are always slight variations in air density, and so many factors contribute to that change." She still looked confused so I tried another approach. "Any factor that raises the needle to 0.5 or below, we do not concern ourselves with because they are not factors that suggest paranormal activity. However, if the needle goes up above 0.5, we may take some consideration to the fact that the density has changed considerably in a short period of time and in one specific area. If I turn away after the needle spikes and it drops back down to 0, we know we have a ghost."

"Oh. And what does that one do?"

"This is the TIS50c. This indicates any change in thermal activity. Let me turn it on and demonstrate. Do you see how anything that emits any level of heat comes up on our screen as some form of bright orange? The more heat an object emits, the brighter the orange. Do you see how anything that does not emit heat is a dark blue?"

She nodded again.

"These are the areas we pay particular attention to. If there is paranormal activity in the room, we will see it on the screen as a very deep, dark purple. It's very hard to detect to the untrained eye, but it's fairly routine for us now."

"Oh. That's all pretty high-tech."

"Yes, it is. It isn't cheap, either. I'm really hoping we find your ghost so we can prove to the department at the University all this money is worth the investment."

"I hope you just find the damned thing and get rid of it."

"Well, that isn't really what we do. Our job is to determine whether or not paranormal activity is occurring on the premises. If so, we can connect you with people who can help exterminate the ghost from your house. Right now, what we are doing is going over every square inch of your house to determine whether or not paranormal activity is ongoing."

It wasn't. We didn't find a thing at the house. Thermal imaging didn't pick up anything unusual and the PDC didn't show any significant change in air density.

Another dead end. We're running out of time.

November 15, 11:30 pm

We didn't receive a single call today.   We don't have time for this. The clock is always against us and we're always racing to keep up. If we don't come up with something quick, our hopes and dreams will be shattered. What to do?

November 16, 10:00 pm

Another day without a call. Time is definitely not on our side. Efforts to obtain specific data are being tremendously hindered by the lack of available data to collect. This is hopeless.

November 17, 10:45 pm

Three days without a call. Not only are we growing more and more helpless but we are growing restless. This total lack of available data to be investigated is taking its toll on the entire crew. Dean is getting ready to pull the plug and I have all but given up. It pains me to think that the realm of the paranormal exists but the lack of evidence is making me wonder if we've been wrong all along. It's as if all the ghosts have taken a vacation or all the insane people calling in the false leads ran out of ideas to deceive us. I'm beginning to wonder if switching from abnormal psychology to paranormal psychology was a wise career choice.

November 18, 8:45 am

Finally, a call. Something, at least. Dean called me at eight this morning and told me to get down to the Brown and Stone Insurance Agency.[15] Preliminary results were negative but I'm not so certain we didn't stumble across something.

November 23, 1:15 pm

Met with Dean to discuss the results collected during the investigation at the Brown & Stone Insurance Agency.
"You say you got nothing but you seem excited. Why?"
"Dean, I think we're on to something."
"Like what?"
"Preliminary results were negative. We didn't pick up anything on the thermal scanner but we did get some really strange readings on the PDC and the EMIC. The density level changed dramatically in one certain area, the area where the witnesses said they felt or saw something bizarre. The needle didn't spike but it was just above 0.7. You know and I know that suggests a significant possibility for paranormal activity."
"What about the EMIC?"
"EMIC went right off the scale. Over 1,000."
"1,000?"
"Yeah."
"But you didn't get anything on thermal?"
"No."
"What about video or audio?"
"That's what bothers me most."

---

15 The Brown and Stone Insurance Agency was built in the 1870s. It was originally an old fire station until, in the 1920s, the town demanded a larger fire fighting force. The unit moved to a larger facility three blocks away leaving the large, stone shell of a building behind to be renovated in the 1930s by the Cartwright Construction Company and turned into an office building which was bought by McAllister, McKlusy and Ayer Insurance in the late 40s. In the early 50s, McAllister, McKlusy and Ayer went bankrupt. The building remained empty for thirty years until, in the 1980s, Brown and Stone Inc. bought the building as a new headquarters for their rising enterprise.

"Why?"

"There's too much margin for error. Anything could have caused the equipment to read inaccurately: a microwave running in the break room or a sudden change in temperature outside; a sudden build up of electrical charge caused by increased heat in the room. But we should have picked something up on audio or video, right? I mean, not necessarily but it would certainly make me feel better. We won't have anything concrete until we go back for the follow-up. It's better than what we've been getting."

Dean smiled. "I'll be excited when the follow-up data is consistent with the preliminary results. Until then, we still have nothing, Hay. Don't get excited yet; it'll only hurt that much more if things don't work out."

He always finds a way to keep me humble.

November 24, 10:15 pm

Follow-up results were negative. My worst fears were confirmed and Dean's suspicions were correct. I should call and tell him but I just want to hold on to that moment yesterday when I told him about the results. It felt so good to have something. Anything. I haven't felt that joy in a long time. I want to keep that moment for just a little while longer. I hate this. Even when things seem to be going our way, they aren't. I should call.

November 24, 11:00 pm

I just got off the phone with Dean. We had a good conversation. He told me not to get too disappointed. He said we should be comfortable with defeat by now. I don't like being comfortable with defeat; it makes me feel worthless. We've decided to take the next four days off for Thanksgiving. We're all going home to our families to unwind and maybe redefine our goals and objectives. We have all sworn an oath that when we return from vacation, we will be rejuvenated and ready to tackle the entire realm of the paranormal if need be but we will not roll over and accept defeat.

Are we fooling ourselves?

November 25, 2:30 am

I can't sleep. There are nights I lie awake and instead of praying for forgiveness or a Porsche or a nice, tall blonde with big green eyes and the body of a model, I pray for hours that sleep will finally come to me and I might get just one night of undisturbed, much-desired slumber. Too much on my mind, I guess. Why should tonight be any different? Except tonight, I find that instead of school and the failing investigations, I am splitting my brain with what to say to my family today when I arrive home. I haven't been home in almost three months. That, I'm sure they could forgive, but I haven't even tried to contact them. I've been so damned busy. I'm not sure they know I'm still alive. I'm nervous about seeing the family and town I abandoned three months ago. What sort of questions are ringing in their minds? I have not told them I am coming home today. I am hoping the shock of seeing me on the doorstep after a quarter of a year will surprise them into forgiving me. I'm family, of course they will forgive me. Home is the one place where if you have to go there they have to take you in. At least, that's what I read somewhere. So why am I so damned nervous?

November 25, 6:45 pm

Returned home about two hours ago. Mom and Dad were excited to see me. The initial shock was enough to get me through the front door at least. I walked through the door and was greeted by Jason and Steven. They looked great. I hadn't seen either of them in years. James went off to college in San Diego to study oceanography and Steven moved to Wisconsin with his wife, we're still not quite sure why Wisconsin, though. We've talked since then but I haven't seen either of them since.

"You remember your sister-in-law right, Hay?" Steven said with a coy smile.

Catherine. Of course I did. Stupid icebreaker questions.

"You look great," I told her.

She thanked me and we all went into the living room. Marcy was there. Little Marcy grew up a lot in three months; I'd forgotten how much of a knockout she was. But, I'm biased. Harry, Kimberly, Sharon and Josh haven't arrived yet but they all promised to be home for Thanksgiving.

After we had all been reacquainted, Mom made a small dinner for those of us who showed up early; the benefits for those who are punctual are limitless. The table was immaculate. Mom always likes everything to look as though the president might just stop by and say hello, but, he never does. I don't know what she was thinking when she sat us children at the end of the table across from each other. That is an accident just looking for a place to happen. We do not see too much of each other but when we do, we are just like every other group of siblings in and world; and as much as it is forbidden by Mom, a food fight is definitely imminent. None of us care too much for vegetables so they are usually the first objects to go flying across the dining room like intercontinental ballistic missiles.

Then, the questions. I hadn't really even had a chance to get the first bite swallowed before the inquisition began.

"So did you forget about your old man and lady?"

"No, Mom. You know I didn't forget about you. Any of you."

"So what's going on? We haven't heard from you in so long, we figured you for dead."

"Well, I've just been so busy trying to get the department to grant us funds for a new program that I haven't even had much time to sleep."

"What's the program?" Steven asked.

"It's a cutting-edge field of psychology. It's not really new but not many schools recognize it in their degree programs so a lot of people don't understand what we're trying to do."

"What kind of psychology?" Even Marcy was getting in on the interrogation.

"Paranormal psychology."

Dead silence.

"You're studying ghosts?" Dad didn't seem too impressed.

"Well, kind of. It's a little more complicated than that."

"What is studying ghosts going to prove?"

"Well, it'll prove a lot of things, Mom. It will answer so many questions about what happens after our death. If we can prove that

there is a life after death, here in this world–well, not in this world–
in another realm of this world, we can solve many of life's great
mysteries."

"How much are you paying to study dead people?" Dad's droll
sense of humor always pops up at the most inopportune times.

I had to agree with him, though. "Too much."

"They should be paying you."

"I know. If we can convince the department to give us funding
and we can find solid proof, they just might pay me."

"Yeah?"

"Big."

"Mom, can I study dead people, too?" Marcy's impromptu
attempt at humor worked like a charm. We all laughed. And that,
as they say, is that. We enjoyed the rest of our dinner catching up on
old times and what was going on in all of our lives. It was nice.

November 26, 10:45 am

Thanksgiving Day. I returned home yesterday and my
nervousness about the homecoming has been short-lived. I hope
they're not just being polite. I know I have disappointed them. I
can't help but feel that I have neglected them. I wish I could tell
them that I'm sorry but I don't know how to. How do I tell them that
my work took precedence over them? It's not that I lost interest in
them or forgot about them, I had to push them aside for a while so
everything else could fall into place. Except things never did and
I just kept pushing them farther and farther aside until, one day,
I felt that contacting them would be a moot point because maybe
they had forgotten about me. What happened? When did my work
become more important than my family? I worry most about Mom
and Dad. I know my brothers and sisters will forgive me. They will
have no choice because when I'm famous, they'll all want to say how
much they love me and enjoy having me around. But Mom and Dad
will give me the "I'm-disappointed-in-you-speech," and that kills
me every time. The one thing I never want to be to my family is a
disappointment. I love them with all my heart and I hope they are as
proud of me as I am of them. I hope dinner today will draw us closer

together. I hope we can mend the ties that seem all but severed. I hope.

November 26, 4:15 pm

I feel much better. Dinner was an eclectic blend of raw family humor and barbaric human behavior with Steven shooting peas from his nose and Marcy almost choking on mashed potatoes while laughing hysterically. This was what I needed. This is what I have been missing for the past few months. Josh and Kim arrived around noon and helped me and Mom in the kitchen with the meal. About thirty minutes later, Sharon and Harry walked through the door. It was great to see them all again. Josh told me that he works for the police, the "good guys," he calls it. Harry works for the town fire department. Sharon has a job at Channel 8 broadcasting the local news. Kim works at Pete's Market.[16] Sometimes, I admire the fact that most of my family stayed in the area. At school, I often feel that things would have been better had I never left. But who knows? It's too late to complicate the irrelevant. Everything was ready around two. All the side dishes and fixings were on the table awaiting inevitable consumption. The chicken was brought out from the kitchen. It was titanic. I don't even know how Mom carried it to the table; she's so tiny. We all said our own silent prayer; which consisted mostly of leering eyes looking around the table to see if everyone else was done praying. Smiles and giggles sneaked out as peeking, wandering eyes caught a glimpse of each other and then nervously averted one another. Dad sliced the ceremonial first piece of turkey and all hell broke loose. Not that this dinner was different from any other dinner. This one was just more special. This is the first time I have been home in three months and I feel like I have never left. I'm not sure I want to leave again. We'll see. I still have two days left. By then, I may be ready to strangle them all. There is no bond quite so frail and tender as the bond between brothers and

---

[16] Pete's Market is a small "Mom and Pop" convenience store. It was established in the early 1970s. Despite rising competition, Pete's Market has been under the same management since it was established.

sisters. I love them dearly but family is family. I am convinced that the Webster's Dictionary's definition of family is inappropriate. It should read: "Family: 1.) a source of frustration and irritability. 2.) a sense of belonging and necessity. 3.) an odd combination of both.

November 29, 10:15 am

Returned to the office today. I think the visit home was exactly what I needed. The time spent with kith and kin has given me the opportunity to re-evaluate the situation. I have decided that whatever is to happen will happen. I've come to grips with the idea that this operation, to prove to the department that we have a legitimate case, may fail. I hope and pray that it does not, but it is understood by myself and my colleagues that bad things happen to good people all the time. This would not be the first or last time things didn't pan out for some deserving individual. I intend to relax a bit over the next few days and hope things fall into place. If not, I know now I can always return home to a family that loves me even if they don't always understand me. For that, I am eternally thankful.

November 29, 8:45 pm

Spoke with Dean today. He seemed to be in good spirts as well. I think the strain of three months of endless, unsuccessful work had finally taken its toll on the crew. This break was what everyone needed to focus and redefine what would be necessary to obtain our goals and objectives.

We met at Mickey's Diner at six.[17]

"How's your family?"

---

[17] Mickey's Diner was a restaurant on Mayfair St. in the early- to mid-1980s. They specialized in keeping the appearance of a 1960s diner. Paintings and pictures on the wall displayed proud rock-n-rollers such as Elvis Presley, Buddy Holly, Richie Valens and the Commodores. Impersonators performed live every evening. Nostalgic patrons would spit-shine their classic cars for display in the parking lot where, every Wednesday night, a contest was held for the most impressive classic car. Their slogan was: "Make every

"They're growing up, Dean. I forgot how much I missed them."

"I know what you mean. We've all been so busy these past few months that none of us has had time to do much of anything except work. I needed this break, too. I feel better about what we're trying to do, don't you?"

"Yeah, I do."

"And if not, we can all take up photography as a second profession."

Dean has such a dry sense of humor. He reminds me a lot of my father.

"What did your family think about what you are doing?"

"They don't understand why I would want to study dead people."

"'Dead people?' Well, that's one way of looking at it."

"I tried explaining to them that it was more than that but I couldn't put it in to words, you know?"

"I know. But don't ever lose focus on the fact that what we are doing has great importance. I've spent the last two years of my life trying to define why I think this is so important and I can't do it. I just know. It feels right. It feels good."

"Amen, Brother Starking."

Laughing and good food are the best remedy for frustration and confusion. I just wish I could do it more often.

December 1, 10:45 pm

A monumental turn of events has occurred. At 8:45 this morning, four individuals witnessed what we believe to be a level three, free-floating apparition. We are very excited! Dean just called with

---

night a 60s night." Vanilla Cokes and chocolate sodas could be purchased at the fully-stocked soda fountain. The waitresses all wore poodle skirts and ribbons in their hair. Although it does seem like an unlikely place for these two men to meet and dine, many loyal patrons say the two men frequented the diner every Sunday. Fun was to be had by both young and old; those nostalgic for the "good ol' days" and those who might want to experience what they never had a chance to. Unfortunately, the diner closed in 1987 due to health code violations.

the details and I am to meet the crew down at the old Detmeyer Building[18] to investigate. I hope this isn't another dead end.

December 1, 3:45 pm

Preliminary results were phenomenal. I arrived at the Detmeyer building at 11:00 am. Jay and Carla were already there with huge smiles to greet me.

I couldn't contain my own smile. "Are we ready to prove the world wrong?"

"Yes, sir, boss," they answered in unison.

"Don't call me boss. Makes me feel old."

"Yes, sir." I felt like I was delivering cadence or ordering a troop of marines to secure a beachhead.

"Let's do this," I said.

We entered the building like the MOD Squad; we were filled with a new found sense of confidence. We were certain that this lead was the lead we had been searching for. We were not blind to the fact that we've had hundreds of false leads before that we were certain were bound to be the lead that would prove our worthiness to the department heads. This investigation just felt different. Everything felt different. The air was heavier, the sounds were amplified and everything felt right.

"Jay, how long before the cameras can be set up and ready to go?"

"Once we get up there, maybe five or ten minutes."

"Great. I feel good about this one, guys."

"Me, too."

---

[18]   The Detmeyer Building was designed and constructed by Vladi Detmeyer, an architect from New York City. This building was originally designed to be an office building when it was built in the 1920s but several tragic accidents forced the building to close in the 1940s. In the 1970s, the building was bought by B&C Construction, the inside was gutted out and it was turned into an apartment complex. Many of the people who live there today say they believe the building to be haunted. They say they can feel the negative energy throughout the building. Many believe that the spirits of those individuals who lost their lives throughout the 1930s and early 1940s still linger in the halls.

"Me, too."

The rest of our journey was trekked in silence. Each of us was wearing a strange smile. We were probably blushing with joy.

The four witnesses each said they had seen something strange in the halls on the third floor of the Detmeyer building. I had not yet had a chance to interview the witnesses so what they saw remained a mystery to me and my crew.

Jay was struggling to carry the equipment as we got off the elevator.

"Here, let me grab some of that." I was already totting the PDC100x and the TIS50c and the EMIC but I grabbed the Nikon camera and the RCA video recorder; which still left Jay with a plethora of film equipment to carry. "Is that better?"

"Not really," he said with a strained grunt, "but thanks." He let out a nervous chuckle. The tension was beginning to mount.

The building had six floors with ten apartments on each floor. We set up cameras in the upper west corner and the lower east corner, diagonally across from each other. This way, we would obtain the optimal range of observation. We used each camera to film activity occurring in the corridors that intersected perpendicular at the cameras.

Jay began filming while I walked the parameter checking for any change in air density with the PDC. I adjusted the knobs to accommodate for any change in temperature, which seemed to be slightly cooler in the corridor running from the lower south side to the lower west side of the building. I still wasn't detecting any significant change in air density.

I could hear the rapid clicking of the Nikon as Carla snapped picture after picture hoping to get lucky and pick up an image on film.

"Jay?" I had to yell to him down the hall.

"What?"

"Can you make a round with thermal imaging? Maybe we'll have better luck. I'm not getting anything on this thing."

"Sure. Do you want me to start over here?" He pointed to the upper west corner.

"Sure."

Countless moments passed. I was beginning to lose that confidence that had been building. I wasn't so sure that this lead was any better than the previous leads. Too many times I have seen one lead ending with the three of us running around in circles with advanced technological equipment that was proving to be useless to us. All I wanted was one lead, one event to occur that would prove me wrong.

Another thirty minutes passed without incident. The three of us sat in the lower east corner looking across the corridor waiting for something to happen.

"Just for the hell of it, let's listen to the audio," I said.

"What? What if we miss something while we're listening? I think we would have heard a voice talking to us."

"Ease my curiosity, Jay. Amuse me. Indulge me, please."

Jay unwillingly rewound the tape. We listened for twenty minutes. We heard the dialogue spoken amongst us for a majority of the tape but for a brief moment, when our conversation had stalled, I heard a faint noise.

"Right there. What was that?"

"I didn't hear anything," Carla said.

"Rewind it. I heard something."

Jay rewound the tape a few seconds. We all turned an eager ear to the speaker. The dialogue had ended, my words being the last. A moment of silence passed and we heard the muffled sound again.

"What is that?" Carla asked.

"Again."

Jay rewound. "I'm taking out as much static as I can and concentrating the noise to the treble. I'll turn the bass down and the volume up. That should help make the sound quality clearer."

The tape played again. The long silence passed, then, in a young, female voice, "Talk to me."

"'Talk to me?' Is that what it says?"

"I'll play it again."

Again, "Talk to me."

"My God, an electromagnetic voice imprint. We did it." Carla was getting excited.

"Relax. Let's not jump to any forgone conclusions yet. We didn't pick anything up on the instruments and we don't know what we have on film. Let's do another round and see if we can't pick something up."

Jay played the tape again. The eerie voice resonated, meshed with minute amounts of static, barely above a whisper. "Talk to me."

I grabbed the PDC and Jay grabbed the TIS. Carla grabbed the Nikon and began snapping pictures as fast as she could, like a photographer at a fashion shoot.

"Jay," I said. "You watch your gauges. If you pick up any unusual thermal activity, you holler. This is it."

I roamed around waving the PDC around in front of me in every direction. The anticipation was killing me. I was so eager to find one more piece of evidence. The voice wasn't enough. The voice could be easily disputed. What we needed was concrete evidence. That evidence would have to come in the form of accurate numbers that we picked up on our instruments.

Jay was walking down the corridor parallel to the corridor I was in and Carla was in the corridor perpendicular to the corridor Jay was in to avoid filming us. The amount of energy emitted from our instruments could possibly be enough to disrupt the image processing on the film if she were to stand to close to the instruments while shooting.

I began to get some strange readings halfway down the hall. The density level changed from .0 to .6, a substantial increase. I paused for a moment, pointed the PDC away from the area where the change occurred and watched the needle drop back down to 0. When I pointed the PDC back in the direction where the change had occurred, again it shot quickly up to .6. This was what I was looking for.

"Jay, Carla, I got something."

"What?" Jay hollered.

I heard their footsteps approaching from around the south corner. Curiously, and without rational explanation, I heard a third pair of footsteps coming up right behind me. When I turned, I saw nothing.

The footsteps were getting louder and still headed in my direction.

I looked around for any sign of life.

Nothing.

The footsteps were directly upon me now. I looked down at the PDC and noticed the needle had spiked at 1.0, which implies intense paranormal activity. I tried to swallow but I was paralyzed with fear. Imagine me, a paranormal investigator, afraid of the paranormal.

The footsteps stopped in front of me. The hairs on the back of my neck began to tingle and a chill ran down my spine. The needle on the PDC was going crazy, spiking at 1.0, dropping quickly to 0 and rising again to 1.0.

"Hello?" It was all I could muster.

"Talk to me."

My legs went weak with exhausting terror and my knees buckled. It was the voice from the tape recorder.

I couldn't even muster a response.

The door to my right swung open quickly. The hairs on the back of my neck settled back down and the cold air was warm again.

The front door of the apartment was now open so I peeked inside. There was nobody standing in the entryway to welcome me.

"Hello," I called out.

Nothing.

The apartment was fully decorated and furnished. It seemed like a nice dwelling. The occupant was not home so I continued into the living room area. The PDC was still spiking at 1.0. I pressed forward awaiting the comfort of my companions.

Outside the door of the apartment, I could hear Jay and Carla approaching.

"Jay?"

"Yeah."

"I'm getting some real weird readings."

The door to the apartment slammed shut leaving Jay and Carla outside. I could hear them tugging on the doorknob.

"Hayden, open the door."

I rushed to the door and began pulling on the knob. I pulled as hard as I could but it wouldn't budge. The door would not open.

"This thing isn't budging." I yelled. "Get the landlord on the first floor. He should have an extra--"

"–Talk to me." The familiar voice echoed from behind me. I turned around in horror at the haunting image displayed before me: a young girl, maybe twenty or thirty, wearing a long, floor-length gown was dangling from a ceiling joist by a rope noose. Her long, curly, auburn hair hung down to her waist. Her skin was almost a pale green.

My heart dropped down into my stomach and my stomach dropped down to the floor.

"What do you want?" I mustered every ounce of courage to communicate with the apparition.

I received no reply.

The young lady turned her head to me. Her eyes were glazed over with an opaque residue, as if she were blind. I stammered backward. "Jay? Help!"

"What do you need?"

"I don't care if you have to kick this door down, get me out of here."

"Stay. Talk to me."

"Goddammit, stop saying that!"

When I turned around, the apparition was no longer hanging from a rope but slowly floating in my direction. I backed up as far as I could, pinning myself against the door. "Jay!"

"I'm trying!" I could hear his boot pounding against the door. I turned around and began pulling on the doorknob again. I was frantic. I wasn't even turning the knob at that point. I was just pulling with all my might. I looked over my shoulder to see the apparition right behind me, arms outstretched. "Talk to me." She kept repeating the same phrase over and over. I didn't want to talk. I wanted to get the hell out of that apartment. I had the information I needed. Now, I wanted out.

I turned around with horrific revulsion to find the apparition was toe-to-toe with me. This was no level three free-floating apparition; this was, without a doubt, a level two free-roaming apparition. I knew she couldn't harm me but the negative energy in the room was beginning to make me nauseated.

I looked her right in the eyes, and she stared right back. The pleasant aroma of flowers filled the air.

And she disappeared. I looked down at the PDC and nothing was registering.

She had vanished completely.

The lock clicked and the door eased open.

"What the hell was that?" Carla asked.

"That, was exactly what we were looking for. Let's grab our gear and get the hell out of here."

December 2, 12:45 pm

Met with Dean to discuss preliminary results from the investigation at the Detmeyer Building.

"This is it, Dean. Not only did we get conclusive data, I saw the damned thing. It floated right up to me. This was no hoax. This was the real thing."

"What do you mean, 'floated up to you?'"

"I followed the readings into Apartment 32 on the third floor; exactly where the witnesses pinpointed the sightings. I was walking the parameter with the PDC and all of a sudden the thing spiked on me. No kidding; 1.0. I couldn't believe it. I yelled to Jay and Carla but before they could even get to me, I started hearing another set of footsteps. I turned around and I swear to you there was nothing there. The footsteps approached and stopped in front of me. You know when you get goose bumps all up and down your flesh and the hairs on the back of your neck start to tingle?"

He nodded.

"Well, that's what happened. I could feel the coolness. Then, the door to the apartment swung open. I went inside and waited for Jay and Carla but before they got there, the door slammed shut and I was trapped inside with the apparition. She kept saying, 'Talk to me.' I haven't been that scared in a long time."

"All the data has been collected?"

"Yes. The equipment has been checked for errors and they are clean. The readings are accurate. I can arrange a meeting with a shrink if you think I should have my head examined."

"That won't be necessary. I believe you. Have you had a chance to interview the witnesses, see if their stories match?"

"Not yet. We're going down today. We're going to try to get some more readings, too. They shouldn't be to hard to find, that building is oozing with paranormal activity. I'd like to check the other floors if you don't mind."

"I mind. One thing at a time, Hay. We have to have all our evidence and proof by Friday. I have to go before the board and plead our case. If the evidence you have collected is, in fact, accurate, they will, hopefully, find it in the goodness of their hearts, if they have any, to grant us the funds to expand the department. If we can do that, we can offer so much more to the public. So what are you waiting for. Time's running out."

December 2, 8:45 pm

Met with Catherine McDouglas.[19]

"Catherine, can you explain exactly what you saw?"

"I was coming out of my apartment to get on the elevator when I saw this lady come around the corner. I knew she wasn't from the building and she looked lost so I asked if I could help her find somebody. She didn't answer me. As she got closer to me, I could tell something was really wrong. Again, I asked 'Are you lost? Can I help you?' She just looked up at me and said, 'Talk to me.' Chills ran down my spine and she disappeared." She sighed deeply. "I haven't seen her since. I was really scared."

"What did she look like?"

"She must have been in her early 30s. She had really pretty auburn hair that hung way down on her back. She had the prettiest hazel-green eyes. She was gorgeous. She was really attractive but she looked so sad and lost."

"What kind of clothes was she wearing?"

"She had on this really long, floor-length gown. It was beautiful. Come to think of it, she was very overdressed, but these days you

---

[19] Catherine McDouglas, moved into the Detmeyer Building in early 1981. She was the first of the four witnesses to call about the strange happenings.

don't question reality you just accept it, you know? But when she vanished right in front of me . . . I called you guys."

"Three other tenants called us claiming to have seen similar occurrences."

"No, I don't really know many people in the building."

"Then how did you know that the lady wasn't from the building?"

"I don't know the names or personal habits of most of the tenants. I do know faces and dressing habits. I'm not stupid." I had definitely struck a nerve; the last thing I wanted to do was alienate and upset her.

"I'm sorry, Miss McDouglas. I'm just trying to eliminate any possibility of a hoax."

"Ask the others, then. They'll tell you the same thing. I'm not crazy. I don't even believe in ghosts. I don't know how to explain what I saw. All I know is that I saw it and it scared me."

"Thank you for your time, Miss McDouglas."

"You're welcome."

We questioned Michael Stone, Jennifer Bishop and Cal Hewes.[20] All three reported similar sightings. They all described the same young female wearing a long, floor-length gown. The female described by all four witnesses was identical to the specter that I had seen in apartment 32. I took all of their written testimonies and all of our dialogues were recorded on my hand recorder.

I scanned the entire third floor again. I did not receive any strange readings except when I was just outside apartment 32. What's so special about this apartment? There must be a connection. What is it?

December 3, 6:45 pm

Jay, Carla and I went over the video tape we recorded at the Detmeyer building. Most of the footage was rather boring. We had

---

[20] All three individuals are tenants on the third floor of the Detmeyer Building and reported seeing strange disturbances on the third floor, close to apartment 32.

almost an hour of nothing but three amateur film junkies wandering around in circles holding out gadgets and scanners. We actually looked quite ridiculous. The moment I was eagerly anticipating was fast approaching. The camera was pointed down the hall, no images on the screen. Dialogue spoken amongst us could be heard. The strange, resonating echo bellowed from the recorder: "Talk to me." I knew the moment was at hand. I watched myself walk down the hall, look down at the PDC, look up, and holler for Jay and Carla. I watched carefully as the third set of footsteps approached.

Streaks of static and jumbled images pressed together on the video. The screen went black.

"Jay, tell me we didn't lose it?"

"I don't know. Hold on."

A long moment in the dark blankness of the screen and finally the video began to display the images again. This time, however, there was a young female with auburn hair wearing a long, floor-length gown approaching me.

"Jay, I swear to God I didn't see her there."

"I believe you."

The specter was no more than two feet away from me.

"Jay, Carla, I'm getting some strange readings here," I watched myself yell.

The apparition stopped right in front of me. I could actually see myself through her translucent body. It was quite an eerie effect. Watching on the screen, the young lady had her back turned toward us but I could tell she was staring right into my eyes. She stood up on her tippy-toes to do so, returned to normal posture then walked through the wall on my right.

"That's when the door burst open." I was starting to shake a little.

"Mr. Walker, is this conclusive evidence?"

"You bet your ass it is."

December 4, 6:30 pm

Met with Dean today.

"Here's the final report. We have four eyewitnesses all with identical stories. We have the data we collected from the preliminary investigation which matched results collected from the follow-up investigation, and we have the video showing the apparition, which is exactly how she is described by four individuals and me. So, tell me, do we stand a chance tomorrow?"

"You never know with the board. They're funny with money. They tend to spend money on things they can relate to and can grasp the concepts and fundamentals of. What we're doing is so cutting edge they might be a little intimidated by our research. But they won't be able to deny these results. You have done such a fine job, Hay. I hope you realize how much this department appreciates you and your efforts."

"Well, I have a dedicated crew and strong, stable support. So I hope you realize how much I appreciate you for allowing me the opportunity to be a part of something this monumental and significant."

"I believe I do."

"Good. Best of luck tomorrow. Let me know the second the decision is made."

"Done. I'll talk to you tomorrow."

More waiting.

December 5, 5:45 am

Surprise, surprise. Another night of tossing and turning. Another restless night of unsettled sleep. I have been nervous before but this morning my stomach is racing laps around my ass. I can't contain the swirling sensation in my stomach and all I really want to do is vomit. Some people complain of butterflies in their stomachs but there must be some huge griffins swarming around in my stomach. My bed sheets are damp with sweat and my nausea is somehow affecting my equilibrium because I have never been this dizzy. I'm very concerned. The members of the board are what we consider old school. I worry they will not be receptive to what we are trying to do. People have a tendency to ignore that which they don't believe because it is easier than trying to rationalize the impossible. But what's so impossible? How can they ignore what they are unable to deny? But people do it every day. It's so frustrating to know that the people who are in control of our future are those same people who would rather turn a deaf ear to the preacher of reason. I feel like we are preaching against the converted or beating a dead horse. It's so frustrating and this waiting is killing me.

December 5, 5:30 pm

Dean called.

"Hay, the board members reached their decision about ten minutes ago."

"They refused our request, didn't they?"

"Not exactly."

"Then what, Dean? Don't keep me in suspense."

"I know how hard you've worked for this and how much you have sacrificed to make this dream of ours a reality so . . .how would you feel about paranormal investigation for a living?"

"Are you kidding?"

"As I live and breathe, Hay. They unanimously accepted our request for funding. They're giving us a one-year probationary period; standard practice. This way they don't put all their eggs in one basket. If they get nervous at any time, they can still pull the plug. We're still going to have to work very hard, maybe even harder than before. Are you up to that?"

"Absolutely."

"One more thing: I want to make you a member of our staff. You've earned it. This will give you the opportunity to teach classes, give lectures and hold seminars on paranormal anomalies if you'd like, or you can keep doing what you're doing?"

"And what am I doing?"

"One hell of a fine job. I'm impressed, son. I must admit, I had my doubts when I recruited you from the abnormal psych program, but you turned out to be one hell of a dedicated pupil. Now, you're bright and intuitive and you could probably go anywhere you want to with this field but I would be greatly appreciative if you stayed here with us."

"Dean, I'm not going anywhere."

"Damn good news, Hay. This is a great day for all of us. Let's celebrate."

December 31, 11:30 pm

1981 has come and gone. In thirty minutes the entire year will be over. Where the hell did it go? This has been, without a doubt, the strangest, most exhilarating year I have ever lived. I find myself alone but that's fine. I've called my family and wished them a Happy New Year. I am physically and psychologically exhausted. Looking back, it was all worth it. I await the coming year with eager anticipation. Hopefully, adventure and good fortune will dominate. I think I've earned it. I know I have. We'll have to wait and see. There's an entirely different world out there waiting to be explored and I am going to be among the chosen few to explore and investigate. What will we find?[21]

---

[21] This entry was the last in this diary. Although there were several blank pages left at the end, for whatever reason, Walker chose to begin the new year with a new diary. Perhaps superstition, perhaps a new year deserved a new diary; anticipating many events to explain and much to write about. We may never know. For explanation or further inquiry about this diary, visit www.basedonatruestory.info.

Diary 2

January 3, 6:30 pm

Dean just called with some great news. The members of the board were so pleased with our results. They want us to begin conducting more investigations as soon as possible. The members are granting us more than $150,000 to our experiment. This means so much. We will be able to buy better, more accurate equipment. No more guessing with the PDC100x. The new version just came out, the PDC450p. I can't wait to try that beautiful piece of machinery in the field. All the suffering and agony and failure has come to an end. We now have a meaning and a purpose: to not fail again. We must not lose focus on the fact that we are going to be in a very strict probationary period. If we do not collect significant, indisputable evidence, and lots of it, the board members will pull the plug on the entire operation and we will be right back where we started: ground zero. I'm so excited. Not only will we be conducting investigations locally, but we'll be able to travel as well. With the amount of funding provided to us by the board members, we will be able to travel just about anywhere in the continental U.S. and conduct specific investigations, run cross-sectional reports, and so much more. There is so much to do and so much to learn. There is so much to teach the world. I hope they're ready, because I'm ready to teach them.

January 10, 8:45 pm

Arrived in Vermont about an hour ago. I checked in at a local motel in Rutland. I'm here to investigate reports of paranormal activity at Katherine's Bed and Breakfast.[22] Katherine and several of her employees have repeatedly claimed that paranormal activity is going on in the house.[23] I have not had a chance to interview

---

[22] Katherine's Bed and Breakfast, owned and operated by Katherine Shueman, was opened on March 4, 1980.

[23] See George K. Peterson's "The House That Jack Built" in *True Hauntings* v. 240 July 1981. The article deals with the first-hand accounts of the employees of Katherine's Bed and Breakfast. Several of the employees have claimed to have seen ghostly apparitions and witnessed bizarre occurrences within the household. Despite claims of fraud or hoax, all of the eyewitness accounts detail amazingly similar events.

any of the employees or the proprietor, Katherine Shueman. I am hoping to arrive first thing in the morning to conduct a very thorough interview session with Katherine and her employees. Later in the day, I will conduct an intense investigation to decide whether or not paranormal activity is, in fact, evident.

January 11, 1:30 am

I can't sleep. I'm so anxious to get down to business. I don't want to be too tired to conduct the interviews or the investigation. I want everything to be perfect. I'm out to prove a point tomorrow: on our first investigation after the committee made their decision, that the choice they made was the right one. I want to prove to myself and the board that they were right to believe in us.

Oh, what to do? I don't even have anyone to call and enjoy my anxious state of mind with. All I have is you, good friend. I guess you're all I need for now. I can tell you anything and you just stare blankly back up at me. I just want to keep writing. It settles my nerves.

I rented a really nice car at the airport: a 1982 Chevy Cavalier. Brand new.[24] It's maroon with maroon interior. I spent a little extra and went with the sunroof. I don't know why. Vermont's so much like Maine. The sun never comes out in January and it's always cold as hell. Why do people say that? "Cold as Hell." It doesn't make sense. Everyone tells you that you can have something or that they will do something when Hell freezes over thinking the idea of Hell freezing over to be preposterous; it would never happen. Yet, at the same time, everyone says that it's cold as Hell whenever

---

[24] Receipts from Hertz Rent-A-Car at the Rutland State Airport verify the fact that Hayden Walker was in Vermont on January 10, 1982 and that he did indeed rent a maroon, 1982 Chevy Cavalier. This piece of the puzzle was very exciting for us. This piece of paper was the first physical piece of evidence, other than the diaries, that proved Hayden Walker actually existed. When Jason called me from Vermont and told me he was holding a photocopied receipt, signed by Walker, in his hand, I almost screamed. This was the first piece of indisputable evidence that Walker existed. The diaries could be pushed aside as a fraud but to have an actual receipt, signed by Walker, verified in his diary, was proof enough for me that Walker existed.

the temperature drops below freezing.   I wonder why people have never picked up on that.[25] I guess it doesn't really matter.

January 11, 3:30 pm

I have just finished conducting the interviews. Many fascinating stories have been told today and I find myself hoping they are all true.

I arrived at around 10:30 am. Katherine Shueman greeted me at the door and invited me in for coffee. I cordially accepted and entered the house. It's beautiful inside. The floors are all hardwood; glossed and waxed to a high-mirrored shine. You can actually see yourself standing on the floor. Fantastic. The decor of the house looks to be early to mid-1800s. The wallpaper in every room is elegant. Mostly floral patterns. The staircase is exceptional. An oak banister spirals exquisitely, winding up from the first floor to the third floor. The stairs are also oak and polished to a shine.[26] I could definitely spend a few nights in this place.

I questioned Katherine Shueman first.

Hayden Walker:[27] Ms. Shueman, are you the proprietor of this establishment?

---

25   This seems to be the first documented occasion where Walker consults his diary as an instrument of comradery. Until now, the diary has been a medium for depicting and portraying everyday activities in Walker's life. However, here, we get a first look into his mind and see what he's thinking and how he rationalizes. I understand this is a very strange rationalization; his inquiry and pondering border on the brink of futility, but the idea that a man of his intelligence has no one to turn to but himself is fascinating. What is more fascinating, is the fact that now we can rationalize *his* rationalizing no matter how bizarre or inconsequential it may seem to us.

26   An interesting side note: I called Katherine Shueman, who still runs the B&B, about a year ago to discuss her meeting with Walker and I mentioned the fact that he constantly remarked on the shine of her floors. She laughed, almost embarrassed and said, "I'm a perfectionist." I asked what she used on her floors and she said, "Murphy's Oil." "That's it?" I asked. She just laughed. "That's it."

27   The initials and bold print have been added by the editor to make reading more fluid. In the original diary, Walker made no indentations nor did he make it easy for anyone to read the diary or know who was speaking. He

Katherine Shueman: Yes, I am. And please, call me Kate.

HW: Ok, Kate, before I ask too many questions, could you give me a quick history of this building?

KS: Sure. The building was built in the mid-1800s by a business tycoon named Jackson Adlebury, an Englishman. Everyone called him Jack. He went through a bitter divorce when his wife left him for another woman. You have to understand, in that time, this behavior was unheard of so you can imagine that Jack was enraged. He sold the house and everything in it. Everything anyone would buy, anyway. He moved back to England where I think he killed himself two years later. The building was left vacant for almost fifty years when it was bought by a construction worker named Jonathon Kingston, another Englishman, not married though. He bought the house in the hopes of finding a woman to marry and have a family with. I have no idea how he could have ever afforded this house, but he did somehow. Anyway, he was killed on a job in Manchester, New Hampshire in 1905. Apparently, he fell off a scaffolding and plummeted one hundred feet to his death. Then, in 1940, the house was rented by Peter and Martha Boyle who later decided to buy the house. He died of heart complications about five or six years ago. Martha died two days later. Nobody knows why. They say it was a broken heart, as corny as it sounds. But it must be hard to lose someone you've been with for so long that you can't remember life without them. Autopsy reports came back negative for heart attack, stroke or aneurysm. She simply gave up.

HW: That's a lot of history.

KS: Yeah, it is. So much tragedy, though.

HW: Kate, are you aware of the fact that some spirits haunt the places they are most familiar with?[28] For whatever reason, ghosts return to the places they remember most.

---

didn't even use quotes. I had an extremely difficult time deciphering where the breaks were in the diary and who was talking. So, to make the reading as easy and enjoyable as possible, I have used bold print to highlight who is speaking.

[28] See Keith Peter's "That Old Familiar Haunt" in *Ghosts* v. 89 January 1978. The article goes into depth about spirits haunting the places they are most familiar with. "Usually, the spirit returns to the place of dwelling where the

KS: I wasn't aware of that. That would certainly explain a lot about what's been happening here.

HW: Like what?

KS: My entire staff and I have all witnessed strange occurrences around here. Several of my staff have complained of personal items being moved around and even stolen from them.

HW: What do you mean by personal items?

KS: All members of my staff live here. It makes it easier for us to be accessible to our customers to provide the best, friendliest service possible. But many of the girls have complained that little knickknacks and things have been moved from where they put them. In some extreme cases, the knickknacks will be hidden or moved to a different room completely. We are a close group of people and when they tell me they aren't fooling around with each other to scare one another, I believe them.

HW: And they all say they have no idea what's going on?

KS: Yes.

HW: What do you think is going on?

KS: I honestly don't know. That's why I called you guys. Things are getting out of hand. I've had two of my girls quit in the past month. I can't afford to keep losing staff. I need to know what's going on.

[Excerpt from interview with Kristen Holcomb][29]

HW: Kristen Holcomb, are you an employee at Katherine's Bed and Breakfast?

---

spirit expressed or experienced the most emotion, negative or positive. Spirits, for some reason, have an innate behavioral instinct to haunt these places. Have you ever wondered why nobody claims to see ghosts in a graveyard or cemetery? Ghosts don't haunt these places. They haunt the places they know and are familiar with. Many believe it is the psychic energy that the spirit expressed emotionally that draws them back." (Page 34).

[29] Due to the length of the interviews, I have cut out certain sections I believe to be unimportant to the pace and progress of the reading. Forgive me for assuming what will and will not be important to you but you must realize

KH: Yes, I am.

HW: According to your employer, many of the staff here have experienced or witnessed bizarre happenings and occurrences. Have you ever witnessed anything unusual?

KH: Yes, I have.

HW: Would you care to elaborate?

KH: I have this trophy I won in third grade for softball . . .and every once in a while, the trophy will be moved across the room. I usually set it on a shelf on the wall but sometimes, when I wake up in the morning, it's on my dresser instead. I asked everyone if they were teasing me or trying to scare me and they all said no.

HW: Do you believe them?

KH: Yes . . .

HW: Have you ever experienced anything else?

KH: Sometimes, late at night, my room gets really cold . . .I can almost feel the covers lift up behind me, the bed moves like someone is lying down beside me, and sometimes I can feel a hand touch the bare flesh on my arm . . .I try to tell myself it's not real and that helps sometimes, but it's happening more and more now. I don't know how much more I can take.

[Excerpt from interview with Kaleb Trent]

HW: Kaleb, have you ever witnessed or experienced anything bizarre in this house? Anything out of the ordinary?

KT: Yes, I have.

HW: Like what?

KT: I've seen a man . . .

HW: What does he look like?

KT: He's an older guy with grey hair; real short, almost buzzed off but not quite. He's always wearing the same black suit. He has one hand tucked in the breast of his jacket like this [Kaleb indicates

---

that, with the volume of information provided to me, I had to be very selective with what I chose to include in the book. Any significant amounts of these interviews that have been extracted will be replaced with an ellipsis(. . .). If you wish to read the interviews in their entirety, Read Peter Tracy's *The Walker Interviews*.

that the man places a flat palm just underneath the breast lapel with the thumb remaining exposed; the hand is near his heart on his upper right breast plate]. He always looks like he's giving the Pledge of Allegiance, or something. He seems like a really classy guy but he always has this intense scowl on his face like he's furious about something . . .

HW: Why do you think he's angry?

KT: Hell, I don't know. He just always looks pissed off. I don't know who he is or why I see him, but I do. Kate's seen him too.

[Excerpt from interview with Kate Blanc]

HW: Kate, Kaleb tells me you have seen a man walking around the halls. Is that correct?

KB: Yes. He's an older gentleman. He wears a pin-stripped suit and seems sophisticated and classy but he seems bitter and enraged at the same time.

HW: How so?

KB: He always has this look on his face. He just looks frustrated and angry at the same time.

HW: Where do you see this man? All over the house?

KB: No. We mostly see him just outside the door to Kristen's room.

HW: Has Kristen ever seen him?

KB: I don't think so. She's never mentioned it if she has. We'd never tell her, though. She'd get scared. I've actually seen him disappear into her room on several occasions. I don't know if he lives there or not, but I see him. And I think he sees me. He scares the hell out of me.

[Excerpt from interview with Rebecca Strout]

HW: Rebecca, how long have you worked for Katherine?

RS: I was her first employee when she opened in 1980. Almost two years now.

HW: And in that time, have you ever witnessed or noticed anything bizarre or extraordinary happen around here?

RS: All the time. We hear noises and see ghosts. We see a lot of things around here.

HW: Do you see them often?

RS: Yeah, it's pretty common, now. Most of us are familiar with the peculiar. What choice do we have?

HW: Have you noticed a gradual progression in the amount of times you see or hear things that are unusual?

RS: Things have always happened so often that we're just kind of accustomed to it now.

January 11, 8:45 pm

I finished the investigation about an hour ago. Being thorough takes time. I must confess, I immensely enjoyed using the PDC450p. What a magnificent piece of machinery. It's a thousand times more accurate than its predecessor.

Despite the claims that these hauntings are a hoax, I found all evidence to be to the contrary. I spoke with Katherine after the investigation and walked her around the house to tell her what I had discovered.

"I found nothing on the first floor which coincides with the fact that none of your staff or you have ever claimed to have seen anything unusual on this floor. On the second floor, I found some really unusual data. I remember two accounts of staff members, I think Kate and Kaleb, telling me they had seen a man in and around the hallway outside Kristen's room. The PDC450p and the EMIC880 confirmed that fact. The density level almost quadrupled in one specific area in Kristen's room. Let me show you."

We walked together to Kristen's room. I pointed toward the upper left-hand corner, as you enter the room. "There is an extreme amount of paranormal density in this particular corner of the room. This is definitely the entity that has been causing you all the headaches."

"How many ghosts do you think there are?"

"At least two, possibly three."

"Where?"

"Third floor."

On the third floor, I told Katherine that the negative energy received by the EMIC880 was insubstantial to the amount of energy detected on the second floor, in Kristen's room.

"If you don't mind, I'd like to call in a specialist."

"Aren't you a specialist?"

"Well, technically, yes, but, this guy is a specialist to the specialist. He's a psychic investigator. He's a very good friend of mine. We've worked together on many occasions. What I do is a more scientific approach to paranormal investigation but he has a unique ability to converse with other realms of this world. He's what we call a psychic medium."

"What's that?"

"A medium is a person who can communicate and channel information from spirits. He can probably tell you which ghost is on which floor and give you a brief history of that ghost before you even tell him the real history. Would that be all right?"

"Sure. Anything that might help."

January 11, 11:30 pm

Kristen was kind enough to let me "borrow" her room for the night. She said she was actually glad to let it go. In a way, I hope I witness what she is so scared of but in a way, I also hope I don't. I don't know why, but this room gives me the creeps. I don't believe what is in this room can physically harm me. The only thing that can be harmed in a situation like this is our own mind. Fear of the unknown is rational paralysis. Fear causes belief and belief can make the most bizarrely inexplicable events seem real. I know this because I have experienced it. I have read about it. I have documented it. Why are people so afraid of what they cannot explain? Simply because they cannot explain it. Rational paralysis.

I called Rick earlier.[30] He should be in by late morning. Hopefully he can shed some light on the subject at hand. I know that this particular room is the root of the negative energy being extended throughout the house but I cannot say why. I hope Rick can.

---

[30] Rick Deeves, psychic investigator. Worked with Walker on many occasions.

January 12, 2:45 pm

Rick arrived around 10 this morning. He had some interesting insight to add to my initial investigation.

I took him directly to Kristen's room. I wanted to hold off telling him what I had observed during the night so everything he would be telling me would be things that he would have no prior knowledge of.

"There is an extreme amount of negative energy coming from this room," he confirmed. "Very negative. This is a very angry spirit. In the upper corner there is his vortex. That's how he gets from his world to ours."

"Can you tell me anything about him?"

"He's an older gentleman; maybe sixty, or so. Very intelligent but very angry judging by the negative vibes he's putting out. Have any of the occupants of this room ever been assaulted by him?"

"I wasn't aware that ghosts could cause physical harm to humans."

"With the amount of negative energy being displayed here, I would say there is a very good chance that this spirit is a level four, free-floating apparition with an extreme capability of harming the living. There have been several documented cases where members of the spirit world have actually caused intense damage to the living world; even death isn't out of the question."

"A ghost can kill a human?"

"If there is enough negative energy, sure."

I must admit that this news came as a shock to me.

We went to the third floor.

"Not so much negative energy here. He's a much younger man; maybe in his thirties. He was a builder or an architect, something like that. He's showing me things that have to do with building. Do you know the history of the building?"

I nodded.

"Did a construction worker die here?"

"Not physically here but he lived here. He died on a construction sight in Manchester, New Hampshire."

"That's him. He's not going to cause any trouble. We can leave him but the other spirit cannot stay here. We need to arrange some means of immediate paranormal extermination. I feel his energy is gaining strength and he may manifest his anger negatively if necessary measures are not taken. Have the guests or staff complained that things are happening more and more often?"

"Some of them have. Some of them say they are so used to it that they almost don't notice anything unusual at all anymore."

"Well, it's going to get worse before it gets better. I'll stay behind for the cleansing and see if that works."

[Following three pages of diary missing][31]

---

[31] The next three pages of the diary have been ripped out for some reason. We know from receipts that Walker was still in Vermont for the next three days. We have no idea if he stayed behind to help with the extermination or if he packed a bag and went off to his next call. His receipt from Hertz indicated that he left Vermont on January 15. But what was he doing during this time? I tried to call Katherine Shueman again but she was unable to be reached for comment. I have not heard from her since.

WHY?[32]

'

---

[32] This is a very unusual entry for Walker; especially in his earlier diaries. Later on, in subsequent diaries, it is not uncommon for Walker to dedicate an entire page to one word or one thought or sentence or paragraph. This is particularly troublesome here because we have no idea why Walker wrote this one word directly in the middle of the page. Jason and I dug for months trying to find even the tiniest of clues as to why, at this time in his life, Walker would be troubled or plagued by something so intensely that he would express his emotion in one word: why? Perhaps we are reading too much into this particular problem. Perhaps he was displaying some form of humor. Perhaps he couldn't think of anything else to write about. Perhaps there is nothing behind this quandary but, perhaps, there *is* something greater involved.

WHY NOT?[33]

---

[33] Is he toying with us? Perhaps he knows that one day the public will read his diaries and they will ponder exhaustively over these two particular entries. Is one an answer to the other or is one a further inquiry? The more I try to rationalize or explain, the less I am able to. Perhaps some day we will know. For now, we must dismiss the matter as an exercise in futility.

January 30, 8:45 am

I've been on the road for so long I don't know where I am now let alone where I was yesterday or where I'll be tomorrow. Who the hell knows? Not me, that's for damn sure. All I know is that Dean leaves a message on my pager, I call him back from the nearest payphone, at my expense of course, and he tells me where I'm going and what airport I need to get there. If it sounds confusing, that's because it is.

January 30, 10:45 am

It probably sounds like a corny bumper sticker, but where the hell is Devil's Lake, North Dakota? I'll find out soon enough because that's where I'm headed. Called Dean and he told me my next client lives on Walnut St. in Devil's Lake, North Dakota.[34] He told me to get to the airport, pick up my ticket and head out as soon as possible. So, I'll finish this cup of coffee, slowly, and eat the rest of this scrumptious bagel loaded with only the finest of cream cheeses and I'll get going when I'm damn good and ready. I'm tired; physically and psychologically exhausted. I'll sleep on the plane.

January 30, 6:45 pm

I arrived on Walnut Street about two hours ago. I approached the apartment I was directed to go to. This tiny lady, who introduced herself as Norma, met me at the door. I went in and had a seat.

"Norma, how are you today?"

"I'm fine, thanks. And you?"

"Very well, thank you."

She had hot coffee ready; Dean must have told her what time I was expecting to arrive. We drank the coffee and shared idle chitchat before I started my interview. She was very strange from

---

[34] Although we never get the woman's full name mentioned in the diary, we did some research and found that a Ms. Norma Kinsgly lived there during this period. She was a mother of two and a widower. Her two children were grown up and her husband had died three years prior.

the start. Her behavior was somewhat erratic and bizarre. I've been around dead people and spirits less bizarre than this lady. She was constantly looking over her shoulder and appeared to be recognizing the appearance of a person or something that I was not privy to seeing. Furthermore, when she left the room, I heard her telling someone or something to shut up when she left the room. While she was in the kitchen preparing the tray of coffee, I observed this odd behavior. I knew something was definitely amiss but I wanted to stay and at least hear her story before casting her aside as a lunatic. Sheer, morbid curiosity, I guess.

"So, Norma, what can we do for you?"

"About three years ago, my Stanley passed away. I swear I can still feel his spirit moping around the apartment. I don't know if he's sad because I'm alone here or what, but I want to let him know it's all right. I'm fine and if he wants to leave he can. I'll be fine. I'll see him soon enough." At this point, I started feeling awful about the way I had perceived her. Perhaps I had mistaken sentimental sincerity for lunacy. Until now, I'd never met anyone who was so concerned about the welfare of a deceased partner enough to want to make contact with them. The gesture seemed sweet and innocent enough but still, I should have known better.

"You want me to conduct a seance?"

She nodded and smiled awkwardly.

"I'll see what I can do. Honestly, this is not my area of expertise. I tend to the more scientific aspects of the business but I know enough to get us by and you seem very sincere in your request. How can I resist honest sentimentality?"

"Thank you so much."

"My pleasure. I'll just need a few of Stanley's personal belongings: clothes, accessories, things he enjoyed; anything you saw him with on a regular basis. When we try to contact him, these possessions will draw him to us and help us communicate."

The first thing Norma brought back was an old shirt. It had originally been a white, long-sleeve button-up shirt with a collar. Now, it was brown and tattered and looked like something had been sleeping on it. Next, she brought out a blue, plastic bowl.

"Stanley used this a lot, did he?"

"Oh, yes. This is what he had breakfast in every morning."

I still didn't think too much of it. So, the man likes cereal. I can buy that. I love cereal, too. Frosted Flakes, but don't tell anyone.

She brought out this strange comb next. It was metallic and looked like it might hurt like hell to use, but I didn't say anything. Then, she brought out a long stretch of rope, knotted at both ends and chewed into a pathetic heap of frayed cloth.

"What did he use that for?"

"He could play with this for hours."

"Norma, could I see a picture of Stanley?"

Before I even had a chance to finish the question, she rushed into the next room, like a child eager to display a new toy. When she emerged from the darkness, she was holding a heart-shaped picture frame, using both hands to clutch it to her chest. The frame was pewter and seemed quite heavy as she appeared to be struggling with its weight. I looked at the picture. If the creature in the picture was, in fact human– not even a man, but a human– I'll be damned for laughing at his misfortune of being the ugliest man to have ever been born, with that giant nose and all that hair.

"Norma, Stanley isn't your husband, is he?"

"Heaven's no," she insisted. "He's my dog."

"You want me to conduct a seance with your dead dog?"

She nodded, grinning a bizarre, cocked lip.

"What would you like me to ask him?"

I had to explain to her that I was unable to conduct a seance with her dog because we have no way of translating "woof-woof" into English. Sometimes, I wonder if this job is worth the trouble.

March 11, 10:45 pm

I actually get to return to the university tomorrow. I'm quite excited. I've been on the road for more than two months without stopping. I'm exhausted. I need this break. I'll get on a plane at 6 in the morning and by 2, I'll be sitting at my desk beside Dean at the university. I have conducted enough interviews and investigations over the past two months to write a novel but I've never been much of a writer. I've always thought it would be great to write a book but unfortunately, my creative skills are severely outweighed by my critical, scientific skills.

March 12, 10:15 am

On the plane. I hate flying. Statistically, they say you're more likely to die in a car crash on your way to the airport than in an airplane, but I would feel safer dying in a car rather than plummeting 35,000 feet to my death in a giant, metal coffin that says "Fly those friendly skies." The skies aren't so friendly today. If you look out the window, you'll see absolutely nothing in front us for miles and miles except for a cloud bank or two, but the plane is bouncing up and down like a knife on a chopping block. Why is that? There's nothing up here but wind. You'd think they could invent a metal strong enough to resist a gust of wind. I've lived through two hurricanes[35] and our house survived both of them. Now, how is it that a bunch of lumber held together by wood and nails is stronger than state-of-the-art metal and tight-fitting screws? Maybe I should be having this introspection on the ground where there is less turbulence.[36]

March 12 10:00 pm

Returned to the "office" today. I already miss being in the field conducting investigations but I could use the rest. I missed Dean. We always have so much to talk about. Today, however, we couldn't find anything to converse about. We tried. Most of it was idle chitchat. After a while, we gave up and sat in silence. I'm tired. I wanted to

---

[35]   Hurricane Kathleen and Hurricane Francis

[36]   This passage was rather humorous to read. At first, the turbulence does not seem all that bad, judging by Walker's writing, but a few lines later, you can actually tell the plane hits a large pocket of turbulence; his writing gets larger, so he can control his command of the pen more accurately but at one point, on the "g" in "fitting," the pen actually skids across the length of the page. Then Walker decides to continue his rant on the ground.

go over the results I had collected during my investigations but he said it could wait till morning. I can wait if he can. I'm quite excited about the results. I'm sure Dean will be, too. He usually shares my enthusiasm.

March 17, 8:45 am

No rest for the inquisitive. I guess if inquiring minds want to know, inquiring minds must pay the price, and that price is countless nights without sleep. So be it. Comes with the job. One of those fringe benefits you're always hearing about. I have to go to a call just up the street which isn't nearly as bad as hopping on a plane and traveling halfway across the country because some crazy, old lady wants to hold a seance with her dead dog.

March 17, 8:00 pm

I arrived at the apartment of Jennifer McPherson, a student at the university. She was very glad to see us.[37] She invited us in.

" . . .I'm starting to get a little worried," she said. "Things seem to be happening more and more lately."

"What sorts of things?"

"Strange noises. Sometimes, at night, I can hear strange, scratching sounds. It's really frightening."

"Is it just the scratching sounds?"

"Usually, but sometimes it's accompanied by deep groaning and wailing sounds. I have no idea where the sound is originating from but it's definitely somewhere in the house. I don't know how to explain it. It scares me to death. There are nights I'll have myself

---

37 "Us": referring to Jay and Carla who both went with Walker on this particular investigation. For what reason, we do not know. We only know that they all went together. We also know that this is the first time the team had worked together since their breakthrough discovery at the Detmeyer building back in 1981; the investigation that started the ball rolling and earned the department the chance to prove itself to the world. Maybe they were hoping for that next big breakthrough.

convinced that whatever is behind the walls is going to get me. I'll admit that there have been nights when I have gone to bed with the covers over my head. I'm ashamed to admit it but that's how scared I am some nights. You know?" The inquisition was more for reassurance than contemplation.

"Yes, Ms. McPherson, I do. The rational mind has a funny way of deducing on its own what is and what is not reality. Even if you think you don't believe in ghosts or poltergeists, or whatnot, your mind can convince itself that the unreal is actually real. It's what I like to refer to as rational paralysis. You cannot explain what is going on, so, rather than succumb to the conclusion that insanity is the only healthy answer, your rational mind shuts down, paralyzes itself so it doesn't have to confront that horrible truth. So, now you're stuck in a physical body that is paralyzed with fear because the logical mind has shut down and no rational answer can be deduced."

"Exactly. And that's rational paralysis?"

"Well, that's just a term I use. I doubt you'll find it in the DSM or any medical textbooks."

She smiled, slowly warming up to us.

"Ms. McPherson, I'd like to ask you a few questions if you don't mind."

"Please, call me Jen. And you can ask anything you'd like."

I was quite taken by her beauty. There was a quiet naivete in her look as she bit down on her lip in confused curiosity. The way her hair looked beautiful even though it hadn't been washed yet and was only up in a ponytail. Her big, brown eyes asked so many questions she couldn't possibly comprehend. She is the most beautiful woman I've ever met. She isn't model gorgeous but she's gorgeous. I don't know how to explain it any other way.

"Jen, is there any history of mental illness in your family?"

"My cousin on my mother's side was diagnosed with Bipolar disorder."

"Was she manic?"

"Yes."

"Was her mother ever diagnosed?"

"I don't think so, why?"

"Depression at a manic level is greatly increased when there is a direct genetic link. If the mother has it, the daughter is more likely to have it, so on and so forth. Does your cousin have any children?"

"A little boy."

"Has he been diagnosed?"

"Well, he's only six."

"Sometimes you'd be surprised to learn that doesn't always matter. There have been documented occasions where children as young as four have expressed manic-depressive behavior. There's nothing more sad than a four-year-old talking about suicide. Those are the lifers, too. They rarely make it back to reality and most cases end with teen suicide. It's really quite tragic."

"Well, I'll tell her. She ought to have him checked."

"It's not guaranteed that he'll have any symptoms but you can't be too careful. Especially with children."

She nodded in agreement.

"I'm going to shift gears here, Jen: are you currently taking any medications for cold, flu, diabetes, viral infections or anything of such nature?"

"No."

"Do you notice the noises at one particular time more then any other time?"

"Actually, I do. I tend to notice them more at night."

"Do you every notice them during the day?"

"I'm usually not home much during the day so I don't really know what goes on when I'm away."

"Have you ever noticed items have been moved around or misplaced that you don't remember misplacing?"

"I tend to be a little forgetful about where I put things. I couldn't answer that with any degree of certainty."

"Do you have any pets, Jen?"

"No."

"Do you have a roommate?"

"No."

Good.

"Just you?"

She nodded.

Great.

"How long have you been hearing these noises?"

"Well, I moved in about three months ago. I never noticed anything while I was here looking around but the first night I moved in, I was unpacking and heard the groaning noise. I was so scared that I ran out of the house and stayed the night at my mother's place. The next night, I returned with Mom and we unpacked together. We both heard the noises but neither of us could explain what it was. I've almost gotten used to it but it seems to be happening more and more. Every night, now. I can't explain it. Rational paralysis, I guess."

"Jen, my team and I are going to run a few tests to determine whether or not any paranormal activity is evident here, okay?"

She nodded.

We broke out the equipment and scoured every inch of the house. We didn't find a damn thing. There were no abnormal density readings and no shift in the electro-magnetic field, either. So, what's going on?

"Jay, are we overlooking the obvious here?"

"We just might be."

I went into the living room where Jen was sitting. "Jen, does this building have a basement?"

"Yeah, let me show you."

We climbed down into the basement, which was more like a giant tomb or catacomb. There was a slate wall and a concrete slab for a floor; it didn't even cover the length of the floor. Where there was no sub-flooring there was loose dirt.

A veined network of conduit piping snaked its way from the ground up the side of the cellar wall and disappeared into a hole in the underside of the floor. "These must be the plumbing pipes here," I told Jay. The pipes seemed relatively new compared to the age of the house. "You think there's air in the pipes?"

"Certainly would explain a lot. One down, one to go. What's the scratching noise?"

"I think I may have an idea."

I asked Jen to show us her pantry; she seemed a little embarrassed but reluctantly led the way into a small room off the kitchen.

She had no reason to be hesitant or embarrassed. She seemed to eat pretty healthy foods: Quaker oats, some honey, some of that Slim-fast crap and a cadre of various pastas.

We found what we were looking for on the top shelf in the upper, right-hand corner; the calling card of a creature that scares me even more than ghosts: mice.

We sat Jen down in the living room and prepared her for the news.

She actually looked quite nervous.

"It's not as bad as you think. The scratching you hear at night is mice. The reason you hear them mostly at night is because mice are nocturnal; meaning they come out at night and scavenge. It's also the safest time for them because you are lying in bed and do not represent a threat to them."

"That's it?"

"That's it."

"What about the groaning?"

"We think probably you have air in your plumbing pipes. It's not uncommon in houses this old. The piping looks like it could be new which would increase the likelihood of there being air and the unfinished basement could be the cause of it; drafts are very common with unfinished basements."

"How do I fix it?"

"I'd suggest you run your water for about a half hour. That should get rid of any air bubbles. If the problems persist, you might want to call a plumber. If that doesn't work, give us another call because that means we've missed something we shouldn't have. But, I don't think you'll have to make that call."

"How embarrassing. I called you guys down here for mice and gastro-intestinal plumbing?" She let out a nervous chuckle.

"Nothing to be embarrassed about. It's that rational paralysis I was telling you about. Usually, the answers are so blatantly obvious that we overlook them for the more complicated, complex answers because they sound better and, somehow, seem more logical and rational. Don't worry about it. I'd suggest you get a cat or bait traps. That might take care of you mouse problems. It's up to you."

"Thank you, so much. I really appreciate you coming down. And, again, I am sorry to have wasted your time."

"Not at all, Jen. It was our pleasure."

My pleasure, indeed.

We left the apartment and returned to the university. I haven't been able to get her out of my mind. Her face is embedded on the back of my eyelids so every time I close them I see her. She's infectious. I can feel her taking over my immune system and systematically taking over every major organ in my body until she reaches my brain. Then . . .it's all over for poor, old Hayden.

I should call her. But what the hell am I going to say? "Hi, it's me. I think I love you. Will you go out with me?" That's so damned archaic and childish. I know I'll be letting something special slip away if I don't seize this opportunity. There's only one thing that bothers me: she never said, "I don't have a boyfriend." What had she said? "I live alone" or "by myself?" Something like that. Never, "I don't have a boyfriend, Hay, would you like to go out with me sometime?" There's really only one way to find out what is not known but this goddamned rational paralysis is starting to get to me, too. It's funny. I can encounter anything that terrifies the reasonable minds of this world but when it comes to things the reasonable mind scoffs at, I turn tail and run, urine dripping down my legs. Why is this so damned difficult?

I'll call. That's all there is to it. I don't have any choice. But it's so late. I can't call up now and profess my love for her. What if she's sleeping? She'll think I'm an inconvenience or bothersome. But what might happen if I wait? It's shit like this that can drive a man insane. What's the right thing to do? Sometimes that's the toughest query of all. Sometimes you can't figure out what the right choice is. Wars are fought, children die, lovers break up and all along that one question constantly remains unanswered: what is the right thing to do?

March 17, 11:30

My heart is still racing. It feels like it's going to burst through my rib cage. I did it. I called her.

"Ms. McPherson? Jen? I need to ask you a few follow up questions. Would that be all right?"

"Oh, sure. Even though I am still a little embarrassed."

"Don't be. It was a perfectly logical mistake. Don't ever question your own judgment. If you can't trust yourself, than who can you trust?"

"True."

"Do you know how old the house is?"

"No."

"Do you have any idea who rented the apartment before you?"

"No, why?"

"Well, I was going to do a background check to see if there might have been any foul play or something like that. Our findings were negative and we're quite certain our data was accurate. We just want to be absolutely certain."

"Okay."

"This may sound a little strange, but do you currently have a significant other?"

"No."

Great!

"Uh, the reason I'm calling, that is, the real reason I'm calling, is that I was wondering– and you're under no obligation at all, but I thought it might be fun if we could have dinner Friday night."

A long pause. At first, I thought she had hung up on me but there was no dial tone rejecting me.

"Jen?"

"Uh, sure. That might be fun. What time?"

"Seven?"

"I'll be ready."

GREAT!

March 19, 5:00 pm

I've been in situations where nerves have played an important factor, and being able to control those nerves has been even more important, but for some reason, tonight, I cannot contain myself. I am so nervous. I haven't been on a date in a long time. I don't even know if I remember how to do it. I guess you can't forget, really. It's like that riding a bike thing; once you learn, you never forget. I just hope I don't blow it. My stomach feels like it's about to explode in a vomitous eruption and my knees feel rubbery and weak. What a wimp, huh? I can challenge the realm of the paranormal and not give it a second thought but I can't take an attractive lady out to dinner. I don't want to bore her with idle chitchat, but I don't want to seem over-anxious, either. I'll probably throw out a few practice questions, see if I can get a bite, if she seems interested, great. If not, I'm in deep shit.

March 19, 10:45 pm

The date went great. She's everything I had hoped she would be. She's great. We went to Le Chateau Devereaux[38] I can't imagine spending an evening with anyone more perfect than Jen.

---

[38] Le Chateau Devereaux is a French restaurant about three blocks away from the campus. The restaurant is world-renowned for its French cuisine and has won ten awards for its chocolate-upside-down-coconut-cream cake; a multi-layered chocolate cake sinfully filled with a unique coconut cream filling. For years, I have tried to get Chef Louis Maten to divulge his secret but, loyal to his cause, he will not. Walker used his credit card to pay the bill. We had to dig through a massive pile of receipts and bills; almost a decades worth, to find what we were looking for. It took six men almost three days, working in three shifts around the clock to find the bill. However, with much effort, in a cause very worthy of fighting for, we were able to find the receipt. We know that Walker and Jen left the restaurant at 8:45 pm. Their bill came to $85.97 plus gratuity. The contents of the meal included two Caesar salads and warm garlic bread sprinkled with mozzarella cheese as an appetizer as well as shrimp cocktail, the shrimp were al a Carte, of course. For the main dish, one of the two had Chicken Cordon Bleu, a tender filet of boneless chicken breast lined with a slice of baked ham and Swiss cheese. The filet is cooked in a burgundy cream sauce and served on long-grain rice to accentuate the taste of the chicken. The other member of the party had La Belle Poulet, which literally translates to "the pretty chicken." Again, this is a whole, breast filet, cooked in a burgundy sauce and served over a plate of vegetables. Of course, for dessert, both Walker and Jen had the world famous chocolate upside-down coconut cream cake. What's a trip to Le Chateau Devereaux without at least trying that delicious cake. Now, I don't know about you, but that usually makes me pretty hungry. I only

We don't really have all that much in common but we have so much in common. I can't explain it. She's a second-year undergrad at the university studying to become a social welfare worker and I'm a staff member at the university who deals specifically with the realm of the paranormal. You want to talk about two worlds which will never collide. One field deals with helping reform living conditions for the socially indigent and one field deals with helping to define living standards for the deceased. What a paradox. I don't care, though. I think that will be our strength. We had so much fun. I think she could listen for hours about my run-ins with the paranormal. Her voice is so pretty, I could listen to her talk about grass clippings for days, just to hear her voice. I can't remember the last time I had so much fun. Probably the last time I was home. When was that, Thanksgiving? Did I make it home for Christmas? No, I was at that convention then got held over in Houston, relayed to Phoenix. Did I even call and wish them a Merry Christmas? I can't remember. Anyway, Jen's great. I look forward to many pleasant evenings in her company. I hope I'm not getting ahead of myself. I know she had a good time. She said she did, anyway. I'll wait for her to call, then I'll know for sure.

---

bring up the ingredients and the fine detail of the composition of the meals because Walker was never known for his great taste in fine cuisine or his insight into foreign culture. I believe, although he never really said this was the reason, that he really wanted to impress Jen. We don't really get to see this side of Walker much before this point in the diaries. Usually, we see the very serious businessman who is only here to do a job and maybe discover a bit of truth in the process. Now, we get to see a side of Walker that is very rare: uncomfortably vulnerable, obviously way out of his league and, for the first time in his life, genuinely worried about how he will be perceived. We've seen him worry about work and his family but never has he gone to such lengths to impress anybody. I think this is very important because it shows his innate vulnerability to this woman who all of a sudden, has become a tremendous focal point in his life. How he knew, this early in the relationship, if you can even call it that at this point, that Jen was the one that he wanted to grow old with is beyond comprehension. He just knew. Deep down, something told him not to screw this one up. And we can see that portrayed in his behavior regarding Jennifer McPherson.

March 20, 8:45 pm

She called. I think I'm in. She told me how much fun she had and hoped that we could do it again sometime. DON'T SCREW THIS ONE UP!![39]

March 23, 10:00 pm

Got together with Jen again. I can't explain how I feel when I'm with her. I don't mind taking the time to figure it out, though. I can see myself spending the rest of my life with her.

March 28, 10:45 pm

Jen has agreed to meet my parents. We're taking off tomorrow and flying to Maine. We should be there by tomorrow night. I'm a little nervous. I'm not sure how they will react to Jen. If they have any of the same thoughts and insights that I do, they will realize in a few moments what only took me a second to realize: this woman is perfect. Not perfect by Webster's definition; there are no perfect people. Nobody should be searching for the perfect person. If they are, they should give up the hunt now; it's as futile as it is impossible.

---

[39] The block print was done by Walker, not the editor, for emphasis. Walker even added a second exclamation mark. Again, I believe this shows Walker's devotion to making a relationship with this girl work. We're beginning to see an almost childlike and giddy behavior from Walker. You almost want to see if you can pass a note for him during study hall. He is noticeably excited about the prospect of a lasting relationship. It's almost "cute", to use a ludicrous, asinine word, to see a man of Walker's stature and, almost glorified persona as a paranormal investigator, become a child again. It's a natural regression to instinct and behavior. I often wonder if Walker, once a behavioral psychologist, ever cued in to the fact that he was applying techniques he knew to be unhealthy psychologically in gaining the attention of this woman. In the long run, the techniques are as insignificant as they are unimportant. For the time being he has thrown caution to the wind, prudence to the lions and wariness to the dogs. And, if his recklessness in winning the heart of his love had in some way enlightened his own heart to new emotions and new feelings, than we should all be so fortunate.

The perfect person doesn't exist. The real secret lies in trying to find the one person who's perfect for you. That's the trick. Stop looking for a figment of your imagination. She's not out there. I firmly believe that there is someone out there, a perfect match, for everybody. Jen is that person for me. She's my light against the dark, my shelter from the wind, my air when I can't breathe, my eyes when I can't see. She's perfect for me. I know it.

But how is my family going to react? I haven't been home since November. They're going to be very upset. I called and told them I was coming. They seemed very excited. They can't wait to see me. I haven't told them about Jen, yet. I want her to be a surprise. If things go awry, I can use her as backup. Sounds like I'm using her as leverage. That's not what I really meant. I want my family to be happy about my homecoming but I also want them to be happy about my new passion in life.

March 29, 6:45 pm

Taxied into BIA[40] about ten minutes ago.[41] Jen has gone to the restroom and nobody has come to pick us up yet. Nothing much to say now, just passing time. I guess I could reiterate my tremendous apprehension about this particular homecoming. I'll know immediately whether or not they like Jen. They'll have that look in their eyes and that weird smirk on their faces. I hope to see both of them. Here they come. God help me.

March 29, 10:45 pm

Jen was still in the bathroom when my folks arrived to pick us up. I actually had to stall them. They're always in such a rush.

"Let's go," they both said to me.

"Just a second. I'm waiting for another piece of luggage to arrive." An out-and-out lie, of course. But what could I do?

---

[40] Bangor International Airport.
[41] Airport records and receipts verify that Walker purchased two tickets for flight 358 on Delta Airline from LAX to BIA on March 28, 1982.

They agreed to wait. I didn't know how long I could stall them there, though. Luckily, Jen didn't take too much longer in the restroom. She walked in our direction, having no idea what my parents looked like, let alone that they were both standing right beside me.

"Here she comes," I told my parents.

They both looked quite confused.

"Mom, Dad, this is Jennifer McPherson."

"Hello," they both said.

"Hi. Please, call me Jen."

"Hello, Jen," my father said.

"How are you?" my mother asked.

"I'm fine, thank you."

"I'm fine, too," I interjected.

As we stepped out of the airport, I could tell that Jen was cold. I took my coat off and placed it over her shoulders.

"First time in Maine?"

"Yes," she said through chattering teeth.

"You picked a horrible month. It never stops snowing. They say March is supposed to come in like a lion and go out like a lamb; we never see that lamb. We got a foot-and-a-half of snow the other day. You're poor father's still trying to shovel the driveway."

"I'll help when we get home."

"You bet your ass, you will." Dad was now finding humor to be appropriate. It seemed to work. We all shared a laugh and headed for my parent's car. They hadn't said anything yet, but I could tell immediately that they liked her. She has that quality. You just want to pick her up and cuddle her.

When we got home, Mom pulled me aside and said, "She's gorgeous. Nice job." Like I picked her out of a panel of top models, or something. I think I even caught my father doing a double-take. But I'm not worried about my old man stealing my lady.

I'm up here now because I don't want to argue with my parents. They have already started in with the why-don't-you-call-questions. I wish I could tell them how busy I am but I know that's just an excuse. There's no reason for why I haven't called except that I haven't thought about it. I'm not proud of that excuse but that's what it is and it's all it is. I'll do better about staying in touch. I really want to.

The evening was a success and the casual pleasantries were indeed that: pleasant. We sat down to dinner at around 7:30. Again, Mom had gone all out with her cooking. She made us a dish that I always loved growing up. I don't even know what it's called. However, it wasn't long before the nosy-parent syndrome kicked into high gear and the questions started.

"So, how did you two meet?" my mother asked.

"Mom, come on. Not the questions." Of course, the effort was futile. I knew it, but I had to try to maintain some sense of burden which insisted her questions were as inappropriate as they were unimportant. But, moms win every time.

"What?" she said throwing her arms in the air like some child who has been caught in the cookie dish just before dinner. "I can't ask questions about my own son? I've got to find out how you're doing through someone because you certainly never call."

The surprise kidney shot, the guilt trip you should see coming from a mile down the road, once again sneaks up from behind and sucker punches you.

"Point taken. It's just a little embarrassing, that's all."

"It was cute," Jen chimed in.

"You don't understand, Jen," I said, "she's sucking you in." I had to smile. My mother had caught her hook, line and sinker, and was quickly reeling her in. "You don't know what you're getting yourself into."

"Stay out of this, Hay," Mom said. Now, I am completely out of the loop. I have absolutely no authority over any event that may transpire in the next several minutes. A tunnel has been formed between Jen and my mother that is impenetrable. Everything Mom wants to know will somehow, even unwillingly, be sucked out of Jen's brain and passed down that tunnel.

"I made a bogus call to the university," Jen began, "because I was hearing strange noises. I thought perhaps it might be a ghost. I remembered seeing a flyer on one of the telephone poles about a division at the university which conducted paranormal investigations for free. I figured it couldn't hurt to check."

"And in walks my boy, radiant and handsome."

"Dad, can't you do something?"

"Don't look at me. If there's one thing I've learned over the years I've been married to your mother, it's to never interrupt her little question and answer sessions." He smiled. "You're on your own, son."

"Then what happened?" Mom asked.

"Well, it turned out that my ghost was nothing more than air in the pipes and a herd of the loudest mice I've ever encountered." She laughed. "I was so embarrassed."

"That's precious."

"Anyway, I was so embarrassed I couldn't even look them in the face when they left."

"So when did he ask you out?"

"Mom, you asked her to tell it. Let her."

"She is telling it. Did he even get to the door?"

"Actually, he made it all the way back to the university. He called me later that night. He was trying to be so suave," she smiled and poked at me in a jeering manner. "He was using this follow-up telephone survey as a guise to milk some personal information out of me." She laughed again. "What was it you said? 'I was wondering if maybe I could . . .' No, it was, 'I was wondering and you're under no obligation at all but I thought it would be nice if we could go to dinner sometime.' I could tell he was oozing with nervous anticipation so I made him wait a minute before I answered. You know, to sort of build that feeling of insecurity and then, of course, I told him that I would love to join him for dinner."

"Where did you go?"

"Dad, you're supposed to be helping me."

"Stay out of this, Hay. Where did you go?"

Jen laughed hysterically.

"How is that relevant?" I asked.

"We went to a nice French restaurant called Le Chateau Devereaux."

"Hay, you surprise me. I figured he would have taken you to Burger King or something."

"Hey! That's a little below the belt, don't you think?"

67

"I'm just teasing."

"Well, try to keep the gloves up, okay?"

As unfortunate as it may seem, the festivities at my expense continued for the next hour or so. The overall atmosphere remained cordial and everyone was having such a good time so the jokes directed toward me were forgiven, due to the general gaiety of the evening's events.

After dinner, I had to beg Mom not to show Jen the baby pictures. It took some real finessing and mind wresting to persuade her but finally, she submitted to my plea.

Shortly after dinner, my parents retired to the bedroom for the evening. I figured that might be the best time to show Jen around the house. That way, I would be able to show her the pictures that were the most appropriate. The baby pictures, though they shouldn't be, always seem to be a point of embarrassment. I'll never understand that: how can a picture of the person you once were, but are not anymore, remain a sensitive point in the minds of those who are looking back at a memory of their former self? Maybe it's because we don't like to look back. It's just easier to keep moving forward, head down, into the future, never looking back, never stopping to access the paths we have traveled and crossroads we've pondered along the way. It's difficult to look back at the helplessness of youth; the days when we needed someone to help us eat, change our clothes, bathe us. To come so far in life, to be reminded of our feeble, vulnerable existence is a shock. So it's easier to not look back. Why shouldn't it be? But for some reason, I desire to show these pictures of the inept child I once was to the woman who was standing beside me. I wanted her to know that same scared, incapable child that was once inside of me, still dwells deep inside of me. Somewhere, anyway. Perhaps only in fleeting thoughts or disregarded memories, but he's in there, reliving the past and waiting for someone he can relate the tales of childhood to.

I think that someone is Jen.

"I remember," I said picking up a photograph from the mantel, "when this was taken." The picture was faded, black and white, and blurry. "This was always one of my favorites." The picture was a close-up shot of four smiling faces. "The one on the left is John. In the back there is Steve. The goofy one in the center is me. Look at that haircut."

"Who's the little one?"

"That's Marcy."

"Why is this one your favorite?"

"Believe it or not, it's the only picture that has any of the children together in it. It's the closest we come to being connected." I smiled thinking about childhood memories that were flooding my mind. All those events that took place that I had tucked away; that I thought were buried, were all coming back. "I'm glad you're here, Jen." I don't know why I said it. It just came out. I didn't even have time to think about how corny or bizarre it might sound; I just blurted it out.

"Me, too."

Reassurance. A long awkward moment of silence passed. Neither of us knew quite what to say. I grabbed another picture from the mantel, trying to break the silence.

"This is a better picture of Steven, newer anyway. This was his high school picture." The picture was a typical hurry-up-there-are-four-hundred-kids-behind-you-photograph. He had obviously not been ready for the shot to be taken: he was looking to the left of the cameraman with his head lightly cocked to the right. His smile was crooked revealing only half his teeth in this snarled, almost evil glance. "My mother thought this one was so funny she had it framed. She wanted to have it copied and sent out as Christmas cards but Steve said he'd disown her if she did. You wouldn't even recognize him now."

"What's he look like now?"

"The last time I saw him, he looked like a lumberjack. He's sprouted this bushy, gnarling beard, which somehow doesn't look bad on him, and he dresses mostly in flannel shirts and Dickies pants. He lives out in the sticks somewhere so he fits right in. Loves it out there."

I showed her a picture of Marcy and one of Kim, both similar to the school picture of Steve accept, of course, the girls were ready for their pictures to be taken.

I yawned widely. "What do you say we retire for the evening?"

"That's a good idea."

I'm watching her sleep and she looks like an angel. She's beautiful.

March 31, 8:00 am

We're heading out today. We couldn't stay for too long. Our agendas require us to stay relatively close to campus. I need to get back and Jen has a test and a term paper due on Wednesday.[42]

"Come back after the next storm. I could use your back to shovel us out again," my father said. My mother laughed out loud. I love her laugh. More of a chuckle/cackle really. She sends me into stitches every time.

"I will."

"It was very nice to meet you, Jen. Come back anytime. You don't even need to have Hay with you. Just come when you feel like it."

"Thank you very much. Both of you. I had a wonderful time. I enjoyed meeting you both."

"Have a safe flight."

"We will, Dad."

"And if you happen to snag a few extra bags of those airline peanuts, send them back to me." He laughed.

"Carl, you know you can't have those things. They're bad for your cholesterol."

"Your mother is such a cholesterol watcher. It's unbearable."

"See you later, Dad. Love you, Mom."

---

[42] See "Cause and Effect of Violent Behavior in Minority Youth" in *Sociology Weekly* v. 3479 May 1982 or *Youth Manifesto* v. 109 June, 1982. This article was first drafted by McPherson for her SOC240 class; the term paper mentioned in the diary. Jen's professor, Mrs. Kathy Hall, convinced Jen to alter some of the format and submit the paper as an article to the National Review Board. Obviously, they accepted her submission. The article gained national notoriety when it was published by the SAA, Sociological Association of America, in the fall of 1982. Jen also gained national attention when her article won the prestigious Sociological Review Board's Article of the Year Award in December of 1982.

"We love you to, hon."

"I'll probably be back when the semester is over. I'll bring Jen with me."

"You be sure to do that. We like her. Keep him in line, Jen, will you? And make sure he calls."

"I'll try. He's quite stubborn."

"He gets that from his father, you know," she whispered into Jen's ear. Dad gave her is "look of death" and she burst out into that chuckle/cackle that always makes me smile.

April 1, 12:00 pm

Everything went so well with my parents. Jen really had a good time. I think my parents really liked her, too. I don't know. Everything's going so well. The candle is burning bright and was ignited quickly. I hope it is not extinguished just as quickly. Back to work tomorrow. Dean has me set up for an appointment with Mr. Steven Crane, head doctor at Wilford J. Magnus Institution. It seems like every institution has some haunted past, some haunted story just waiting to break out. So much tragedy must take place behind those walls, behind closed doors with nothing to quiet you but the night, and maybe a few hundred Valium and shock treatment. I should probably be more sympathetic. I just can't imagine being insane. I can't imagine having my own thoughts conspiring against me; to know that what I am thinking is so outrageously misguided and outlandish that no one else believes me.

It would be pretty lonely being the only person to believe the words that are coming out of my mouth. I think that the realm of the paranormal is much like the realm of insanity: people are afraid of it simply because they do not understand it. So what happens when the realm of the paranormal and the realm of insanity collide? That prospect scares the hell out of me. I will go to the institution tomorrow Hayden Walker, paranormal investigator. I will be as convincing as possible. I will present an air of professional authority and do my best not to show even a modicum of trepidation. But deep down, I will be as scared as a child lost in the woods on a stormy night. I know it. And it's that knowing that can cause even the slightest inkling of doubt, and doubt will splinter even the strongest of minds. I can't let that happen. Things must revolve, progress, and continue. As sure as day will forfeit its reins to night, as sure as life relinquishes its grip to death, rational, cognitive thought will continually dissolve away to fear. And that's when the sane mind goes insane; when insanity becomes the majority and sanity becomes the minority. We'd all be locked away in padded rooms wondering what happened to us. These are the thoughts that can drive a man insane. So what am I to expect when I confront a realm of the paranormal I have not yet dealt with? What do the two realms share in common? Do they share anything?

It makes you question your own invincibility. We all have this protective armor we are engulfed in; or at least we think we do. We believe in one, immutable, universal truth: nothing's going to happen to me. When the real truth is as obvious and evident as the air we breathe; we believe that nothing is going to hurt us, to happen to us, even, God forbid, KILL us; but we're wrong. I know that. I'd have a hard time convincing a nation of that thought. Hell, I can't even convince them that the realm of the paranormal exists. How can I convince them that they are going to die someday when they don't want to believe me?

That answer is simple: I can't.

So I won't.

I'll keep doing what I'm doing and saying what I'm saying and I'll be one of the few who believes the words I am speaking.

April 2, 8:00 pm

I just don't understand what the hell happened today. I've been doing this for almost two years now and I've never seen anything like that. I mean, you see that kind of shit in the movies all the time and never give it a second thought. I didn't think stuff like that really happened. That was the scariest, craziest experience of my life and, hopefully, I will never again experience anything so awful. Jay's dead. I don't know exactly what happened to him out there today.[43] All I know is that I hope I never have an investigation go so awry again ever. I remember Rick[44] saying that if there was enough negative potential and kinetic energy that it would be possible for spirits in other realms of existence to make contact with us. But, I never thought it would be like that. Jesus Christ, he was only 23. I know it wasn't my fault but I feel like it was. I could have done something. But what? This changes everything. This experience gives us enough conclusive data to prove that two different realms of existence can inhabit the same area in a symbion or hostile relationship. And that changes everything. Services for Jay will be held tomorrow. I should go but I don't think I can bear the guilt. He was so damn young. I'm beginning to question whether or not I can ever go back into the field after this. It's a goddamn tragedy.[45]

---

[43] Coroner's report indicates that Jay Munson, then only 23, died due to complete heart failure. With no previous record of heart complications, it seems unlikely that a man as young as Jay, and as relatively healthy as Jay, would even have heart problems.

[44] Rick Deeves, psychic investigator at Katherine's Bed and Breakfast.

[45] At first, this particular entry seemed incredibly vague. We knew that Jay Munson had died of a massive coronary failure as indicated by his death certificate, but what we didn't know was how. As I said before, for anyone that young and healthy to die from heart failure is almost impossible. The heart would have to be under incredible strain. Now, what strain could have been so powerful and overbearing that it could seize the heart of a 23 year old man? We had no idea. After several meetings by phone and in person, I convinced a member of the Archives Department at the university to look for a video that may have been shot by Walker on April 2, 1982. I was hoping there might be something in the tape that would reveal some form of information that could help us understand what happened that day. One tape was found. I convinced the man to let me watch it. What I saw turned my stomach. I couldn't believe what I was seeing. I have seen many hoaxes in my life but I know this was not a hoax. Why would Walker, a paranormal investigator, falsely submit evidence to the department when so much rested on the amount of indisputable evidence submitted? Why would he take that chance? The video was perhaps the most disturbing twenty minutes of film I have ever seen. What I'd like to do, even though the video is not a diary entry, though it does bear some pertinence, is to detail for you what was displayed on the screen when I sat down to watch the film. This will give you a chance to see the man at work and the horrifying reality that took place that day.

73

The camera blinks to life revealing a rather large office. The camera is focused on a man who is rather tall, maybe 6'3". He has short brown hair, parted on the right and combed to the left. He is very clean shaven and wearing a suit, proudly displaying himself before the camera.

"I'm Hayden Walker," he announces.

"I'm Carla Leveque." The young lady beside him is fairly short and unattractive. She has curly, dark hair that hangs down over her shoulders. She is wearing dark-framed, thick-rimmed glasses that make her eyes look like giant black marbles. She has a goofy smile that reveals buckteeth and sharp incisors.

"And I'm Jay. Jay Munson." Jay, like Walker, is tall. He has an olive complexion and short, dark hair. He is well built though he is obviously not a body builder.

"We're here to investigate the bizarre happenings that have been documented at this institution. Before we begin, we're going to record a brief history of the Wilford J. Magnus Institute for the Criminally Insane from its current head resident, Mr. Steven Crane. Mr. Crane, can you describe the history of this institute and offer a few comments on what you or your staff members have seen over the years?"

The camera focuses on a man sitting behind a desk. He is rather old; maybe 68 and he has a bushy mustache. His stare is vacant and distant as he begins his speech. "The Wilford J. Magnus Institute for the Criminally Insane was named for its architect and first head resident. Magnus was a rich doctor from Germany who came to this country in the late 1800s. He designed the plans himself and funded the construction. When the building was finished in 1886, Magnus resided as chief doctor here. For years, Magnus' unorthodox techniques were questioned. However, nobody could prove that he was in to foul play. He was never recorded doing anything unethical to his patients. However, for years, the basement has been a source of discomfort for all my staff. I have been chief resident here since 1978 and I have witnessed some very bizarre, unexplainable events down in that level of the building. I assume, as so many others, that Magnus had some sort of private office down there where he conducted all sorts of experiments. The basement is the only place strange things have ever happened. We've never seen anything in any other parts of the building, which suggests that there is an extreme amount of paranormal activity on that floor. How much and how to go about stopping it is why we called you. What can you do for us?"

The camera focuses back on Walker. "We'll run some tests, see what we can find. After we get the results, we'll come talk to you and let you know what's going on."

"Fine by me. I wish you the best of luck."

For a brief moment, the camera cuts to black then blinks back to life. When the images on the screen are restored, Walker is descending a large staircase. Carla is behind him and we have to assume that Jay is running the camera.

"You may want to turn the light on, Jay; it's dark down here." Instantly, a bright light illuminates the stairwell; it seems to go on forever. Even with the light on, the stairs go past the light and disappear into the darkness again.

"We're getting our exercise today," Jay says from behind the camera.

Carla and Walker laugh.

The staircase ends and the camera pans around the basement. It's enormous. It too seems to swallow the light of the camera. We can see approximately twenty feet before the dark drops down like a curtain, blinding us.

The three investigators wander around the basement level for a few moments closely examining the area. The basement is obviously used only for storage and supplies. Boxes and shelves litter the area. It is not unkempt, like you would expect; it's rather the opposite. Boxes are clearly marked and stacked neatly in piles of four or five. None of the boxes seem to go much above head-level. The shelves are immaculate; again, everything is clearly marked and placed neatly, not haphazardly strewn about the place. Someone must spend a great deal of time down here for things to be in such neat order, or, nobody comes down here at all and it remains in the same order it was left in years ago. Walker approaches a shelf and runs his finger across it. He holds his finger up to the light. "Dusty," he says. "Nobody's been down here for a long time." Which answers our question.

The three continue their initial tour. Jay follows behind a good ten feet so Walker and Carla are both in the frame of the shot.

BANG! The camera shakes violently and turns at a dizzying pace. It looks inquisitively back and forth into the darkness searching for the root of the noise. "What was that?" Jay whispers.

"I don't know. Hello?" Walker yells. "Is anybody there?"

No response.

"Come on," Walker insists, heading back toward the direction the noise originated from.

"I'm not sure this is a good idea."

"Relax, Jay. Nothing's going to hurt us."

The camera picks up pace and doesn't stay nearly as far back as it has. You can barely make out Carla's hair to the right of the camera, which means Jay is very close to her. They continue forward, lighting the darkness as they progress.

They walk all the way to the back end of the basement.

Nothing.

They turn and head back. Again, Jay stands farther back allowing the frame to include both Carla and Walker. Jay seems to be re-threading a stitch of courage through his invisible sheath of fear. Carla and Hayden are both holding instruments out in front of them and panning them side to side.

"You getting anything?"

"No," Carla says.

"Me, neither."

With disappointment etched on their faces, they reach the other end of the basement.

"Did you get anything?"

Carla shakes her head.

The camera again jerks quickly around as a strange scratching noise echoes through the basement.

"What the hell is that?" Jay yells.

No reaction from Carla or Walker.

The scratching noise intensifies, a cacophonous sound. Jay yells something but it cannot be distinguished above the ear-splintering sound of the noise. The camera twirls around violently several times. Jay breathes heavily. Again, he yells but cannot be understood. The quality of the picture begins to disintegrate; static fills the screen followed by strange colored lines that appear then disappear. The color of the picture is traded for a morbid black and white, for a brief moment, then returns to color. It looks like something you would see from a store security camera during an earthquake. Jay yells, "Something strange is happening to the camera." He takes it off his shoulder and we are almost plunged to the floor. He is holding the camera by the top handle and all we can see are the three investigators from the knees down as the camera continues its bizarre odyssey of confusion. We watch legs twirl around in circles trying to determine the origin of the sound.

SCRATCH! SCRATCH! SCRATCH!

Confusion.

Louder and faster: SCRATCHSCRATCHSCRATCH!

Finally, one long, loud SSSSSCCCCRRRRRRAAAAATTTTTTC CCCCHHH and it's over.

The film returns to normal, the noise is gone and all that remains are three very confused, scared paranormal investigators standing in a dank, dark basement wondering what the hell just happened. They stand there silently for a long time, catching their breath and quelling their undoubtedly rapid-beating hearts.

"What the fuck was that?" Jay yells.

"I don't know. The PDC went right off the scale. What about the EMIC?"

"Over a thousand, boss."

"Oh, we've done it now," Jay says.

"Relax, Jay."

Walker looks around, perplexed. He seems to notice something off in the darkness to his right. "Jay, shine the light over here." He points his finger at the far wall of the basement. The light focuses in on what appears to be a pile of boxes. Jay walks closer to them. As we get closer, we can just barely make out the frame of a door around the stack of boxes. Walker lifts the first box off the stack. When the light focuses, we see a little gold plaque that reads Wilford Magnus, Office.

"*Jesus Christ,*" *Jay whispers.*

Walker quickly removes the rest of the boxes then tugs at the doorknob.

It doesn't budge.

He pulls as hard as he can with the same result. He puts his right foot on the wall to the right of the door trying to gain leverage.

Nothing.

"*Jay, help me here.*" *Jay hands the camera to Carla; we are pulled awkwardly sideways as Carla grabs the camera from Jay and places it on her shoulder. Jay walks over to help Walker. Both men pull with all their might; straining and grunting as they tug. Finally, with one last heave, the wooden frame releases its grip and almost explodes outward as the door swings open violently. Quite unready are Jay and Walker as their momentum hurls them both backwards into somersaults coming to a halt at Carla's feet. The camera jeeringly peers down at them then returns its focus to the door, a flume of dust just beginning to settle in the doorway.*

Strangely enough, the camera, which usually lights about twenty feet in front of itself, seems to only be able to light up to the door. It's almost as if the light doesn't dare to cross the threshold. Even as Carla walks closer to the door, the light refuses to illuminate the darkness.

"*It's really dark in here,*" *Carla mutters.*

The camera turns around and shows Jay and Walker dusting themselves off. Carla laughs a little as both men look up at her, unamused.

"*What's in there?*"

"*I don't know. The light doesn't seem to penetrate the darkness. It's real weird.*"

"*Let's have a look.*"

"*Hay, I'm not sure about this. I've got a real bad feeling.*"

"*Don't worry. You take the camera, we'll do the investigating. Okay?*"

Jay grudgingly takes the camera from Carla; again, a weird transcending moment through space and time as the camera reverses its angle, finally resting upon Jay's shoulder. "Let's go," he says.

Walker and Carla stand nervously in the doorway. They pause for a moment, cross the threshold and disappear into the darkness. Jay follows quickly behind them. The room continues to have a strange effect on the light of the camera. Instead of lighting up twenty feet of the room, it seems to light only two or three feet. Just enough to see Walker and Carla walking around.

"Is the bulb going on that thing?"

"No, I don't know what's going on."

The three delve deeper into the darkness having no idea where they are or how deep the darkness really is. The light radiates a bizarre orange glow adding to the creepy ambiance of the moment. The light dims sporadically in a rhythmic pattern throughout the remainder of the film, almost pulsating to the beat of a heart.

Dim. light. Dim. light. Dim. light.

The camera focuses in on a large, oak table with a vinyl-upholstered pad lying across the top and tied to the legs. The foam stuffing has begun to pop out of a tear in the upper right-hand corner of the pad. The camera pans the length of the table and back again.

"What is this?"

"Looks like some kind of operating table. Look."

The camera tilts up to show a strange metallic contraption fastened to the ceiling and hanging just above the operating table. It's rather large and dome-shaped with a giant metal probe that is capable of coming through the top of the dome.

"Magnus must have used this for lobotomies."

"Lobotomies?"

"Yeah, it's a technique that was developed during Medieval times and pioneered by doctors during the late 1800s and early 1900s. They thought that by drilling into a skull and probing around certain areas of the brain, they could strike certain neurons responsible for causing mental problems and thereby cure the problem."

"Did it work?"

"Oh, it worked. To an extent. Except, instead of curing the problem, the patient was usually left brain-dead. Poking and prodding around in the brain can cause serious damage; enough so that it can be irreparable, leaving the patient brain-dead for life.

The practice was band decades ago but it was quite common in early psychology."

The camera seems to drift off to the right. Carla and Walker go with it; they almost have to because the camera is the only source of light. As we get closer to the wall, we see something very disturbing. There is a large piece of wood nailed into the wall; screwed into the wood are several different types of manacles. The closer we get to the manacles, the more we can make out tiny indentations in the wood. The camera gets extremely close, almost curious as to what it is looking at. There are literally hundreds of indentations on the wood and there are at least as many on the tile floor.

"What do you suppose these are?" Jay inquires.

"Fingernail grooves."

"What?" Jay asks, bewildered.

"It's where the patients were chained before the operations. They were clawing to get away. It's very common that you see these marks in institutions such as this. I mean, would you want a giant metal rod drilled through your head? Hell, no. You'd probably do everything in your power to get away. So, they tried to claw themselves away. Oh, yeah. There is a plethora of negative energy flowing through this room."

The camera focuses in on Walker.

"Do you notice a draft?" Jay asks.

"Yeah." A puff of air can be seen drifting away from Walker's mouth. The temperature has suddenly dropped below freezing. Carla and Walker rub their arms for warmth. Jay noticeably shivers as the camera shakes. We can hear his teeth chattering.

"What the hell is going on?"

"LEAVE!" Another cacophonous sound bellows through the room. A draft picks up in the room and loose leaflets of paper drift by quickly.

The camera again twirls violently around in circles.

"What was that?"

"How the hell should I know?"

"Hay, let's just get the fuck out of here. Please!"

"Just a minute. Who are you? What do you want?"

"LEAVE!"

"*Hay!*" *Jay shouts.*

"*Just a minute? Who are you?*"

"*Please, Hay!*"

"*In a minute! What do you want?*"

Jay screams wildly as he is pulled backwards. We see this as Carla and Walker, who are standing still, are swallowed by the darkness as the camera is pulled away from them.

"*Help, Hay!*"

"*Jesus. Jay!*"

We hear heavy footsteps as Carla and Walker begin to chase after Jay.

"*Something's got me!*"

We see Carla and Walker catch up to the fading light of the camera then disappear into the darkness as they try to keep up.

"*Please!*"

The camera moves smoothly backward; not like someone is running, in which case the camera would be bouncing up and down. In this case, the camera glides, moving absolutely smoothly backwards, like Jay is being dragged; he doesn't even seem to be on his feet.

"*Hay, Help me!*"

The camera, and Jay, exit the room. The door frame comes into the frame of the camera.

Carla and Walker almost make it to the door when it slams shut.

The camera falls from Jay's hands and drops to the floor landing on its side. It films the last moment of Jay Munson's life as he screams wildly.

"*Get this thing off me! Get it off!*" *We cannot see anything physically assaulting Jay but he is shaking violently like he is being punched in the stomach. He is trapped on his back. Something has him pinned to the floor.*

"*Please, stop!*"

"*Jay? Jay, buddy, we're coming!*" *Walker screams from the other side of the door. We can hear Walker and Carla banging and kicking the door, trying to break it open.*

Jay lunges up into a sitting position then is slammed back down onto the floor.

"Stop! Please!"

"Jay!"

"Oh, God, stop!" *He is literally crying at this point.*

"Jay!"

Jay frantically tries to ward off something we cannot see, something we are uncertain of whether or not even he can see. He waves his arms blindly in the air, trying to stop whatever assault is being inflicted.

"HELPMEHELPMEHELPME! Please, Hay, help me!"

Silence.

The struggle is over. Jay lies unflinching on the floor. His head is cocked toward the camera and he stares blankly into it, dead.

"Jay? Come on, buddy, answer me," *Walker yells.* "Jay! Goddamnit, answer me!"

We hear the door creak open and Carla scream.

They rush to their fallen comrade. Walker lifts Jay's head and upper torso into his arms. "Jesus, Jay. Wake up, buddy. Come back to us." *Walker checks Jay's pulmonary pulse.*

"Jesus Christ. He's dead."

We see Walker lay Jay down on the concrete floor of the basement and crawl toward the camera; hand outstretched, reaching for the power button.

The screen flickers to blackness.

April 3, 8:00 pm

I wish there was something I could do to bring Jay back. I wish in some ways I could take his place. I should have listened to him. He was so scared. But I couldn't leave. I couldn't. I had to know. And now, Jay's dead and I still have no idea what happened. I have no idea what ended the life of the nicest young man I know. I wondered what I was to expect when the realm of the paranormal and the realm of insanity collided. Now I know.

And I wish I didn't.

How did this get so screwed up? We were sent there on a routine investigation. This wasn't even supposed to be a spiritual cleansing. We were just supposed to determine whether or not supernatural activity was occurring. So why were the spirits so belligerent? Why were they so hostile? We meant them no harm.

So what happened?

We'll have to go back, of course. There's no way we can let this escalate. Who knows what else could happen. I talked to a priest today who is willing to try an exorcism. He said he would see what he could do.[46]

---

[46] Father Sinclair, a Catholic priest at St. John's Church on Watters St. was the exorcist Walker mentioned. We know from the sign-up sheet at the institution that Father Sinclair was at the institution on April 6th. After the exorcism, many of the staff members at the Wilford J. Magnus Institution for the Criminally Insane still complained of bizarre, supernatural happenings. We can assume that the exorcism was a failure. We can also assume that the institute claimed its second victim in just under a week. Father Sinclair left the institute on his own accord but was weakened. Later that night, he checked himself into a local hospital where he slipped into unconsciousness and later died. The coroner's report seemed to indicate heart failure as the cause of death. See Angela Pete's "Priest Dies of Heart Failure" in *Daily News* April 7, 1983 (sec. E, pages 8 and 9). Also, see James Killian's "What Do They Want?" in *Possessions and Hauntings* v. 981, May, 1983. This article deals specifically with the happenings and bizarre accounts detailed by staff members at the Wilfred J. Magnus Institute. It actually chronicles the "botched investigation of an amateur team of paranormal investigators headed by their fearless leader, Hayden Walker," in which, "one man was left dead and one man's image was left dead" (Pg. 42). The article was very unsympathetic to Walker and the turmoil and grief he was experiencing due to the untimely death of Jay Munson. I actually found the article to be very misleading and unintelligible. The author had absolutely no idea what had happened on that tragic day and had no business tramping on a man's emotions. His information was obviously fabricated by those few members of the staff who saw Walker that day. Dr. Crane refused to talk to the author, which, in my book, makes him the only decent human being at the institution. Killian was obviously hoping to gain attention by smearing the reputation of a good man, who was becoming a pillar of the community by this time, in hopes that the mere propriety of smearing such a well-known figure would gain him notoriety. I actually called Killian to confront him on the issue. I told him his article was bogus and that he should be ashamed for printing such rubbish in such a highly respectable magazine as *Possessions*

April 9, 10:00 am

I'm hoping Jen can cheer me up some. I'm so depressed I can't even smile. I need a better mood. I haven't left the house in three days. I just can't do it. Now that I know Father Sinclair has passed,

---

and Hauntings. The fabrication of truth is not only an assault on those who read the article but also on those who the article was about. When I finally reached Killian on the phone, I realized why he would write such garbage. He was a bitter, cantankerous old man. He still maintains that what he printed was as accurate as he could depict.

"Well, I hope you never have to save anyone's life in court," I said, "because the way you depict events is as poor as the way you write. You could have at least spell checked your article before submitting it. Do you have any idea how many spelling and grammatical errors were in there? It was ridiculous to the point of offensive."

"There's no need to be hostile," he said.

"So, it's okay for you to be hostile but it's not okay for people to be hostile to you? Is that the way it works?"

"No. Not at all– "

"–Then how can you justify smearing the reputation of a man you don't even know? Because you don't know him? Is it easier for you to be a coward and hide behind words that are false to make yourself feel better about who you are and what you are?"

"No."

"Then how do you justify it?"

"I don't. I write what I write and people read it."

"Exactly. People who knew Walker read that article. You don't think you ruined his image in the eyes of those who knew him? Next time you decide to stab someone in the back, make sure they're turned around." I was so angry I slammed the phone down on the receiver. Some people's kids. How ignorant can you be? Two men were dead, tragically, and all Killian could do was cattle-prod Walker for his botched investigation.

I often wonder what people are thinking when they insult another person. I don't understand how that resolves anything. Here was poor Hayden Walker, mourning the lose of a friend, obviously crushed by the experience, and this nobody named Killian, a man Walker never had a problem with, didn't even know, was verbally accosting him for his shortcomings. That's as ignorant as it is cowardly. If you're going to insult someone, do it to their face; don't do it in some magazine where everyone can read it. That's a losers way out. At least man up to your insults. Have enough pride and dignity to say what you want to say to whom you want to say it to.

I feel that was my fault as well. I could have prepared him for the power he was going to confront but I didn't. I was so disoriented when we spoke that I didn't think to do it. I wish I had. Another death on my conscience, more blood on my hands. "Out, out, damn spot." Lady MacBeth felt this guilt, too. She wasn't responsible for the actual deaths but felt the blame should fall directly on her.

So do I!

So where does that leave me? I guess I could chuck myself out the window but what would that prove? That would prove nothing except that I could not accept the guilt. I don't want people to think of me that way. I want people to think of me as the man who was beaten down and got back up. Not only got back up but got back up and told his assailants to fuck off. I know people think harshly of me now. They think I wanted those two men to die or that it was my cold-blooded nature that lead to their deaths. The truth is, if Hayden Walker could have given his life to save theirs, he would have.

I would have in a heartbeat.

But I can't. Those two men are dead and this lump of depressed flesh is all that's left. I have to live with that. If that isn't guilt enough, then I say guilt be damned because I don't know how much more I can take.

God, I hope Jen can cheer me up.

April 9, 10:30

I can't say that I am a changed man, but I'm feeling better. I told Jen I didn't feel like going out anywhere. I told her that if she wanted to get together maybe we could stay in either at my place or hers. She had different plans. She practically dragged me to her car.

"Where are we going?" I asked.

"It's a surprise."

"I hate surprises. Come on, where?"

"I can't tell you."

"This better be good."

"It is."

We drove for almost an hour before we pulled into the parking lot of Big Boys[47] and grabbed a bite to eat. When we finished eating, we left and got on the highway. The sun was going down and we just drove for hours, into the sunset, like Gene Autry or John Wayne in some cheesy imitation cowboy move.

"Do you want to talk about it?" she asked several miles into our adventure. It was perfect; she waited just the right amount of time for me to get comfortable before bringing it up. She didn't just blurt out, "What the hell happened?" when she came through the door. There is a time and place for prudence and Jen seems to know exactly when that is.

"I think so."

"You don't have to. Just know that I'm a pretty good listener and if you need a shoulder to lean on, I know one that just might fit that stubborn head of yours." She smiled.

We drove for about twenty minutes longer before I said anything.

"What am I fighting for?"

"What?"

"What am I fighting for?"

"Hay, you're doing something special. You're a part of something extraordinarily different. You're documenting supernatural experiences. The interest has been there for years, of course, but the ability to approach this scientifically has never been greater then

---

47 Big Boys is an old-fashioned diner. The waitresses all wear red- and white-striped skirts and shirts. You never have to leave the comforts of your car. You flash your headlights once when you are ready to order and a waitress pops out of nowhere wearing her uniform and roller skates. It's really a fantastic restaurant. I went there once when I was doing some research. If you ever get the chance to go, order the Galactaburger. This beast must way over a pound. It's topped with lettuce, pickles, bacon, hickory-smoked cheddar, mustard and ketchup. Of course, you can order it pretty much any way you want; according to taste. And, if you can masticate your way through that half a cow, I would suggest you try the gravy fries. They bring this appetizer out in a giant bucket, fries literally spilling over the top and saturated with a beef gravy that would put any old grandmother to shame. If you make it that far, I suggest you try the milkshake. Truly, a feast for the taste buds. It's almost worth the trip just to eat at Big Boys.

now. Doubt will be resolved and interest piqued . . .because of you and people like you. I know people who would kill to be in your position. Nobody wants to sit on the sidelines and watch the truth unfurl. They want to be right in the middle of it like a photographer developing truth as it is established. If I wasn't such a wimp, I'd do it. But I am. So are a lot of people. It takes a strong, confident, capable person to do what you do. I admire that about you."

"Is it worth it, though? Jay's dead. He's dead, Jen, and I couldn't do a goddamned thing to help him. I keep asking myself, over and over, is it worth it?"

"What's your answer?"

"In the end, it's all worth it. But in the short run, it's not. As glorious as it sounds, as fun as it sounds, as adventurous as it sounds, I'd give it all up to have Jay back. I'd give it back in a second."

"Jay's dead, Hay. Don't make a martyr of him. What happened was tragic, yes, but you have to move on. Don't you think Jay would want you to continue the hunt, to pursue his passion . . .and yours? Don't you think he'd be more upset if you quit than if you didn't? I know I would be. I'd find a way to come back from the dead and haunt you for the rest of your natural life." She offered another one of her beautiful smiles.

I think I love this woman.

When we got back to my apartment, she walked me in. I invited her to stay for coffee but she had to write a term paper for one of her classes. I can understand that. She stayed for a few, quiet, awkward moments. Neither of us really knew what to say or do. We both knew she was right. She always is. When my voice of reason becomes mute, she steps up to the microphone and belts out her reason, which is just as strong as mine. I almost told her I loved her right there but I wasn't sure if the time was right. Things had happened so quickly, I didn't want her to think I was jumping to any exaggerated conclusion. I wasn't sure if she was feeling the same way about me as I was about her.

Our eyes met as she crossed the kitchen toward me, never taking her eyes from mine. She crossed the invisible plain of my territorial bubble and reassured me with a kiss on the lips and whispered softly into my ear, "I love you, Hayden."

[The diary entries for the rest of April, all of May and June have been removed from the diary.][48]

---

[48]   Three very important months have been removed from the diary for some reason. We really couldn't find a whole lot of information about this period. We know from credit card receipts that Walker flew to Phoenix, Arizona on April 28th, Gloucester, Massachusetts on May 15th, New Brunswick on May 19th, Palm Springs, Florida on May 28th, Presque Isle, Maine on June 3rd, Raleigh, North Carolina on June 18th, Oklahoma City, Oklahoma on June 21st and Springfield, Massachusetts on June 29th. What he did while he was at these destinations or why he was there in the first place is still somewhat of an enigma. I spoke with Dean Starking several times to see if he could find some information on what assignments Walker may have been on during this time frame but he said, "[There were] so many [assignments] that we stopped detailing why we were there and just focused on the data and information we could collect while we were there. You have to understand that Walker was everywhere. He didn't even have enough time to keep me posted. I tried to keep in touch with him as much as I could. I called his pager about a million times trying to contact him. Sometimes he'd call back, sometimes he wouldn't. You never knew with Hay. I don't think I've ever met a greater man than Hayden Walker, but his people skills, as you've probably uncovered in your research, weren't all that great. I looked forward to the times he would return my pages but they were definitely few and far between. He was just so damned busy all the time. I guess that was my fault. I tried to get more help so Hay wouldn't have to do all the work but nobody was willing. Hay was one of the only people I could convince to do this line of work, other than people already enrolled in the program. And he usually insisted on being at every investigation, whether he was heading it up or not."

Starking was able to give us some information. We know that Walker was investigating a haunted water works system in Springfield. We know nothing of the data or information that was compiled at this investigation. We know from credit card receipts that he stayed at a Best Western in Carolina for three days. We do not know what he was sent there to investigate. We know that he spent his birthday in Palm Springs. We do not believe this trip was for business purposes. Airline records show that Jen flew into Miami on May 27th. We can assume she was there to meet Walker. The two stayed in a condo on the waterfront. They spent three days there. What they did we can only speculate.

From the end of May to the end of June, we have absolutely no idea what was going on in Walker's life, other than the places he had traveled. We do not know what he was investigating or whether or not he was able to obtain any valuable information or insight into the realm of the paranormal.

To Jen[49]
When fear has been extinguished,
Replaced by placid thoughts
Of calm tranquility,
Will you be there to enjoy it with me?

When doubt has been resolved,
Replaced by the understanding

Of one unified conscience,
Will you be there to share it with me?

When anger has been whisked away
By the gently blowing breeze,

I can't help but wonder why particular pages of Walker's diaries have been removed. Was it something Walker did? Or was it something someone else did so we wouldn't know too much about Walker? It is such a puzzle, and such a daunting task to try to piece together the life of a nomad. Walker was all over the country in 1982. Most instances we can account for but what about those instances we cannot account for? What was he doing? Why was he there? Why were the pages that correlate with these periods removed from the diary? Someone, somewhere, doesn't want us to know. Why? What's the point? Who does it benefit and why?

[49] As strange as it sounds, it seems that Walker, along with being a paranormal investigator, also fancied himself a poet. It's not uncommon for a man or woman to express his or her emotions in verse. Hell, I do it all the time. I don't expect that anybody else will ever read my poetry; I'm sure as Hell not going to put it out in the public eye to be ridiculed and condemned by literary critics and self-professed poetry scholars. My poems are for me. They are a way of releasing built-up emotion; not negative emotion but positive emotion. I think it is very healthy; and who the hell is it going to hurt? I want you all to try it sometime. Just sit down and write a poem about someone or something that is important to you. Don't worry about rhyme and meter and all that useless crap. Save that for the self-professed poetry scholars. Just write in verse form and enjoy yourselves. Don't worry about whether or not words rhyme because, in the end, the finished product is all that matters; and that finished product is a spewing, if you will, of your heart and your emotions on a piece of paper. That product is you in paper form and I think that that is something special in itself. It is obvious that Walker is no poet Laureate, but he is a hopeless romantic and I enjoyed the poem for its quality.

Replaced by warmth and gentle nature,
Will you be there to feel it blowing through our hair?

When the statue of youth
Has been chiseled into an aging figurine
Replacing the comforts of immortality,
Will you be scared with me?

The world revolves around the sun
And life revolves around the world.
Time marches on whether we want it to or not.
Will you be there in the end?

Of course, I know the answer.
I can see it in those eyes of yours.
You talk to me without even opening your mouth,
And open your heart to mine.

What does your heart say to me?
Does it desire to spend eternity
With someone like me?
I hope so.

Because I would trade every day
From this day till death
For that one chance to say I fell in love
And spent my life with you.[50]

---

[50] I asked Jen if Hayden ever showed her his poetry; there are several more poems in these diaries about her, and she said no.

"Deep down, I knew he felt that way, of course, but he never showed me these. They're beautiful. Hayden wasn't the type of person who expressed himself verbally. It was the quiet, subtle attempt that made him Hayden, that made him mine," she said.

By this time in the diaries, we cannot deny Walker's love for Jen. These poems are just one more attempt to prove this. It may not be a beautiful poem to anybody but Jen, but that is who the poem was intended for, and if the person it was intended for was deeply moved or touched, as Jen was, than the poem served its purpose. And *that* is beautiful.

July 28, 7:00 am

En route to Madison, Indiana to investigate claims of an alien abduction. I have to admit that the prospect of running into a tiny martian out in a cornfield somewhere in Indiana terrifies me. Up until now, the investigations have all been routine hauntings. This is something entirely different, entirely new.

And entirely frightening.

I almost hope the claim is a hoax. But I have seen enough and been involved in too much over the past two years to be naive, to be blind to the possibility of extra-terrestrial existence. I've never been an extremely religious man. If evolution is the key to human existence, we cannot overlook the prospect that evolution has been occurring all over the galaxy for the past 200 billion years, just like on this planet. Somewhere, in a distant galaxy, a race of beings could be out there; perhaps millions of races of beings, pondering the eternal question, "are we alone in the universe?" Well, are we?

January 28, 10:45 pm

Arrived at the house of John and Genie Mills around 5:00. He seems like a nice enough guy, your typical country bumpkin with the ratty beard, flannel shirt and green John Deere hat cocked slightly to the left. He actually reminds me a bit of Steven. Genie is the homemaker and John seems to handle the financial end of the business. They own their own farm with five fields of wheat and corn. And in the middle of one of these giant fields of wheat is where our little adventure took place.[51]

"I was getting ready to come in for the night," John began. "I was out late taking advantage of the full moon. I only had one more row to harvest when I seen this bright light in the sky. It was way over to my left so I didn't give it much thought. I just thought it was a plane or something. All of a sudden, it's right above me. It ain't flying or nothing, it's just hovering there above me. That's when I tried to scream for Genie to call the police, but I couldn't scream. I

---

[51] For further detail, read *Encounters With the Beyond* v. 8, Chapter 5, pages 52-57.

couldn't even talk. It's like my voice froze. It didn't hurt but it was like someone pushed the mute button on me.

"All of a sudden this ray of light shoots down at me and I feel this strange sensation, like being pulled but I wasn't going nowhere. I tried to scream again but nothing come out so I tried to get off the tractor. I figured, if I could run for it maybe the thing would lose me in the field. I'll be damned if I couldn't move; I was paralyzed. I couldn't budge an inch.

"Suddenly, I get jerked off the tractor. Nothing had me though. I was just floating there, like the space ship was. I was lying on my back, like I would if I was asleep. I turned my head and I could see the tractor about ten feet below me. I was so scared. I looked up and the ship was getting closer, or I was getting closer to the ship. I looked back down and the tractor was about twenty feet below me. I looked back up at the ship and saw a door slide open on the bottom, and that's all I remember. I blacked out after that. Genie found me about three in the morning stumbling through the field as naked as the day I was born. I didn't even know where I was. She got me inside and calmed me down. I passed out again. I was exhausted. That's when she called you guys."

"You don't remember anything that happened once you were inside the ship; or even if you were in the ship at all?"

"Nothing. I remember seeing the door open and the next thing I knew I was in the middle of the field, almost a mile from my tractor. I don't have a clue."

"John, I want to try something with you. I want to try to put you into a hypnotic state. Sometimes, the unconscious mind blocks certain material from the conscious mind because the truth can be too damaging to the conscious mind so it kind of hides it there. It's there but camouflaged. I'd like to try to get some more information from you. I believe you will remember things better from an entranced state. Would that be all right?"

He nodded.

Fifteen minutes passed before he fell under to the hypnosis. Then, I started a very thorough interview.

"John?"

"Yes?"

"The night is July 25th. It's a warm night. The moon is full and you're out later than usual harvesting wheat. Can you remember this?"

"Yes."

"Good. You see a bright flash in the sky off to your left. Can you see it?"

"Yes."

"Now the light is above you. You now see that the bright flash was a flying spacecraft of some sort. Can you see it?"

"Yes."

"You're being pulled up to the ship by some mode of teleportation, yes?"

" No." He was shaking now and almost crying. " I don't want to go."

"Relax, John. Nothing's going to hurt you now. The worst is over. All you have to do is tell me what you remember. They can't hurt you now."

"I'm scared."

"I know you are, John, but we're here with you now. Me and Genie. You're safe. Can you tell me what happened?"

"Yes."

"What happened?"

"The doors opened. I was lying on the floor for a long time before I was approached."

"Who approached you?"

"Them."

"What do they look like?"

"They're ta– " He broke away again, trying not to cry. "They're tall. Real tall and real skinny but they have these enormous heads with giant, black eyes. They're awful." Now he began to cry again.

"You're safe, John. Relax. What happened next?"

"Two of them put me on a tray and carried me into a huge, open room. They put me on a table. I waited for a long time till . . .oh, God, here he comes. Help me! HELP ME!"

"Relax, John. You're safe. What happened next?"

"Another one came out; just appeared out of nowhere. He stood over me, watching me with those hollow, black eyes. He started poking me. He pulled this giant tube out from underneath the table somewhere and he," his voice wavered and cracked, "he crammed it down my throat, oh God! I tried to kick and get him off me but I still couldn't move. I can still taste the hose. I want to throw up but I can't."

"Then what?"

"Two more appeared and they all stood around me. They pulled the hose out of my mouth and I tried to tell them to stop but I still couldn't talk. They grabbed a smaller hose and shoved it up my nose. I swear it touched my brain. It hurts so bad. It hurts so bad!" He erupted into violent, unconsolable fear. "Please. Get me out of here. I want to leave." He began bawling at this point. He was kicking and squirming trying to get away from what he was seeing in his mind. "Please! Get me out of here!"

"Stop it, for Christ's sake," Genie finally yelled. "Please, stop it."

"Okay, John? John, I need you to calm down and listen to me. When I count backwards from three you will wake up and remember nothing of this conversation.

"1 . . ."

His breathing became heavy and sedated.

"2 . . ."

He was slowly finding calmness.

"3."

He was awake and lying on the couch in his living room again, not on some cold, sterile exam table in an alien spacecraft. His eyes were still moist from the tears.

"John, are you all right?" Genie asked.

"What happened?"

"You don't remember?" Genie seemed perplexed by his complete lack of recollection. The fear had seemed so real to her that she thought for sure he would remember.

Instead, he just shook his head.

"Let's leave it at that," I said. "We'll pick up where we left off tomorrow."

July 29, 12:00 pm

John took me out to the point of abduction.

The tractor was no longer in the field but it was obvious where it had been. There was a large portion of burned wheat; it was perfectly symmetrical except for one area which was a perfect outline of a John Deere tractor.

"This burning is something you do here?"

"Nope," John said. "It was like this the next morning. I come back here with the missus after I'd collected my bearings. Do you think the ray of light burned up all my wheat?"

"I don't know. I'll have a sample analyzed. You say this wasn't like this before the encounter?"

"Nope. I swear. I got no reason to lie."

"I believe you, John. I'm just contemplating the ifs."

I took a sample of the burned wheat and we walked back to the farmhouse. I packaged the sample to travel through the mail and Fed-Ex'ed it back to the lab for analysis.

Awaiting the results. More waiting.

August 2, 9:45 pm

Still at the farmhouse. Received an interesting phone call from Stan.[52]

"Did you get the sample?" I asked.

"Yes. Where did you get it?"

"I'm in Madison, Indiana. Some wheat field, why?

"Is there anything unusual about the area? Any radioactive sources out there, maybe a power plant or something?"

"There is nothing out here, Stan. Nothing. If it weren't for the long grass, you could probably see me with a telescopic lens from where you are. Nothing but flatland, here. Why, did you get something?"

---

[52] Stanley Philbrook, specialist in combustible gases at the laboratory at Stanford.

"Well, we picked up trace amounts of carbon, probably from the scorched wheat and the computers came back with twelve other elements they can't account for."

"What does that mean?"

"The elements in this sample didn't match up with any of the elements on the periodic chart which is very strange. It's also very interesting."

"Why's that?"

"Because it means the elements are not terrestrial."

"What?"

"These elements do not seem to be earth-based. Either we've discovered twelve new minerals or those same twelve minerals came from somewhere other than Earth. I'm not calling Guiness to gloat about a new discovery."

"No shit? They're from outer space?"

"Looks that way."

"There's no way it could be a hoax?"

"No. If the farmer had some pranksters burn his field, there would be excess amounts of accelerating liquids; gasoline or propane or some kind of combustible agent. Every combustible agent is known to scientists. These aren't known to anybody. This is genuine and legitimate. I'm confounded by the results myself. I half-expected the results to come back indicating arson being the reason for the burned wheat but this is beyond me. This is your sport. The ball's in your court now. Good luck to you."

"Thanks, Stan. You're the best."

I couldn't believe it. Actual proof that aliens exist. This is a whole different realm we need to investigate. There are so many possibilities. We'll have to get another team together. They'll have to start researching immediately. I hate to have to move on but I have my orders like everyone else. I'll call Dean and let him know what's going on before I head out.[53]

---

[53] I wish I could tell you that Walker further detailed the investigation but he was true to his word. He allowed another team to investigate while he went on to his next assignment. The team that investigated after Walker, headed by John Stevenson and Claire Miller, found evidence to be conclusive and indisputable that the materials and elements in the charred remains of John

September 8, 6:40 pm

What next?

Why is it that some assignments run as smooth as silk and the assignments that get botched up so bad, leave you wondering if the good assignments are worth the loss? And why are the consequences so much more severe.

How many people under my authority are going to die? This shouldn't even be happening.

What the fuck is going on?[54]

Mills' wheat field were, indeed, extra-terrestrial. John has not indicated to any member of the staff at Stanford that he has been abducted since. And, although he suffers from intense migraine headaches since the abduction, he has not complained of any other serious physical problems as a result of the encounter. What was the purpose of the abduction? What did those instruments do? What effect did they have on John? We may never know. Walker went along with business as usual spending the next few months on routine investigations. Nothing major happened until the next diary entry when everything, once again, takes a turn for the worst.

[54] Again, another very somber entry that leaves us wondering what the hell is going on. Who died? I had to go back to my friend at the archives department at Stanford and beg him to look for another video tape that may have been taken on September 7th or 8th. It took me almost a week of convincing but he finally searched the vault. He came back with three video tapes. One tape was shot by Walker, one by Carla and one by a man who I have yet to identify. We never see his face and his voice just isn't enough to go on. I tried to run a comparison of who was on the staff to see if any member seemed to qualify for this particular assignment. I came up with three possibilities. The first choice was Gabriel Marquez, a second-year undergrad at the university. He had all the qualifications to handle this type of assignment but the voice leads me to believe it is not him behind the camera. Second choice was Daniel Look, a first-year undergrad at the university. Again, his voice would have been too young for the voice on this tape. Which leads me to believe that the mystery man is Greg Taggot, a first-year grad student at the university. He met all the qualifications and was old enough to have the voice that is heard on the video. Of course, this is merely speculation. The voice could easily have been that of Gabriel or Daniel. I don't want to sleight credit were credit is due. I admire the courage of all these men for their ability to operate under such conditions. Therefore, I will not say for certain who the third camera operator is. I honestly do not know and staff members at the department cannot recall who went on what team on an investigation that happened almost two decades ago, so I won't ask them to.

[film footage courtesy of Archives Depatment]

Hayden's camera:[55] *The camera flickers to existence while we are midway up a long flight of wooden stairs. We can hear Walker's footsteps eerily echoing as he ascends the staircase.*

"I'm going into the attic of Norman Bates' house.[56] He has complained of strange noises and bizarre incidences here in his house. Primarily in the attic and basement. Carla's in the basement and I will go to the attic and see what I can observe there."

As we ascend the staircase, a door comes uncomfortably into the frame. It is strangely lit by the glow of the bulb on the camera and looks ominous and overbearing as we approach. As we get closer, the details of the door come into focus. It is a large door with four panels, all separated by what appears to be a cross; the two panels on top are much smaller than the panels on the bottom to create this effect. The "cross" is incredibly intimidating; even though it is not really a cross at all, merely the framework of the door.

What I would like to do, like before, is offer you the chance to see what actually happened on that day. This will be a bit different. I don't want to seem like I am overplaying it or overdramatizing this incident, but I believe it to be very important. What I will do is offer you a montage of what is going on through the vision of all three cameras simultaneously throughout the house. As much as I don't want this to seem like a book rather than a diary, I do want to share with you this horrific and tragic experience.

55   To help you better envision this experience, I will provide for you which camera the viewpoint is coming from. When you see "Hayden's camera," obviously we are watching from the viewpoint of Walker's camera and so on and so forth. Since we do not know the true identity of the third cameraman, though we know it was a man, you will simply see "Camera 3," when I am referring to that particular viewpoint. I hope this does not make this experience too confusing. I will warn you now, what you are about to witness, vicariously through writing, is unpleasant.

56   Obviously this is not the house of the real Norman Bates from Hitchcock's *Psycho*, but it is an incredible coincidence. Norman Bates lived in this house for several years before the disturbing incidences became too much of a problem and he moved. I must admit, though, I was looking for a mad axeman to come hurdling at the camera wearing woman's clothing and speaking in an unusually high-pitched voice. Of course, it never happened, but . . .you never know.

Hayden's hand reaches out in front of the camera, grabs the doorknob and pushes the door open. It creaks loudly. Walker stands in the doorway for a moment pondering whether or not he should enter. The camera wobbles oddly back and forth for a moment then Walker holds the PDC out in front of him. It is a strange looking instrument; the handle seems freakishly long and slender and sprouts into a large, cumbersome box that seems too large for the handle. A scale from 0 to 1 sprawls across the face of the box. For now, the needle rests steadily on 0.

Walker enters the attic. The camera peeks down momentarily at the PDC then back to the expanse of the room in front of him. The attic is very typical: there are several 2x6s supporting the frame of the roof and a slew of cardboard boxes. We walk from one side of the attic to the other sneaking a peek at the PDC every few feet.

Nothing registers on the PDC.

"Well, this place is as haunted as my underwear. There's nothing up here." We again wobble oddly for a moment. "Carla, are you there?" he says into his walkie-talkie.

"Yeah, what?" The voice is very unclear through the static.

"Where are you?"

"In the basement. Why?"

"Are you getting anything?"

"No. Not a damn thing. You?"

"I didn't get anything."

Carla's camera: We're looking at a dingy tomb. The sub-flooring has been completed, but barely. The walls are slimy from some unknown residue. The only source of light is coming from a dim light bulb somewhere above Carla's head.

"What do you want to do?"

"Keep looking. Maybe we'll get lucky." This time, it is Walker's voice that is hard to be heard over the static.

"How about you, new fish? What have you got?" Carla asks.

Camera 3: We are looking at a large dining area. The camera is at one end of an enormous oak table and seems to extend forever. It is polished with a dark walnut stain and the glare is reeking havoc with the camera. On one wall, a large picture hangs regally. We can assume that this is Mr. Norman Bates, but we are unsure. The table is not set and seems cold, like there haven't been too many dinners here.

"I haven't picked up anything unusual, except this guys eating habits."

The camera pans in a full circle at a pace that is just shy of dizzying.

"Keep looking." Hayden's voice again crackles through the walkie-talkie.

Walker's camera: "You got it, boss." We're in the attic again. Now we are looking back through the door and down the staircase. We slowly descend the staircase, again, the footsteps produce a chilling echo.

Carla's camera: The basement seems small compared to the size of the dining area, which is indicative of the rest of the house. She pans around and we can clearly see that this portion of the basement is strictly for supplies and the water system. She pans back to the short staircase that ascends to the ground floor, the light coming in from the kitchen shines in brightly.

The door at the top of the staircase shuts right in front of us. The camera jerks wildly as Carla screams.

"Girl, you are losing your mind." She looks down at her walkie-talkie. "Hayden, that's very unoriginal."

Walker's camera: We are finally reaching the bottom of the staircase.

"What's unoriginal?"

"Slamming the door on me."

"I didn't slam the door. I just got out of the attic." Which is confirmed by the camera.

"Well who shut it, then?"

"Maybe your 'new fish' is playing a prank on you."

Third camera: "Wasn't me." The camera is in another large room which is obviously not the kitchen; several stuffed animal heads hang from the walls. This room appears to be a study of some sort; rows of books line the shelves and a large desk sits in the corner.

Carla's camera: "Then what's going on?"

"Can't help you, hon. Sorry."

The lights flicker momentarily then extinguish.

"Guys, come on. This isn't funny. What are you doing?"

Walker's camera: We're standing at the top of another staircase looking down.

"Are you all right, Carla?"

Third camera: "Carla? Carla, are you okay?"

Carla's camera: We are in complete darkness.

"You're telling me that you guys aren't doing this? You have no idea what's going on?"

"Carla, if I were playing with you, I would have stopped by now. You sound really upset. What's going on?"

"I don't know. The lights just went out. I can't see a thing."

"Calm down, Carla. I'm coming."

Walker's camera: We pick up pace as Walker quickly descends the staircase.

Third camera: We pan around and exit the room, moving quickly. We cross through another room and then another room. We are back in the dining hall when the camera stops, uncomfortably wavering from side to side. "Hay, where are you?"

"Third floor. You?"

"Second."

"Get down to the kitchen. I'll meet you the—"

Carla lets out an ear-piercing scream which hauntingly resonates from the crackle of the walkie-talkie.

"Carla!" Walker screams.

We move at a pace that must be running now. The camera is bouncing up and down. "Carla!" the man yells. "We're coming." We haul ass across three rooms and come to a long hallway. He runs halfway down the hall and turns right revealing another staircase. He takes the camera off his shoulder and carries it by the handle as he descends the stairs. We're being jerked from side to side. The camera bangs into his leg sending us upside-down at one point.

"We're coming, Carla. Hang on."

Walker's camera: Walker is breathing heavily as he races down a long hallway. The camera has been taken off his shoulder and we are again racing alongside the man carrying the camera. It bounces and jerks all around causing a very strange effect for the viewer.

"We're coming, Carla. We'll get you out."

"Help me!" *she yells again.* "Help me, please!"

Carla's camera: We are in total darkness. Carla is crying uncontrollably and sniffling loudly. "Get me out of here," *she says between suffocated breaths.*

Camera three: We finally arrive in the kitchen. The man places the camera on the floor facing away from the door. We cannot see a thing except the bottom of a counter.

We hear the man try to turn the doorknob but the door does not creak open. He pulls the knob hard then pounds on the door "Carla! Open the door, Carla!"

"I can't," *she screams from the other side of the door.* "It won't budge."

Moments later, we hear a second set of footsteps race into the kitchen. A dark shadow passes by the camera.

We hear Walker's voice now. "Carla, we're here."

Walker's camera: Walker has also set his camera down facing away from the door to the basement so we cannot see from this point of view either. All three cameras are useless at this point. All we can do is sit and listen to the event.

Carla's camera: We are still in absolute darkness. We can hear Walker and the other man pounding on the door and yelling to Carla but we cannot see a thing. We can still hear Carla crying and sniffling.

She screams wildly, and even though we are in complete darkness, we can tell that she has kicked the camera over on its side as we hear the frame scrape across the cement sub-flooring. She screams again.

"Something's got me," *she screams.*

"Carla! What's going on?" *Walker yells.*

"Help me, Hay! Help me!"

We hear the pounding intensify.

"Carla, open this door!"

"Help me!" *This time, the voice seems faint and very far away; farther away then the confines of the basement should allow.*

"Carla!" The door swings open violently and we see the silhouette of two men standing in the doorway. They both descend the staircase.

"Carla? Where are you, hon?"

No response.

"Carla, say something."

Still, no response.

The lights flicker back on casting a strange shadow on the two men standing there in complete silence. Walker crosses the basement toward the camera, which has been abandoned on its side, picks it up and turns it around revealing the room to be absolutely barren.

"Where'd she go?" the man asks.

"I don't know."

The camera flickers to blackness.[57]

September 9, 8:00 pm

Things are just getting out of hand. I don't know how much more I can take. Two of my crew are dead. Not just two of my crew but two of my friends. Am I next? What the hell is going on here? I don't understand. Things were never supposed to be like this. I didn't want any of this to happen. We started out with

---

[57] This is the last known observance of Carla LeVeque. Walker waited the mandatory 48 hour period then filed a missing persons report. To this day, no one has seen or heard from Carla. It's strange. It's like she disappeared off the face of the planet. She just seemed to have been swallowed by the darkness. Any information regarding this matter would be greatly appreciated by her family who have offered a cash reward for information that might lead to the recovery of their daughter. They are obviously heart-broken from the entire ordeal. I talked to them a few years ago and they still haven't given up the search.

"The search isn't over until she's found," her father, Jason, told me. "Whether she's dead or alive, we will not rest comfortably until we know what happened." The incident made national headlines when it debuted on an episode of Unsolved Mysteries in 1989. "We'll search till we find her. It's that simple," her father said on the program.

Again, if anybody out there has any information regarding this incident, contact her family members immediately. Any information would be greatly appreciated.

good intentions. The best intentions. But, they say the road to hell is paved with good intentions. I'm beginning to believe that. I need a break. I can't take it anymore. I'll go to Dean in the morning and ask to take a sabbatical. I don't have any choice. Either way, this job is going to kill me.[58]

December 31, 10:45 pm

Another year has come and gone. What a strange, strange year. Moments of utter astonishment mixed with fear and excitement and, of course, regret. I still can't believe that Jay and Carla are gone. It makes me sad sometimes to think about them and the time we shared. I am so appreciative of the time I was allowed to spend with them. They were both extremely unique individuals who had so much to offer the world. I wonder sometimes what they might have offered the world had they lived and I had been the one to die. Would they mope about like I have been, mourning my passing, or would they have honored and avenged my death by fighting for the cause? I would hope the latter. I'll return to the fight when I am ready. Right now, I just can't do it. I need more time to mourn and regress. The time will come. I know it. Right now, I'll focus on Jen and my family and hope everything works out in the end. We'll see what fate has in store for Hayden Walker this year.[59]

---

[58] On September 10th, Walker submitted a leave of absence form on Dean's desk requesting a one year sabbatical. I asked Dean if he remembered the incident.

"Very well," he said. "I tried to talk him out of it. But he was right. He needed a break. We were working him so damned hard that year. He was only home for about a period of one month that entire year. So, I gave him the break. Why wouldn't I? I told him to relax but not to forget what was important. He promised me he wouldn't forget anything. He said he just needed some 'down time.' That's what he called it, 'down time.'"

[59] This is the last entry in this diary. It leaves us with many questions. When will he return to the hunt? Will he return to the hunt at all? This particular entry is very somber but very promising at the same time. He seems to be in healthy spirits and willing to return to the chase. The only questions are when and how

Diary 3

March 10, 8:45 pm[60]

I wish I could spend the rest of my life like this: no work, no worries, no stress. Just me and Jen in quiet bliss. We've decided to move back to Maine for the summer. I told her she wouldn't be disappointed. A blatant lie, of course. Maine has no summer. Winter seems to last all the way through spring and spring bleeds directly into fall, then we repeat the cycle. It's a vicious cycle when you think about it. We normally have about one week of summer. It's the week prior to the coming of August. Mom is famous for saying, "summer was on a Tuesday this year." I miss her. I can't wait to see her. I can't wait to tell her the good news. I have to make sure there is good news to tell her first. I am ready to commit. I haven't seen anything that would suggest that Jen's not ready. All I have to do is ask. That's the hard part; the scary part. I have to find a clever way to do this. I don't want to be the guy who proposes in a restaurant making the woman feel obligated to say yes. If you propose in a restaurant, everybody will be watching the woman and if she says no, all of a sudden she's the bad guy; which works quite well for the man because the woman is then pressured by guilt into marriage. I don't want to spend the next forty years of my life in therapy with a wife who can't stand me and holds a grudge over my head because I "forced" her into marriage. It has to be private. That way, no one is hurt and nothing is lost, except for pride. My pride, of course, but we all have to make sacrifices, right?

---

[60] This diary, the third of five that I received, is a relatively dry period in Walker's life. However, there are several important events which took place during his one-year sabbatical that will be of some relevance; mainly Walker's first disappearance later in '83. We'll cross that bridge when we get there. In the meantime, please bear with me. I understand that most of this will be incredibly dull for some of you; especially for those of you who skip around to the parts that seem more tense. You know who you are. Like I said, these few events that I will document are very important in understanding the mental anguish and despair that Walker continued to experience throughout his professional career. This is all a means to an end. More than that, it's a means to justify the end; good or bad, like it or not.

Shane Layman

March 17, 2:00 am

Yes! She said yes. My heart is still racing. I can't believe it. She said she would marry me. The prospect of spending the rest of my life with her fills me with a sense of belonging and eternal gratitude. I just can't believe it. This is one of the greatest days of my life.[61]

---

[61] Walker dedicated many days to the presentation of his proposal and then speaks nothing of how he did it. When I spoke with Jen, I asked her if she would tell me how he went about proposing to her; how he went about asking the love of his life to spend the rest of *her* life with him.

"It was actually quite romantic. I didn't think Hay could be that romantic." She was grinning widely while dwelling in pleasant recollection. "It was exactly the way I had dreamed it would happen. His technique was nothing like I was expecting but the romantic aspect of it was: the privateness, the attention to detail, the work and effort involved were all so romantic. I cried that entire day. I'm so glad he didn't do something cold and unoriginal like asking me to marry him in a restaurant. I would never want that pressure on me. But the way he went about it was so private and affectionate that saying no would almost be mind-numbingly inappropriate."

"What did he do?" I asked.

"I was still asleep while he was assembling his little plan; while he was scheming. When I woke up, sometime in the middle of the night, there were two candles burning on the dresser in front of our bed. It was so early. It must have been around one or two in the morning. Anyway, by the light of the candles, I could see a trail of silver leading out of the room. Then, I noticed a folded piece of paper beside the candles. It said, "the path laid out before you is a path we'll take together. Follow the silver trail and discover what awaits you." I was a little nervous. I knew he wouldn't do anything to hurt me so it was all so romantic."

"What did you do then?"

"I followed the path."

"What were the silver things?"

"Hershey Kisses," she giggled. "A whole trail of chocolate kisses. They're my favorite."

"Where did the path lead to?"

"Into the bathroom, of all places." She began to laugh.

"The bathroom?"

She nodded.

"What was in the bathroom?"

"The trail led to the shower which was filled with all sorts of flower pedals. On top of the flowers was another folded piece of paper."

"What did that one say?"

"It said, 'I would kiss the ground you walk on and shower you with flowers if you'd spend the rest of your life with me.'" A tear raced down the side of her face.

"That's beautiful."

"Yeah, it was. He wrote a poem for me, too."

"Do you still have it?"

"Are you kidding? I committed it to memory. Do you want to hear it?"

"I wouldn't miss this opportunity for the world."

She smiled and said,

> "'When your hopes and dreams are shattered
> And lay in pieces on the ground;
> When everything you've wished for
> Seems like it can't be found;
> When all of your desires
> No longer seem to matter;
> When everything you wish to say
> Turns into nervous chatter;
> When your love of living life
> Is extinguished in the night;
> When all your goals and standards
> Seem to be far out of sight;
> When everyone you've ever loved
> Has turned their backs to you;
> When all your precious moments
> Have been dwindled to a few;
> When you entertain the thought
> That no one cares or loves you;
> When you sit at home and wonder
> Where the time has gone to;
> When you feel worn down by life
> And have nothing left to give;
> Even if you feel sometimes
> You no longer wish to live;
> Remember this, if nothing else:
> If you need a hug, a smile, a kiss,
> If you ever could be happy
> With a love as true as this;
> When you're searching for a person
> Who can set your spirits free . . .
> Call off the futile search, my love,
> You can always count on me.
> And I'll love you forever
> If you'll let me.'

May 28, 7:45 am

Flying home today. I'm a little apprehensive. I've already introduced Jen to Mom and Dad but this time the whole family will be there to meet her. I'm certain that they will receive her warmly, like my parents did. Jen is the woman I will be spending the rest of my life with. She's the woman who will be attending the reunions and birthday parties and holidays from now on. So they'll have to like her. I'm still nervous, though.[62]

May 29, 8:45 pm

Flew in yesterday. I almost hyperventilated on the plane. Jen was great. She spent the entire flight trying to get me to breathe steadily. I just couldn't do it. I couldn't muster the strength in my lungs to breathe right. I was so nervous. Of course, I had nothing to worry about. My family is great at making people feel welcome.

The entire family was at the airport waiting for us.

"Hay!" Of course, an entire airport turns when someone yells, "hey." They have no idea that "hey" is actually "Hay." It's my curse. Steven was yelling across the terminal. "Hay! How you doing, you stud?" He was smiling. Everyone was still perplexed about who the hell this guy was talking to. I think he was excited. We haven't seen each other since Thanksgiving. He was racing toward me. We always got along best, out of all of us. I don't know why. We just

---

"Underneath that he wrote, 'Will you marry me, Jen?'"

"And, of course, you said yes."

"Of course I did. Hayden was the most important person in my life. The idea of spending the rest of our lives together was a prospect I was very interested in. So I said yes."

62 I asked Jen if she remembered that day.

"He was so nervous I think he was actually sweating. I had to calm him down all the way to Maine. I was the one who was supposed to be nervous. I was the one leaving my home state for an extended period of time, for the first time in my life, meeting a new family, a family I was uncertain would like or care about me, but he was so nervous that I didn't have time to be. He was nervous enough for both of us. The entire flight was spent trying to get Hay relaxed."

have. I love them all, of course. Steve and I just have some kind of connection.

"Steve!" I yelled. "What's going on, buddy?"

"You're looking fine today. And who is this elegant young lady you're wearing on your arm?"

"Steve, this is Jen. Jen, Steve."

"Nice to meet you," she said.

"The pleasure is all mine," Steve said suavely, then kissed her hand.

"All right, Don Juan. Hands off."

He smiled and laughed.

"Everyone is awaiting your arrival. Shall I announce your presence?"

"Thank you, Jeeves. Oh, and could you bring the car around, please." I attempted my best English accent; which was actually quite horrific.

"Hay!" Mom yelled from across the terminal. Of course, heads turned everywhere.

"Mom. How are you doing?" I hugged and kissed her. "Dad. Everything's good?"

"Sure is. How about you?"

"Great."

I could tell Jen was getting a little uncomfortable, tightening her grip on my arm. Perhaps the overwhelming amount of people she was confronted with made her nervous. I felt some introductions were in order.

"Everybody, excluding Mom and Dad and Steve, this is Jen."

[Walker dedicates almost an entire page to the casual pleasantries passed between Jen and the Walker clan. He is painstaking in his attention to detail, mentioning what people are wearing, the looks on their faces, the general gaiety of the moment. I feel, though maybe some of the more morbid readers would take pleasure in the fine-tuned details of this segment, general rules of pace and rhythm cannot allow me to supplement this segment of the diary entry. For those curious, Walker introduced Jen to every member of his family, one by one, making sure to state that hands were shaken and smiles

were exchanged along with several comments in between. Why Walker went to such great lengths to reproduce the feeling of the moment is unknown. Why did he write half of the details he wrote? We may never know. However, to maintain the pace of the story, said entry has been removed. We continue several paragraphs into the same entry, after the family has left the airport].

My palms were sweating all the way home. I was still nervous about telling them about me and Jen. I had already decided to wait until dinner. That would give me plenty of time to drop the bomb on them.

With the stage set, the opportunity was evident. All I had to do was muster the courage to tell them. We shared idle chitchat for about thirty minutes. Pleasant conversations about life and where everybody's at. Marcy is going to modeling school next month and her agent seems to think she has potential. James is still in San Diego. Steve is still in Wisconsin. Both are doing great. Harry is going to become a lieutenant at the fire department in the fall. Sharon is still giving the forecast. Kim is managing Pete's Market for the time being. She hopes to go on to bigger, better things but for now, she says, this job will get her by. Josh is still patrolling the streets. He's up for a promotion in another year. I hope he gets it. So much promise and potential for this family. I am so proud of all of them. And through all of this, this little voice in my head is screaming, "Tell them, you idiot. Tell them now or you'll never do it."

"Everybody," I said, standing up from the table. "I have an announcement to make." My knees were so weak, I could barely stand up. "I wanted to wait until we were all together. I love you all so much and I am so proud of all of you that it wouldn't be right not to share this moment with you."

"You're flying us all to Disneyland?" Steve always planted humor wherever he could and we all laughed.

"No. As you all know, Jen and I have been together for some time now and we have agreed that it's time to elevate the level of commitment. I have asked Jen to marry me and she has said yes."

"Really?" James seemed quite surprised.

"Can you believe it?"

"That is so great. Congratulations," Steve said.

Everything else is a blur. I really don't remember much after that. I was still so nervous. Everyone seems excited about the idea.[63]

---

[63] Over the next few months, Walker was able to give his family the attention he believed they deserved. He was able to spend a lot of time with his family as they helped him and Jen prepare for their upcoming wedding. Jen was also becoming very friendly with the Walker family.

"Every Friday, the females in the Walker family would all get together and help me plan for the wedding. I was so grateful for that. I didn't really know the area that well so I didn't know where to go to get flowers or invitations or a dress, even. I was a mess when Norma came to me and asked if there was anything she could do to help. So, every Friday, we would get together and work on plans for the wedding."

"I figured Jen would need some help," Norma told me. "And I was more than happy to volunteer my time. I really liked her. Her and Hayden were perfect for each other. I still like her, of course. And I still think they're perfect for each other. Life just has such a bizarre sense of humor. Of course, Hayden would come to me," she began to laugh, "to make sure we weren't planning anything he didn't feel comfortable with. He didn't act concerned at all but deep down he was very concerned."

"Everything was great that summer," Marcy told me. "Everyone was happy. We all kind of missed Steve and James but everybody else was right here in Maine. We were always together. We were a family. It was great. It felt good. For the first time in a long time, it felt really good."

"I took Hay on patrol with me a few nights so we could talk," Josh told me.

"What did you talk about?"

"Whatever, really. We'd just talk all night. Whatever came across our minds."

"Did he ever talk about Jen?"

"Constantly. He was absolutely smitten with that girl. He was so excited about the wedding and moving back to Maine so he could spend time with us. It was the first time in a long time I remember seeing him truly happy. And that made me happy."

I think it is abundantly clear that for that summer, the family was very happy. They were all accessible to one another; with the exception of Steve and James. Walker finally had what he wanted; the comforts of kith and kin accompanied with a relationship that was not only sprouting but blooming. This curious combination was not really new to Walker but very acceptable and very welcome. For the previous two years, or so, Walker was always sacrificing something. At the university, he had Jen, the love of his life, but he was thousands of miles away from his family. Before he was at the

June 8, 3:30 pm

We've rented a beautiful house for the summer. In fact, we are planning on having the wedding here in the back yard. I can't believe we are actually staying in this house. It's fantastic. If the weather holds out, this will be the perfect spot for the wedding.[64]

---

university, he had his family but he was missing that one key element in his life: love. Of course, he loved his family very much, I think this is indicated clearly throughout his diary entries. But no one is truly complete until they find that one person who completes them; who complements them perfectly. He found that person in Jen. Of course, while he was at home, before he went to Stanford, he did not have Jen. Now, Walker was living this ultimate, utopian experience of having the best of both worlds and I believe, for the first time, he was truly happy.

64   I took a trip down to see this house and Walker's right; it's fantastic. It took me a few moments to convince the current occupants that I was not trying to rob them before they would allow me to enter the house. It was almost embarrassing. I had to tell them about the book and how important it was for me to be able to see this place so I could accurately detail the aesthetics of the house. Finally, they conceded and led me on a quick tour.

    The layout of this place was phenomenal. The house wasn't huge by any stretch of the imagination, but it was still a fantastic presence to behold. The ground floor had three rooms: a nice, full-sized kitchen stocked with all sorts of different accessories and gadgets; a relatively large dining area and a massive living room. This room was gigantic. It has to be 30x30. I didn't take the tape measurer to it but take my word that it's huge. There were giant bay windows on each of the two walls that faced the outdoors, providing a panoramic view of the dense forest that surrounds the house. I don't know how Jen and Walker had this room decorated or furnished but the current occupants obviously had cash to have furnished this huge living room the way they did. They had a big screen television that took up the majority of one wall. A fantastic set of Pioneer speakers was fastened to the wall on each side to provide ample sound quality; we're talking hi-fidelity. They had a very nice Pioneer stereo as well; which was hooked into the television providing surround sound through the room. This place was fantastic. I wanted to pitch a tent right there in their living room and never leave. I almost did. But, I had promises to keep. I swore I would only need a minute.

    The second floor was equally as stunning; again consisting of three rooms: a master bedroom, a spare bedroom and a lovely bathroom. The master bedroom also had a large bay window overlooking the beautiful forest. The spare bedroom wasn't nearly as big as the master bedroom but was equally as quaint.

I could go in to detail about the bathroom but some things are best left private. The tour continued as we went downstairs to the back door. It swung open letting in the brilliant radiance of the sun and my mind flooded with hundreds of images and comments I had ingested from Walker's friends and family about the day of the wedding. The door I had just exited was the same door Jen had exited to the back yard where she and Walker were married.

"It was all so beautiful," Norma recalled. "She came out the back door and walked towards us. There was this wonderful flower garden (which is still there to this day): lilies, and daffodils, though their time had already passed that late in the season, roses, pansies, tulips. It was beautiful."

"It was a great day," Steve told me. "The sun was out and the temperature was right around 70 degrees. It was perfect. It had rained that morning but by the time of the wedding, the lawn had dried. They say that it's good luck, though: rain on your wedding day. I guess. I don't know. Hay wasn't much for having good luck. That was the happiest I had ever seen him. Everybody was so happy. It was a beautiful day. Absolutely perfect."

Jen's mom, Caroline, flew in from California along with a handful of Jen's friends. She recalled that "Jen kept telling me all day, right up till the wedding, how perfect everything was. 'This is exactly the way I envisioned my wedding day to be like,' she told me." Caroline began to cry as she recollected. "She was so happy. And that made me happy."

And all along, I was standing there in the back yard envisioning all of this. I stood there, baffled yet strangely excited, looking out at an audience whose collective attention seemed to be focused on me. They sat uncomfortably in white, foldout chairs; very attentive, staring at me. Most of them were smiling and laughing; some gasping and gazing in awe at the radiant beauty that was walking towards them and, of course, many were crying. I felt like I was inside Jen's body, seeing what she saw on the day of her wedding. Feeling her emotions, sharing her anxiety; which was strange for me, being male, but the feeling was so overwhelming that I didn't even try to ignore it. I let it overcome me, like a tidal wave and I embraced every nerve-racking moment of it. The scent of flowers was overpowering. The sun was penetrating through the mighty evergreens which were standing tall and proud like dutiful watch guards. Along the path, there was an array, a bouquet, of assorted flowers. I could see Norma Walker and Caroline McPherson looking at me, teary-eyed. I almost wanted to cry. It was the strangest feeling.

As I got farther down the path, I could see Hayden at the makeshift alter, which, in itself, was quite beautiful: a white, arching trellis, dark green shoots of ivy crawling steadfastly up the sides and intertwining with the latticework. It was stunning. On the other side of the trellis was a man garbed with a robe; he was holding the Bible in one hand, a strange smile on his face. I could see Hayden perfectly. He was wearing a giant smile and it was quite obvious he could barely contain his emotions. He held his hand

July 8, 9:00 pm

Tomorrow's the big day.[65] I am so nervous and excited. I feel like a schoolboy who has finally gotten the chance to go on a date with his schoolgirl crush. Tomorrow, I am going to marry the most

---

out to me and I was so nervous. I looked behind me to make sure it was me he was reaching out for and there was nothing there.

I turned back to face him and they were all gone. Everything was gone. The rickety, white foldout chairs were replaced by wicker furniture sitting on a deck that was just beginning to show the first signs of wood rot; shards and splinters of wood were shooting up from the surface and the elegant, natural wood color had long since been replaced by that odd grayish-green color that comes only after years of loyal service. The flowers were beginning to die too; most of them anyway. The proud evergreens remained, of course, and would remain for as long as time allows them. The rest of the forest looked scattered and emaciated. Those once plush trees had shed the years coat, truly separating the forest from the trees. All that remained of these poor victims of nature were stingy, slender trunks sprouting a few weak, naked branches that seemed to be reaching out for salvation or redemption; or something else altogether.

It was quite depressing, really. That very spot was a joining ground for two people who were very special to one another. Now, all that remained of this sacred, hallowed ground was a vacant, hollow lot; almost barren, save for the proud evergreens and the stubborn perennials which refused to relinquish their grip to the bitter hands of Old Man Winter. But, in the end, we are all powerless to stop the inevitable.

I stood there, on that early October morning, the air just cold enough to freeze my breath. The mighty pines stood erect and at attention. I stood in the middle of that lawn that morning and I wanted to cry. I had envisioned what was probably the happiest moment of this couple's life and, like their marriage, it slipped away. The couple who found it in their untrusting souls to allow me to tour the house must have taken me for a lunatic. But they didn't know what I knew; and that made me very upset. It always makes me sad to revisit that point in time, and will probably haunt and plague me forever. Happiness be damned.

65 Walker dedicated two pages of his diary to talking about the wedding. However, I believe I have detailed enough for you. His writing is rather dry and, although it is very heart warming and sentimental, what I have given you should be adequate enough to show the perfect setting of the day and how happy everyone was on that day; which is basically what Walker rambles on about for the better part of two pages. I'd like to skip right over his details and move on to the next important turn of events in Walker's life.

wonderful woman in the world. I am ready to spend the rest of my life with her. I can't imagine endeavoring a journey like this with anyone else. Jen is perfect for me. I don't know if it's fate or blind luck that we ended up together. Maybe it's both. I wouldn't have met Jen if I hadn't gone to school at Stanford, or if I hadn't decided to switch from an abnormal psychologist to a paranormal psychologist. The cards must have been stacked in my favor this time. So many times, the cards have been stacked against me. It's nice to finally be winning a hand. I'm so nervous I can't even concentrate on what I'm writing. That's not important. Tomorrow is. And I can't wait.

September 2, 8:00 pm

This has been the worst/best day of my life. I don't even know where to begin. I'm not sure which news outweighs the other. Or are they equally compelling? They are both so important to the rest of my life. Jen told me that she's pregnant. Which makes me the happiest man on earth. The prospect of starting a family with the woman I love is very worthwhile to me. We had planned to wait until after she graduated from college to start a family but fate had other plans. And, on this day of joy and happiness comes some of the worst news I have ever received: Dad was diagnosed with cancer. They don't know how bad it is yet, but I don't want him to die. Not like that. Not in some hospital bed clinging on to life by a thread, hooked up to some goddamned machine like an android. He deserves better than that. He deserves to be able to enjoy his life. Every time something good happens in my life, something tragic happens to compensate the gain; combat the good. Why can't I catch a fucking break? I need to stay calm; for everybody's sake. We don't know how bad it is yet. They say there is a seventy-five percent chance the tumor is benign and that he'll be fine after an operation and chemotherapy. Let's hope.

September 9, 9:00 pm

A break. Initial results indicate that Dad's cancer is operable. Not only is it operable, but, in a few months, he'll be back to his normal self again. I do not envy him the battle he is embarking on, but I have so much faith in him. I think his strength, his courage, and of course, his stubborn ignorance will pull him through this ordeal. I don't doubt it a bit. The words from the doctor are both promising and extremely reassuring. I hope everything goes well. We have to go back to California. School starts back up next week. We leave in three days. I hate to leave at such an inopportune time but what choice do we have? Mom understands, though. She has everyone else here to help her. I'll call and write and visit as often as possible. I just have to go away for a little while. When I come back, this will all be over. Like a bad dream.[66]

---

[66]   Over the next two months, Walker came through on his promises. He kept in close contact with his family. He called his mother once a week and wrote once a month. Old telephone records indicate that Walker talked with his mother, on average, by telephone, for almost an hour a week; which is good considering he was all the way across the country. Carl's cancer did go into remission and he spent the next few months in chemotherapy. For Walker, in California, life went on. Jen was doing well in school, according to her transcripts. Walker was enjoying his sabbatical. The two purchased a house four blocks away from the university; a small home but very quaint and perfect to start a family in. Walker spent his days fixing up the house and maintaining the lawn. He even built a nursery for their unborn child. He was living the American dream. Of course, he knew he would have to go back to work eventually, but for now, he was content being Hayden Walker, upstanding citizen, loving husband and father-to-be-extraordinaire.

     "Everything was so perfect," Jen told me. "He was excited about the baby and being a father and I was excited, too. I couldn't wait until we were a family. The three of us in our dainty, little house were going to be inseparable. Then, things got strange. He'd disappear for long periods of time. I'm not talking about hours, either. Sometimes, he'd be gone for days; weeks even. He wouldn't tell me where he'd been. It was like he just gave up on all of our hopes and dreams. I started hating him for that. He didn't talk to his family anymore. I talked with them more than he did during those last few months of 1983. I didn't know what was going on. Everything was perfect. . .then it wasn't. It was so damned frustrating. I think he wanted to tell me what was going on, but, obviously he couldn't at the time. I don't know. I think he was frustrated, too. We'd get in these awful arguments which usually ended with me crying and him disappearing for another extended, undefined period of time. It was hard on both of us."

     "When did he start acting like this?"

     "He got a call from Dean in November. Dean said he 'only needed him for one job.' That was what he said, anyway. He left that night and it was

November 3, 3:30 pm

Dean called today. I thought I would be happy to hear from him but I can't say that I am. The phone rang this morning and my heart dropped. I didn't know who was on the other end, but something told me not to answer it. But, what can you do? What if it was Mom or Dad?

"Hay, Buddy. Am I glad to hear your voice." He sounded very serious.

"Dean. What can I do for you?"

"I need you, Hay. I know you're on sabbatical but I've got a real live one here. Nobody else is qualified. Not since Jay and Carla departed us, anyway. I need you, buddy. One job. That's all I need you for. Can you do it for me? Please."

How could I refuse?

November 4, 8:00 pm.

En route to Roswell, New Mexico. Jen isn't too happy about me taking on this assignment but Dean is my friend and friends help each other. I must admit, I am a little nervous about this one. Dean told me this assignment was on a strict, need-to-know basis. And, at present, Dean and myself are the only two people who need to know. I feel like a reconnaissance missionary sent on a black-op mission; if you are captured or killed, this outfit will deny and disavow any and all knowledge of your existence. How the hell do I get myself into these situations. Why couldn't I have chosen a profession that didn't require secrecy and anonymity?

I'm going to Roswell to investigate what is probably a bogus claim of encounters with XXXXXXXXXXXXXXXXXXXXXXXXX XXXXXXXXXXXXXXXXXXXXXXXXXXXXXXXXXXXXXXXX XXXXXXXXXXXXXXXXXXXXXXXXXXXXXXXXXXXXXXXX XXXXXXXXXXXXXXXXXXXXXXXXXXXXXXXXXXXXXXXX

---

two weeks before anyone heard from him again. When he came back, he wasn't the same Hay I knew. He was, but he wasn't. You know what I mean? I don't know what happened to him on that assignment but it changed his life. . .our life. And it was hard."

XXXXXXXXXXXXXXXXXXXXXXXXXXXXXXXXXXXXXXX
XXXXXXXXXXXXXXXXXXXXXXXXXXXXXXXXXXXXXXX
XXXXXXXXXXXXXXXXXXXXXXXXXXXXXXXXXXXXXXX
XXXXXXXXXXXXXXXXXXXXXXXXXXXXXXXXXXXXXXX
XXXXXXXXXXXXXXXXXXXXXXXXXXXXXXXXXXXXXXX
XXXXXXXXXXXXXXXXXXXXXXXXXXXXXXXXXXXXXXX
XXXXXXXXXXXXXXXXXXXXXXXXXXXXXXXXXXXXXXX
XXXXXXXXXXXXXXXXXXXXXXXXXXXXXXXXXXXXXXX
XXXXXXXXXXXXXXXXXXXXXXXXXXXXXXXXXXXXXX.[67]

November 5, 8:30 pm

Outside the gates of XXXXXXXXXXX, XXXXXXXXXXX. I just saw the strangest thing: the sun dug itself into the horizon hours ago, the black cloak of night has nestled in for the evening yet, on the horizon, a fabulous light glows brightly above me, all around me. It's breathtaking. Bright, incandescent and neon lights are swirling about the evening sky like giant kites. Then, momentarily, the lights will dim. What I saw was enough to rattle the toughest of nerves... even mine. Gliding across the night sky, like a dreamscape canopy were two XXXXXXXXXXXXXXXXXXXXXXXXXXXXXXXXXX
XXXXXXXXXXXXXXXXXXXXXXXXXXXXXXXXXXXXXX
XXXXXXXXXXXXXXXXXXXXXXXXXXXXXXXXXXXXXX
XXXXXXXXXXXXXXXXXXXXXXXXXXXXXXXXXXXXXX
XXXXXXXXXXXXXXXXXXXXXXXXXXXXXXXXXXXXXX

---

[67] This particular passage was blacked out with a magic marker or something similar. I have spent countless hours trying to read through the block; all of it was wasted time. I have no idea what is written under these black lines. What could be that important? Why would someone go through the trouble of editing this diary, a private diary, which was never intended for public viewing before allowing the public to view it? There are several more passages in this diary, and many in subsequent diaries, with similar markings. Somebody, somewhere doesn't want us to know why Walker was in Roswell, New Mexico on November 4, 1983, or what he was investigating. In future passages, I will use the same technique to show you what sections were blacked out. It is really quite fascinating when you think about it: somebody doesn't want us to gain access to some of the information hidden in the many pages of these diaries. Why?

XXXXXXXXXXXXXXXXXXXXXXXXXXXXXXXXXXXXXXXX
XXXXXXXXXXXXXXXXXXXXXXXXXXXXXXXXXXXXXXXX
XXXXXXXXXXXXXXXXXXXXXXXXXXXXXXXXXXXXXXXX
XXXXXXXXXXXXXXXXXXXXXXXXXXXXXXXXXXXXXXXX
XXXXXXXXXXXXXXXXXXXXXXXXXXXXXXXXXXXXXXXX
XXXXXXXXXXXXXXXXXXXXXXXXXXXXXXXXXXXXXXXX
XXXXXXXXXXXXXXXXXXXXXXXXXXXXXX. I don't believe it. I have investigated this sort of thing before but I have never seen anything like this.[68]

November 17, 8:00 pm

I haven't been home in almost two weeks. I don't know what to tell Jen. I can't tell here where I've been. The XXXXXXXXX won't let me. So what do I do? Lie to my own wife? I don't know if I can do that. But if I don't the XXXXXXXXX will kill me. It's like the Hotel California: you can check in but you can't check out. Not in the physical sense, anyway. I hate this. I don't want to lie to Jen but if I don't tell her something, she'll assume the worst on her own. What the hell am I going to do?

---

[68] Whoever was proofreading this diary to filter whatever information we were not intended to know, made a terrible error here. I believe, from all of my studying and research, that Walker was sent to Roswell, New Mexico to investigate extra-terrestrial communications. Think about it: in all the diaries, the only thing Walker has investigated without actually physically encountering anything during his investigation, was the alien abduction of John Mills in Madison, Indiana. He was sent to Indiana but never made mention of actually seeing or encountering extra-terrestrial life. And, in this diary entry, Walker makes reference to a gate. Now, this is strictly speculation and may be stretching the statutes of imagination, but what if he was standing outside the gates of Area 51, the much-fabled government operation that caused so much publicity back in the 40s and 50s? What if he was standing outside the gates of Area 51, investigating extra-terrestrial communications with government officials and was discovered sneaking around? Wouldn't those same government officials be inclined and obligated, not only morally but in the interest of saving their own careers, to make sure that what they were doing, their top secret assignments, did not get out to the public? It seems to be a fantastic coincidence. One which cannot be ignored.

November 21, 10:00 pm

I hate the fighting. I hate the lying and the sneaking around, too. I get calls from Mom and Dad every other day wondering where I've been. I lie to them, too. I can hear the concern in their voices and I lie to them. I hate myself for that. But what can I do? The XXXXXXX won't allow me to tell the truth. Not yet, anyway. They promise me that one day I will be able to look my wife in the eyes and proudly tell her the truth. But when will that be? And will it be too late? These are the questions that keep me up nights wondering if it's all worth it. I could run; take Jen and run. We could change our names and identities but I refuse to spend the rest of my life looking over my shoulder wondering if every suit I see is an XXXXX; or if around every corner the XXXXXXXX is waiting for me. So, I'll do what I'm doing, for now anyway. Maybe someday I'll get the courage to stand up for myself. Maybe.

November 28, 12:00 am[69]

I'm drunk. I cant do this anymore. Im gone for days at a time and when I get back I cant say where I've ben.[70] She's doubting my loyalty and im not sure I even trust myself. What happened to me? Why cant I just [word illegible] like normal people? Why does everyone hate me? Why do I hate myself? Nobody likes me anymore. Im [sentence illegible]. [Word illegible]. I want to go back. Back to the days when I was Hayden Walker, child. Can I do

---

[69] The entries from November 23 to 27 have been removed from the diary. For what reason, I do not know. I also do not know what he was doing for those five days. I looked for months. I couldn't find a single trace of the man. Whoever was financing his travels knew how to keep him hidden. They didn't take any chances and they didn't want anyone to know where he was. Why?

[70] Walker must have been incredibly intoxicated when he wrote this entry. All of the spelling and grammatical errors are due to Walker's inebriated state. I have replicated his writing exactly the way it appears in the diary to allow you to experience the moment for yourselves. Also, many of the words in the passage were illegible. When I get to a word or sentence I was unable to translate, read or even comprehend to try to make a sentence of, I will simply write [word/sentence illegible].

that? Can I just go back and [word illegible]? Id like that. Id like that a lot. I would. Id love to be young again. Just not even have a care in the world and just be myself. Do whatever the hell I want to. I could [words illegible] or I could start over. Could I do that? Id like that. I would. Cause I hate this. I hate my life. I don't know if I can take much more of this.

November 29, 4:00 pm

Where the hell was I last night? I can't even read my own writing. I missed Thanksgiving. That's all I know. And now, I have to face Jen, look her in the eyes, and lie to her. I have to make up another bullshit story about run-ins with the law. I know she's talked to Dean by now. I can't use him as an alibi anymore. I've seen him less than I've seen her in the last few weeks. She's going to put two and two together eventually. And then, she'll know that I've been lying all along. Will she be able to forgive me? I hope so. I love her more than anything in the world. I don't want to lose her but I think if things keep going on like this, if I have to go on lying, Jen and I will not be together long enough for me to witness the birth of our child. I really want to be there for that. Nothing is going to stop me. Unless Jen and I have a falling out, nothing short of death will keep me away from the hospital room that day. That will be one of the greatest days of my life and I WILL be there to enjoy it.

December 25, 11:00 pm

Home for Christmas. Thank God for small miracles. The XXXXXXX didn't need me on assignment. I had a feeling that if I missed Christmas like I missed Thanksgiving that would prove to be the end of Mr. and Mrs. Hayden Walker. I couldn't go on with the lying. I had to tell her the truth. Part of it, at least. I owed her that much.

"Jen," I began. "I have to tell you something. Something that could seriously change things between you and me."

She sat on the sofa, patient, bracing herself for the bad news.

I couldn't find the right words. I stumbled over a few false starts and stuttered incoherently. "This is, uh . . . this is harder than I thought it would be."

"Just say it, Hay."

"I've been lying to you."

"I know."

"You know? How could you know?"

"I talked with Dean. What's going on, Hay?"

"I want to tell you. I do. I want to tell you everything is going to be all right. But I can't."

"What can't you tell me, Hay? You don't trust your own wife enough to keep a secret; is that it?"

"Jen, you know that's not true. I would trust you with my soul in Las Vegas. But I cannot tell you. Don't you understand? They will kill me."

"What the hell are you talking about, Hay?"

"Nothing. Forget it."

"No. There's no 'forget it' now. What have you gotten yourself into?"

"Nothing. Something." I sighed and composed myself. "It's not a bad thing. It's just a secret thing."

"A secret thing?"

"A top secret thing."

She lowered her head. "Please, Hay. Don't do this to me. The lying and sneaking around have both been hard enough to overlook but now you pull this Cloak and Dagger bullshit. What's going on?"

"I promise you that when the time is right, I will tell you everything. Right now, I really need you to trust me. I'm going through a really rough patch right now and I need to know you're behind me. I love you more than life itself, I hope you know that. I would never leave you or do anything to hurt you. Do you believe me?"

She nodded and began to cry.

"Okay. I promise you that I will be more honest. This thing I'm involved in is a lot like work. I can't tell you whom I work for. Not yet, anyway. That comes later. I'm doing the same line of work I was doing at the university except these cases are a lot stranger. A lot. I'm not sure I like it but I can't get out now. Once you're in, you're in for life. They're funny that way."

"Who?"

"I can't tell you that right now. I can't." There I was promising to be more honest with her and in the same breath I had been dishonest. "I'm not cheating on you. I'll never leave you. I will love you until the day I die. Do you believe me?"

She nodded.

"Do you trust me?"

"No." She smiled. "But I'll work on it."

"I love you, Jen." I hugged her. We spent the rest of the day wrapped in each other's arms. It was wonderful. It's been one of the happiest days we've spent together in the last two months.

December 28, 4:00 pm

The XXXXXXX has demanded that I resign my position at the university as head investigator of the paranormal psychology department. I hate to do it. Dean and I have been together for so long. What am I going to tell him? The fucking XXXXXXX is going to be the death of me. All of this shit is really getting to me. They're systematically deleting my past and writing my future as we go along.[71]

---

[71] On December 29, 1983, Hayden Walker resigned his position as head investigator of paranormal psychology at the university.

"He didn't really say why," Dean recalled. "He just said 'personal reasons.' What was I going to tell him? No, you can't resign? I refuse to let you go? Of course not. I let him go. I put up a fight but he was very insistent. I hated every minute of it but I let him go. Hay was one of the best, brightest students I have ever had the opportunity to teach and it was my honor and pleasure to have worked with him; even if it was just for a short while."

"Do you ever think about him?" I asked.

"Occasionally, yeah. I always wondered what actually happened to him. Now that I know what I know, it blows my mind. I can't believe something like that would happen to Hay. It was a tragedy. The world of parapsychology lost a good investigator and the world lost one hell of a great man that day."

December 31, 11:00 pm

Another year has come and gone. I find I am filled with mixed emotions about its passing. Some of the best moments of my life happened this year: my marriage to Jen, finding out we are going to start a family, beginning my life again. That was all great. But then, those great moments were rivaled by some of the worst moments of my life: finding out Dad was ill, lying to everybody I held dear to me, resigning my position at the university and losing one of the best friends I've ever had. So, what will happen to me next year? What does fate have in store for me? Sometimes, that thought is so overwhelmingly mind-boggling it gives me migraine headaches. I find, despite the hardship I have endured, I am welcoming 1984 with an open mind. I think my career in the XXXXXXX will progress and get better. I will finally be able to tell Jen and my family the truth; about everything. No more lies. That will lift a huge burden from my shoulders. Right now, all I can hope for is the best and hope the best has my best interests in mind.[72]

---

[72] This is the last diary entry in this diary. You can't help but feel sorry for Walker. This particular year was so important for him yet all of these terrible events played a horribly significant role in his life

Diary 4

January 3, 8:45 pm[73]

I had hoped I would have more time with Jen before heading out on my next assignment but life doesn't always work out the way we want it to. I've been paired with a man who, for some reason, is referred to as Jakes. I'm William. They call me Bill. I'm assuming they just call you by your middle name since William is my middle name. Nobody in the Agency[74] uses their real name. Our contact man is simply called Mr. E. How bizarre is that? If anonymity is

---

[73] We can be thankful that the person who was kind enough, and brave enough, to pass this diary on to me, was not as thorough in his/her editing and filtering process as the editor of the last diary. For the most part, this diary is in full. However, there are several sections that have been blacked out and even ripped out, for whatever reason. The information that is most often censored from us appears to be people's names and names of locations. Whoever the silent hero is who delivered this parcel to me, I am forever grateful and indebted to you. Perhaps, one day, this silent rogue will come forth and claim his debt from me. Perhaps not.

What follows in the pages ahead is a bizarre blend of absolute chaos and utter horror combined with a very bitter blend of raw human emotion. Reader be warned, the following encounters are not for the faint of heart. Some of the strangest, scariest things I have ever read are held within the confines of this diary. I think the reason this is so intriguing and startling is that it *is* real. I've read a lot of scary books and stories in my life, but when I read this diary for the first time, I slept with the lights on. I didn't actually think things like this happened. I've seen things in movies like the things I read in this diary, but those were just movies. But they say movies are art imitating life. What you see in movies is what you see in life. I never believed that until I read these diaries. They somewhat opened a new door connecting imagination with reality and blew the hinges off, distinguishing the difference between the two of them. I've discovered, as I hope you will, that the line between reality and fantasy is much thinner than we originally anticipated it to be. In fact, it's almost non-existent. These diaries have redefined reality and reality has redefined itself. Fantasy is reality, reality is fantasy, and never the two shall part, so to speak. That thought, and these diary entries, have kept me up more nights than I care to remember.

[74] This is the first instance where we actually see the word "Agency" appear in Walker's diary. In the previous diary, whenever Walker made mention of the Agency, it was always blacked out with a magic marker. In this diary, not only is it not blacked out, we are able to understand that Walker is actually working for this particular agency. I have spent years trying to find any possible information about the existence of this Agency. I wanted to know

a precious commodity, I can understand using the middle names. But the idea that he is Mr. E holds too much coincidence. Mr. E, "mystery"; what's the connection? Why are there so many secrets? What are they hiding from us? Strangely enough, only the highest officials use their real names. I still can't figure that out but then again, maybe it's not supposed to make sense. The rest of us aren't supposed to know each other, I guess. That won't last. I ask too many questions. I'll get Jakes to warm up to me and tell me a bit about himself.

In the meantime, we're en route to XXXXXXX, XXXXXXXX. Why, I do not know. We'll be briefed when we get there. Until then, it's a waiting game. I hate waiting.

January 4, 6:00 pm

We've been briefed. We know our assignment and I have to say I'm a little nervous. The last two times I've investigated houses that we're supposed to be haunted I lost a friend. I don't really consider Jakes a friend, but what if it's me who doesn't make it back this time?

We arrived at the XXXXXXXX around 3:30. A man, who remained nameless, of course, met us at the door.

"Welcome, gentlemen. We have a real live one here." He seemed really excited about the news he was about to give us. "I think you'll both appreciate this particular assignment and find it very intriguing."

The three of us walked to a tiny room. It was very uniform: flat, gray walls with no markings or posters of any kind. Very plain and ordinary. A gaunt podium stood lonely in the center/front of

---

what they did, other than the obvious. Who were the highest officials? Where did they get their funding? Who sponsored their research? Years of countless man-hours produced negative results. I couldn't find one damn clue. This agency does not exist; not to the public, at least. I searched high and low for even a crumb, something I could work with. I can't find any evidence that it exists; no W2s, no work profiles, no job descriptions, nothing. I even called the Better Business Bureau and they couldn't tell me what the Agency is. They had no record or any official documentation declaring the Agency as a real agency.

the room. In front of this emaciated piece of lumber sat two silver-colored foldout chairs. The man walked to the podium and invited us to sit down.

"As usual, gentlemen, this operation is strictly need-to-know and nobody but the three of us and a select few above us, need to know. I'll leave time for questions after the briefing, until then I would appreciate your undivided attention."

The man made me uncomfortable. I'm not used to receiving orders. I'm usually the one commanding the troops. Here, I'm just a pawn in this game of chess: used, abused and totally unappreciated. But, what can you do? Life has a funny way of kicking you when you're down.

"Your assignment, gentlemen, is a spiritual cleansing. There is a rather large house on XXXXXXXX St. which has an unusually bloody history. The house was built by a rich aristocrat named Wesley Ashbury[75] who purchased the tract of land from England in return for his loyalty to the king and the expansion and exploitation of the New World. This guy was old money, very rich and he had a lot of ties with local clergymen and politicians so when he decided he liked a piece of land, no time was wasted in making sure he received it.

"The land had originally belonged to a tribe of Native Americans. When the English arrived, the natives were slaughtered and buried on the land the English were building on. Two years after the land was taken from the Natives, the house was finished and the Ashburys moved in. We know from his diary that strange things began happening shortly after the family moved in. He detailed bizarre sightings and, what he called, 'hallucinations.' Four weeks later, Ashbury's wife and three daughters were dead. The constable found Mr. Ashbury huddled in a far corner of his home, clinging to a loaded musket. The constable tried to talk Ashbury out of his

---

[75] Why this name was not removed I'll never know. After some considerable digging, we discovered that Wesley Ashbury had a house built on Westmore St. It was built in the mid-1600s; the documents were too old and tattered to extract an exact date. At the time it was built, Ashbury had a wife and three young daughters. On paper, this family was perfect but after reading mystery man's briefing, I discovered otherwise.

shock but, before he could be convinced, Ashbury shot himself in the head.

"Unfortunately for Ashbury, the bullet only grazed the side of his head and rendered him unconscious. The constable took him into custody immediately. A month later, Ashbury was hanged for 'being of unsound mind and body, and probable affiliations with witchcraft and demon possession.'[76] To the day of his death, Ashbury denied the charges and swore his innocence. He claimed he didn't remember a thing; that he was asleep and when he awoke, his wife and three children were dead and he was holding a musket that was not only still warm, but still smoking.[77]

---

[76]   Taken from the death certificate of Wesley Ashbury. For further reference, read *Witchcraft: The Manhunt*, pgs. 105-113. The book details several stories, many believed to be fables, of demonic possessions and the nature of witchcraft in early Colonial America. Pay particular attention to the section entitled "The Devil Followed Them From England." This section deals with Ashbury and his account with demon possession. Edmund Weiss, an historian on witchcraft in early American Colonialism stated that, "Ashbury's complete lack of ability to recollect or ascertain any remembrance of the situation clearly makes him an outstanding candidate for demonic possession [because] many persons who cannot remember certain events have experienced a traumatic schism with reality. In that altered state of reality, one allows himself to be subjected to all sorts of manipulation and exposes himself to any number of dangers. A demon is more apt to seduce the mind of a person who has a weakened capacity to reason than to try to seduce a mind that is rigid and stern. The demon knows it does not stand a chance in a mind like this; the odds just do not add up. Therefore, it can be reasonably deduced that Ashbury was, in fact, possessed at the time of the murders."(pg. 108)

[77]   I was able to obtain the diary of Ashbury which details many bizarre accounts with what appears to be paranormal anomalies. Too many to be ignored. The similarities documented by future occupants of the house are more than coincidental, I believe. I often wonder if Ashbury might have been possessed while writing his diaries.

June 13, We've been here less then a fortnight and already we are experiencing difficulties with living conditions. Bizarre noises and unexplainable hallucinations plague my slumber. Horrific images of savages brutally slaying my wife and children. I awake most nights with cold shivers and drenched with perspiration. Not a fortnight has passed and already I regret inhabiting this dwelling.

June 17, Witnessed one of my hallucinations during the light of day. These images are escaping my dreams and haunting my waking hours as

"It's almost thirty years before the house becomes occupied again. This time by Mr. and Mrs. XXXXXXX.[78] They lived in the house for approximately one month, similar to the XXXXXXXX.[79] The two complained to neighbors about strange noises and bizarre images but were unable to explain any of them. According to reports, the neighbors heard a loud noise around two in the morning. Almost

---

well now. Standing in my bedroom, looking into my mirror, I noticed a man I was not familiar with standing behind me. He was obviously a savage; long dark hair and skin. He stood remarkably still, arms crossed the entire time he was staring at me; those dark eyes penetrating my very sanity. He spoke not a word to me. He merely stared at me. And then he vanished, right before my own eyes. Am I mad or are these visions real?

June 30, These haunting images plague me still. I feel I am losing control of my body. I am uncertain of what I am capable of. I fear for the life of my wife and daughters. I fear these visions will force me to do something I would not normally do. What? This thought haunts me more than the visions.

The next day, the bodies of Ashbury's wife and three daughters were found lying slumped over one other, left where they fell. The one detail which bothers me about this entire event, other than the fact that five people lost their lives, is that Ashbury must have shot all four of them at the same time. A musket is nothing like a modern-day shotgun or any semi-automatic weapon for that matter; you don't have rapid, automatic fire. With a musket, after each shot, the shooter must reload. It takes a good rifleman almost ten seconds to load a new bullet into the muzzle, pour in the gun powder, pack it down and aim for his next shot. Which means the four women all stood around while Ashbury shot them. If you think about it, after the first woman was shot, the other three would have had a full ten seconds to run, and probably more than that if Ashbury was unfamiliar with the workings of the musket. Ten seconds! That's a lifetime. Ten seconds to run. The loading process would have been hindered further if Ashbury was forced to reload while running. So why didn't anyone run? There was ample time. Instead, they all stood there, like lambs at the slaughter and watched as Ashbury picked them off one by one. This phenomenon is still unexplained and will probably remain unexplained for eternity.

[78] Again, since I was able to track the house down, I was able to follow its progress. The house was next purchased by Mr. and Mrs. Keith Henry. The couple was elderly and had a relatively large nest egg set aside to retire on. The couple married in 1665 and until their brutal deaths, the two never had so much as a lover's spat; at least, I can't find any evidence to support such a claim.

[79] Ashburys.

thirty minutes later, the neighbors heard another loud noise and went to investigate. The front door was unlocked so they went inside. They walked around for almost twenty minutes and then approached the master bedroom on the third floor. When they opened the doors, they found an absolute bloodbath: Mrs. XXXXXXX[80] was lying on the bed, face down, shot once in the back of the head. The white sheets were drenched with blood. When they turned to exit the room, they found Mr. XXXXXXXX[81] hunched awkwardly on the ground and his brains splattered all over the wall; another single gun shot wound. The event was reported as a murder/suicide but according to neighbors, the XXXXXXX[82] were a perfect couple who never fought or argued. They were as happy as anyone could be after so many years of marriage. So why the deaths? Unexplained.

"The house remains vacant for the next hundred years or so when it is rented by Mr. and Mrs. XXXXXXXX.[83] They have three children, like the XXXXXXXX.[84] Except this family has two boys and a girl, the girl being the youngest child. They're there for a month, just like the other families. At the end of that month, like every other family, they are all found shot to death. The two young boys were found lying on their backs with one gunshot wound in each of them. The young girl was found in her room with a gunshot wound to the chest. The mother was found the same way. The father, who was responsible for the killings, was found on the kitchen floor with the shotgun by his side and a gunshot wound to the head.

"Fast forward to 1976. The XXXXXXX[85] family bought the house. He was a school teacher, third grade. She was a city councilwoman. They had two children. A month goes by and, surprise, surprise, we've got more dead bodies on our hands. Very

---

[80] Henry.

[81] Henry.

[82] Henrys.

[83] Strangely enough, I could not find the name of the family who owned the house at this point. There were never any records from the bank indicating a down payment or a mortgage, so the names of the occupants were never revealed. All I know about this particular family is what I read in the briefing documented in the diary.

[84] Ashburys.

[85] In 1976, the Wilkens family purchased the house.

similar circumstances; all victims killed by single gunshot wounds. The wife was found shot in the back of the head, the young boy and girl were found shot in the back.

"The police received a phone call around 2:30 am. It was Mr. XXXXXXXX.[86] He said he'd shot his wife and kids and actually asked if they could come arrest him. Of course, they arrested him immediately and charged him. He'd already admitted to the murders. What he never told anybody was why. We still have no idea. What made him, a school teacher and pillar of the community, shoot his entire family still remains unexplained.[87] Any questions?"

Jesus Christ, I thought. All that murder and death in one house. "One: why are we here? These appear to be homicide cases. What's paranormal about them?"

"We believe these deaths are connected, not just by the fact that they all happened in the same house but by the fact that they are almost identical cases. The occupants were never informed of the history of the house. They were never told what happened there yet every time, the same horrible results. We believe this goes back to when the house was built in the 1600s."

"How?"

"Native Americans have a different culture from ours. When we bury our dead, we bury them all facing up, so they can go to Heaven, good or bad. Let God decide the judgement. In some Native American cultures, the bodies of individuals believed to be evil or possessed were buried face down, so they could never reach the spirit world. The good souls were buried face up. In our culture, like I said, everyone is buried face up; so when the English slaughtered the Native Americans and buried them, they would have, most probably, buried them all face up: good and bad. If an evil spirit was buried face up, it would be able to surface. And if an evil spirit was buried face up underneath a house, it would probably haunt that place for eternity."

"So, you're saying this house is haunted by some sort of demon?"

---

[86] Wilkens.

[87] Anthony Wilkens is currently serving three consecutive life sentences; one for each of his victims.

"That's exactly what I'm saying."

"So, what do you want us to do?"

"Judging by your highly successful careers as paranormal investigators, I am quite certain that both of you know how to cleanse a house of evil spirits."

"An exorcism?"

"Yes."

These things can be incredibly problematic. Demons have much more negative energy than ghosts. Things always go wrong. I don't know if I'm ready for this. I can sense that Jakes is as nervous and concerned about this assignment as I am.

January 5, 10:00 pm

They have us shacked up in this cheesy motel called the Bluepoint. The wallpaper seems to be circa 1900 and is peeling away at the corners. Water stains cover the ceiling and carpet. It's probably roach-infested but I'm not about to turn the lights off and find out.

They don't let us share a room. Even though there are two beds in here, they have us in separate rooms. I don't know why. Maybe it's so we don't talk about the assignment. More than likely, though, it's so we don't talk about ourselves. The Agency doesn't seem to want us to know anything about each other. Even though the bond between investigators is incredibly important, especially during a cleansing, they keep us separate. I don't know if I can trust this guy and he has no idea if he can trust me. If there is no trust, this assignment will fail. And fail miserably. It could result in one of us getting really hurt or worse, dead. So, why, when they know the importance of trust and bond, do they keep us apart?

January 6, [time illegible]

Today's the big day. I've attended and conducted dozens of these cleansings[88] in the past but this particular cleansing has me

---

[88]   This point proves that there are other diaries in existence. Of all the material I have read, the only time I came across Walker possibly attending an

worried. I've never had to face a demon before. That sounds so corny: a demon. People equate demons with horrible, half-animal, half-human beasts. They're not though. Demons are just fallen angels. They have much the same qualities as anybody walking the earth. Except they usually have a huge chip on their shoulders. They're still pissed about that "God created man in his image" thing. I guess they didn't like the idea of being replaced. The Bible says something about those who were not going to be replaced so easily being banished from Heaven. Now, they walk the earth, much like us, awaiting the apocalypse and doing what they can to hurry the process along.

The problem with trying to exorcize a demon, rather than a ghost, is that a demon is stronger. They can and do manifest themselves differently than ghosts. They can appear physically, in human form, or they can be invisible. They have the ability to be seen or not seen. And it's when they decide not to be seen that we have problems. Which seems to be the case here. The demon has, in the past, infected the human inhabitants forcing them to do things they wouldn't normally do, which is fun for them. What happens if the demon gets inside Jakes and I can't tell if it's him or not? How can I trust him with my life when I don't even know him?

January 6, 3:30 am

Returned from assignment. I'm exhausted but I want to write all this down while it's still fresh in my mind. I don't want to forget anything. Not like that is possible anyway. What a fucking mess. If I never have to exorcize another house again for the rest of my life I will die a happy man.

We entered the house around 11 this morning. We didn't get two feet through the door before our gauges and instruments went

---

exorcism was at Katherine's Bed and Breakfast with his co-worker, Rick Deeves. I hope that one day I will find these diaries or perhaps the diary entries. I have pondered whether or not some of the entries which were torn from the diaries contained some of these exorcisms. Perhaps some day we'll know.

crazy. This place was teeming with paranormal activity. They were everywhere. They weren't all bad, but they weren't all good.

"How much activity are you picking up on the EMIC?"

"Off the chart," Jakes said. "It's phenomenal. I've never seen so much energy in one place."

"The PDC is going crazy too," I said.

I still wasn't expecting anything problematic until we had to confront the evil spirit inhabiting the house. Many of the apparitions were just that, apparitions; the trapped souls of those individuals who had the unfortunate predicament to live in that place of evil. They would be easy to convince. Sometimes, all you have to do is tell them that it's time for them to move on. More often than not, the apparition will leave if you ask it to. If it doesn't, then you have to get a little physical.

"Spirits," I yelled. "We can understand why you are here. And we can appreciate your unfortunate position. But, it is time to move on. It is time to go on to a better place. This place, this house, has no more use for you. You are free from any and all ties that bind you here."

A child's voice giggled behind us. "I see you."

I turned around quickly but there was nothing there.

"Hello?"

Nothing.

"Jakes, you getting anything?"

"You better believe it."

"Hello? What's your name?"

Again, that spine-tingling giggle. I walked toward where the sound was originating. A cold chill shot through me. I could hear another giggle. This time, it faded away down the hall in front of me.

"This is going to take a long time. We should split up."

"Are you insane? This place is huge. What if something happens?"

"If I need help, I guarantee you'll hear me screaming across the house. People in the next town will hear me. Don't you worry about that."

We split up. I took the second floor and Jakes took the first floor.

I tried to remember everything I had learned up until that point about cleansing houses. It's not a terribly difficult thing to do, but it can be exhausting. And it can take hours, days even.

"Little girl? Hello?" I walked up the stairs trying to be as quiet as possible. I don't know why. If the spirits were aware of my presence, they wouldn't be concentrating on the noise I was making. That's their advantage: they can see you but you can't see them. You could walk right by a ghost and, other than a strange feeling of coldness or a weird nauseated feeling, you'd never know they were there.

"Hello? Is anybody here? I would like to make contact with you."

I entered a room at the top/right of the stairs. Immediately, the PDC spiked.

"Whoever is inhabiting this room, you have been requested to leave. I am here to help you move on. I am here to help you cross over. But first, I must make contact with you. If there is anybody in this room, knock three times."

Knock. Knock. Knock.

"Are you a child or an adult? If you are a child, knock once. If you are an adult, knock twice."

Knock. Knock.

"Can you speak to me? If yes, knock once. If no, knock twice."

Knock.

"Will you?"

Knock. Knock.

"Please. I am here to help you. I understand you may be scared or nervous but I am here to assure and reassure, there is nothing to be nervous about. Do you understand?"

Knock.

"Good. I am here to tell you that you don't have to stay here anymore. This house has no more use for you. You can be happy and you can be free but you cannot stay here. Do you understand?"

Knock.

"Good. Will you leave?"

Knock.

I looked down at the PDC, and like that, the needle dropped quickly back to 0. I breathed a sigh of relief.

One down.

Before I knew it, the sun was setting and darkness was quickly consuming the interior of the house. I met Jakes by the front door. We went to the truck and grabbed our flashlights.

"Can't somebody just turn the power back on for the evening? I don't want to do this in the dark," he said.

"It's our lot in life, pal. No breaks. We don't need them. To hell with breaks. To hell with all of them. We can do this in the dark just as well as we could if the place was lit up like a Christmas tree."

"I'm glad you're so confident."

"Aren't you?" I smiled and forced a laugh.

"I have to tell you: I'm a little nervous about taking this thing on. I mean the others were easy to get out. But, I have a feeling this one's going to be tough."

"You can't be nervous. You can never let it know that you're afraid of it. That's its strength and your weakness. You have to be absolutely certain that this thing is no match for your superior ability."

"How do you do it?"

"Easy. I lie to myself."

He laughed.

"All right. Let's get this over with."

We walked back into the house, no light except for the dim ray of our flashlights.

I was terrified.

The two of us stood in the center of the living room. We panned our lights around the cavernous living room. The ceiling had to be at least fifteen feet high and the walls were at least thirty feet apart, maybe more. There were actually pillars supporting the structure of the room.

"Evil spirit," I yelled. "You are no longer welcome here. We'll give you one chance to leave without incident. Can you hear me? Knock once for yes, twice for no."

Knock.

"You have been asked to leave this dwelling. You are no longer welcome here. Will you leave?"

Knock.

"Good. I thought this was going to be--"

KNOCK! The sound was so deafening. I had to cover my ears to dilute the noise.

"GET OUT!"

"That's funny," I said. "We just said the same thing to you."

"Bill, are you out of your fucking mind? This isn't game and I'm not playing. Just do what you have to do and let's get the fuck out of here."

"Relax, Jakes. You have to let these guys know you're not intimidated by them."

Of course, I was lying. I was whimpering on the inside. I didn't want Jakes to know I was scared, though. I wanted him to think that I was confident that we could beat this thing. At the time, I didn't think there was a chance in hell of beating it. But I wasn't about to tell Jakes that.

I continued my taunting. Don't ask me why. "Why are you here, anyway? Nobody wants you here. You're not welcome. You never were. Why don't you leave?"

"LEAVE!" It was like he was imitating me. Except he was commanding me at the same time.

"No. No, I think I'll stay awhile. How about you, Jakes?"

"Don't do this," he whispered angrily. "Please. I don't want to die."

"Relax. He's not going to hurt us. He may rough us up a bit, but other than that, he's harmless. And he knows it. DON'T YOU?"

"GET OUT!"

"I think we've been over this and I believe I've been very clear on this issue. Our position is this: we have been assigned to make sure you no longer take up any type of residence here. Now, in order to carry out that assignment, I'll tell you this: we're not leaving until you leave. If you don't leave, hell, we just might move in. Do you like Judas Priest and Metallica? I could listen to them all day. Real loud, too."

"Stop fucking around. I don't want to do this. I say we get the fuck out of here. Now."

"And leave without acquiring our objective? Come on, Jakes. We can take care of this worthless sack of shit. He's nothing."

I felt a sudden, hard jab in my side, like an invisible battering ram smashing into my rib cage. I thought Jakes had gotten tired of my antics and decided to smack me one so I shot an awkward glance in his direction.

"I didn't fucking touch you."

"I think we pissed him off."

"We? What the fuck? We? I didn't do shit!"

"I may have made a mistake."

Another hard jab, this time in my back. I spun around looking for something to swing at but I knew I would just be punching air. Suddenly, I wasn't so sure of myself. I wasn't nearly as confident. I was beginning to think that not only was this thing more powerful than I had expected, but it was capable of inflicting immense harm upon us.

Another jab to the chest. I fell backward and the hit the floor with a dull thud.

A kick to the side. I rolled over onto my stomach and mustered what little strength I could to get to my knees. I coughed, gasping for air.

Another kick to the side. This one knocked me flat on my back.

"For Christ's sake, help me."

"What do you want me to do?"

"Reason with him." I was joking, or course. I still don't know how I was able to crack a joke when I was getting the shit pounded out of me. It must have been nerves.

A cold hand grabbed me by the throat and actually picked me up off the floor. Another jab to the stomach. I coughed out another precious gasp of air.

"Stop! Please, stop!" I yelled.

What had me by the throat stopped hitting me. I could still feel the cold hand wrapped around my throat, though.

"GET OUT!"

I was gasping for air, kicking at nothing in a desperate attempt to hit something–anything.

The grip on my throat released and I fell to the floor.

"I think we should leave," I said, massaging my throat, trying to ease the pain.

"Me, too."

We hurried to the door, not looking behind us. I grabbed the doorknob. A maniacal laugh echoed through the room.

"Dammit!" The door was locked. I tried unlocking it but the lock wouldn't budge. "We seem to be in some serious shit here. Did you see another way out?"

"There has to be."

We ran through the downstairs floor searching frantically for a way out. All the while, the same, evil laugh echoed through the house.

"We're not getting out of here," Jakes said.

"Why not?"

"Because it doesn't want us to."

"I am not going to die here. Not here, not like this. I've got a wife with a baby on the way and I will get home to them."

We searched desperately for what seemed like an eternity but in all reality, probably only fifteen minutes had elapsed. There wasn't a single exit other than the front door.

"Let's try upstairs."

When we got to the second floor, the strange became stranger. A series of dimly lit ceiling lights blinked out at us even though the power supply to the house had been cut off.

On. off. On. off. On. off. On–

The laugh once again bellowed through the hall. The sound was quickly drowned out by the banging of doors, every door leading out into the hall opening and shutting in unison. The sound was deafening.

"Jesus, we've got to get out of here."

"We'll go out a window." I went into the first room we came to. A giant window overlooked the neighbor's yard. I grabbed a chair from the corner and threw it at the window. In mid-air, just before impact, the chair stopped, slammed to the floor and shattered into pieces. In desperation, I charged at the window, trying to knock it out but something grabbed me from behind and pulled me back.

I thrashed outrageously trying to free myself. Whatever had me, had me. The grip was so tight, I was losing circulation in my arm.

"Let go!"

Whatever had me, released its grip and I fell to the ground.

I looked over and Jakes was lying unconscious on the floor. I had no idea what happened to him but I had to get over to him. I crawled, still a bit shocked from what had happened.

"Jakes, are you all right?"

No answer.

"Answer me." He opened his eyes and stared at me.

"I see you." It wasn't his voice but it was coming from his mouth. "I see you," he said again in that same childish, elfin tone. He giggled and got to his feet. "Do you want to play a game?"

"What are you talking about?"

"I want to play a game," the child's voice demanded. I tried to crawl away from him. "I want to play! I want to play!" the child demanded again in a whiny tone.

"Okay. Okay. What do you want to play?"

"Hide and seek."

"Hide and seek?"

"Yeah. You hide and I'll find you."

Jakes' body toppled to the ground like a collapsing building. He wasn't dead; I could still see his chest rising and falling but other than that he wasn't moving.

"Jakes, wake up." I slapped his face trying to wake him.

"1 . . ." the elfin voice cried out.

"Get up!" I yelled.

"2 . . ."

"Please, I can't do this by myself."

"3. Ready or not here I come."

I ran. I didn't even know where I was going. I just ran for my life. I ran down the hall; lights were still flickering and doors were still slamming. I wanted to cry. I wanted to ball up in a corner somewhere and cry.

I heard a door open behind me. I ran harder. I didn't really have a plan; I was just running. My legs felt like lead weights. The harder I tried to run the heavier they felt. I tripped over a lump in the carpet and catapulted myself down the hallway smashing my head against the wall. Blood trickled down my forehead and splattered on the carpet.

Blood had been drawn, and like sharks, whatever was behind me could smell it. I heard another evil giggle come from somewhere behind me.

"Where are you?" The voice asked.

My head was spinning and the pain seared through my forehead like a tidal wave crashing against the shore. A knot had already started to develop and swell. I pressed my hand to my forehead trying to stop the bleeding. Somehow, managing to muster what little strength I had left, I picked myself up off the ground.

I turned down hallways left and right. I had no idea where I was going. Completely lost and beginning to lose what little sense of courage I had left, I turned left again and started ascending a giant staircase. I don't know why. I knew that if I was a floor higher that I would be one floor farther from escape, and at least ten feet higher if I could find a window to jump from.

Something was drawing me to that floor.

I turned left at the top of the stairwell, still having absolutely no idea where I was going or why. Another long hallway spread in either direction. I proceeded forward, praying for a way out. I was close to tears now. The lights continued to flicker on all sides of me, doors banged around me. The elfin voice yelled again from somewhere on the floor beneath me.

I ran faster. The sound of my shoes pounding off the wooden floors resonated against the walls producing an awkward sound, like hearing someone bang on a hard surface under water. My ears felt clogged and my sense of hearing was beginning to dull. I shook my head, stupidly hoping this would reinstate my hearing.

"Come out, come out, wherever you are!" the voice yelled; this time from the same floor as me.

I darted into a room on my right and slammed the door behind me. I searched frantically for an exit. Nothing, not so much as a window to crawl out of. There wasn't even a closet to hide in. I paused trying to gather my composure. I was beginning to hyperventilate. I clutched at my chest feeling the beat of my heart and lungs all but burst through my rib cage. My throat was beginning to swell from the overburden of heavy breathing.

Knock. Knock.

I jumped away from the door. Whatever had knocked was standing on the other side of the wall. Until that moment, when I turned back around, I hadn't seen her. I simply hadn't noticed her lying there on the bed.

"Ma'am," I said with a quiver in my voice. I pressed forward, reaching out to her as she lay on the bed in the center of the room. "Ma'am, can you help me?"

Knock. Knock.

"Please, ma'am. I need help. I don't know how you got here but I'm in serious trouble. Please."

The door burst open behind me jarring the woman from her sleep. She looked at me . . . that's not true. She almost seemed to be looking through me. She was an older woman. I have no idea how old, but in that split second, I could see a look of terror in her face. I turned around, expecting to see the little girl. Instead, an older man was standing in the doorway. He was bulky and holding . . .I don't know what, but it was the biggest fucking gun I've ever seen. The barrel alone was almost two feet long.

"Sir, I don't know what the hell is going on but whatever's wrong we can work it out."

He raised the gun to his shoulder and aimed it at me.

"Sir, don't do this!"

The sound of the bullet exiting the chamber echoed loudly in my ears. I could see the smoke rising from the muzzle and trigger as the bullet hurdled toward me.

Time had slowed to a crawl.

I could literally see the bullet splitting the air as it tore through my clothing and passed through my body. The bullet should surely have killed me yet, strangely, I felt nothing. I turned around to see the bullet continue its rampage and plant itself in the back of the lady who was lying on the bed. She howled out a sound of extreme pain and fell silent.

Mouth gaped open, eyes as wide as oceans, I stared at the woman as blood poured from the open wound and flowed down her back in little rivulets draining off into a mini-delta on the mattress. She lay motionless on the bed, color already beginning to drain from her body.

I turned back to face the man, knowing what was next. What I was seeing had to be the ghost of any number of the poor inhabitants of this house who had met a horrible fate on the night of their deaths.

The man placed the barrel of the gun in his mouth and pulled the trigger. His brains splattered bizarrely against the wall and his body crumpled to an uncomfortable, hunkered-down position.

Again, I gasped for air; searching for answers that really had no questions to precede them. I collapsed to the floor and sat cross-legged, cradling my head in my hands and rocking back and forth. I started to cry.

"What the hell is going on?"

"Mr. Walker?" Gooseflesh ran up and down my spine. I jerked my head up and looked spastically in every direction.

"Who's there?"

No answer.

Again, I yelled, "Who's there?"

"We are," came the reply.

"We? You and I?" I asked, hoping for some reason to produce itself.

"You and us."

At that moment, the head of the corpse which was, until just recently, hunkered down on the ground with what was left of his mind splattered on the wall behind him like a Jackson Pollack print, stood up and looked right at me.

He brooded menacingly over me. Legs kicking wildly, I tried desperately to push myself away from him. Backed against the bed, I was trapped. I pressed my hands to my face.

"This isn't real," I said over and over again. "You're not real."

"But we are, Mr. Walker. We're very real."

A cold hand slid slowly across my shoulder grabbing my neck. Paralyzed with fear, I prayed for my life. "Won't you join us?" came the female voice from behind me.

The man again raised his gun to his shoulder. I could see right through the hole in his head, the eerie patten of splattered blood showing through. He pulled the hammer back, ready to fire. Again, I kicked wildly and broke free from her grasp seconds before the gun went off. I rolled away from the bed in time to watch another bullet enter the woman on the bed, blowing the right side of her head off.

I rose to my feet and darted out the door. I looked over my shoulder as I ran from the room. The man seemed unfazed by what he had done. He too turned and followed me into the hallway.

Another gunshot rang out, echoing through the hallway. A light on the wall to my right shattered from the impact of the bullet as it zipped passed my head. I ducked as flames and sparks erupted from the detonating socket. Turning left, I headed back down the stairs, tripping over ever other step, the weakness in my legs increasing with each passing second. When I reached the bottom of the staircase, I turned left down the hallway, the same way I had run to get to the stairs. All I wanted was the front door. If I had had ruby slippers, I probably would have tried clicking them together. I was desperate at this point. All I wanted was out. Out of that house.

Lost, I stopped for a moment trying to regain my bearings. I looked back to see if anyone was behind me. No spooks or specters in sight so I stood still for a moment and caught my breath.

Tiny footsteps clicked on the hardwood floor in a room to my left so I darted into a room on my right.

"Come out, come out, wherever you are."

I balled up behind a couch in the corner, crippled with fear.

The lights in the room extinguished but I could see the light in the hall caressing the outline of the door.

"Come out, come out, wherever you are."

The door creaked open. Nobody was there. I stared as the crack widened and then shrunk as the door closed. I was encapsulated by darkness. I was beginning to sweat and shake uncontrollably.

"Where are you?" the voice asked.

I bit my sleeve to keep from making any type of sound.

I felt a cold breeze sweep behind me.

A giggle erupted from behind me in the darkness. "I see you."

I bolted upright and dove over the couch. I struck my leg on the coffee table and pain seared through my body. I dragged myself up and lurched forward toward the door.

"Ha, ha. I see you," came a jeering taunt from the darkness.

I fumbled along the wall trying to find the doorknob but it wasn't there. The lights flickered back on, momentarily, to show me there was no doorknob, then extinguished again. Almost to tease me and show me that the room was nothing more than four walls without an exit.

"Jesus, please!" I began pounding on the wall hoping for help from Jakes.

"Help me! Somebody help me! Please!"

"Bill? Where are you?" I could hear Jakes on the other side of the wall. His voice was faded and faint but it was him. It had to have been. Nobody else would have been stupid enough to be in that house.

"Jakes, get me out of here. I'm trapped."

Suddenly, a ray of light pierced through the darkness and a door opened. I looked up and saw a brass doorknob, which hadn't been there before, lit by the light coming in from the hall.

"Bill?" Jakes entered the room. I was on the ground, cowering. The little girl was gone now. Or if she was there, she wasn't making her presence known.

Jakes grabbed me and we ran down the hall racing passed pictures of the Christ child in a manger, passed pictures of angels, passed crucified lords and martyred saints. Blood oozed out of light fixtures mounted on the wall and slowly crept down to the floor, covering it in a thin, runny layer. We slid as we ran, trying to stay on our feet.

We made it to the blood-soaked staircase. The lights began to flicker again and doors continued to open and slam shut. We quickly descended the staircase.

The railing was covered with blood making the descent very difficult. From the bottom of the staircase, I looked back up. I don't know why I did it. At the top of the stairs was a man wearing a long, feather headpiece, his face marked with some sort of black paint. His arms were crossed as he stared at me. He didn't say a word, he just stared at me and pointed at the door.

The door immediately swung open. We didn't think twice. We dove outside and didn't look back. I don't even remember the drive home. I'm still shaking but I wanted to write it down while it was all still fresh in my mind. Even though shit like that is pretty hard to forget.

What happened to me out there? It's been years since I've lost my composure on an assignment like that. I don't understand it. There was so much negative energy it was suffocating.

Jakes is still pretty upset and shaken up. He won't even talk about it. But I want to talk and I can't. The only communication I have right now is you, dear friend. I guess you'll have to do for now. But soon, I will need solace from an actual human being; someone who can give back what I put in. Not now, but soon.

Very soon.

January 25, 8:00 pm

It's been more than three weeks since I have had any contact with my family. I hope that Jen has explained to them the seriousness of the situation I seem to have fumbled along into. I hope they understand that I am not ignoring them. I'll try writing to them. Maybe the Agency will allow me that much. I spoke with Steven Dunnett[89] yesterday and he said I could write a letter but that I couldn't make mention of any work I was doing here at the Agency. I guess I can

---

[89] As hard as I tried, I could not find a single shred of evidence to prove this guy even exists. In his past journal entries, Walker mentioned that only the highest ranking officials in the Agency used their real names. What I can't figure out is how a man of his power and stature can be invisible in the system. How does he hide? He should have bank records, old W2s, tax returns. Someone somewhere knows the real identity of Mr. Dunnett. There has to be at least one person in this world who knows who this man is. Whether or not they will ever come forward to prove that remains uncertain. Until then, Steven Dunnett does not exist. But I believe he's out there somewhere.

do that. For the most part, anyway. I'm not doing a damn thing right now. I'm waiting for the next assignment. I'll try to write to them all tomorrow.

January 26, 1984[90]

Jen,

I can't tell you how much I miss you. I wish I could hear your voice but they won't let us use a phone here. My only contact with you will be through these letters. I'm sorry. I miss you so much. How is everything going with the baby? It won't be long now before little Hayden Jr. is introduced into the world. I love you. From the bottom of my heart, I love you. I hope you believe that. I'm so sorry things are hard right now. They'll get better. I promise. They say when we are not on assignment that we may return home for a few weeks. Otherwise, we're stuck where we are. And I never know where I am or where I'm going. It's confusing. One day I'll be in one place, and the next day I'll be in a totally different state. I don't know how to explain it. This line of work takes its toll on the nerves. I've been privileged to work some strange cases, but these are the strangest yet. I don't know how much longer I can hold out. I want to see you. I want to hold you in my arms and tell you I love you. Soon enough, Jen. I promise. Soon enough.

I love you

Hay

P.S. Give little Hay Jr. a big kiss for his daddy.

---

[90] This section of diary was actually ripped from the book. Most likely not by the Agency but by Walker. It is a rough draft of his letter to Jen. Evidently, he wrote rough drafts of ever letter he sent. So, for future reference, any selected diary entry that has the year after the date, instead of a certain time of day, it can be implied that it is a rough draft letter he is sending to his wife or family.

[Crammed into the same page of the diary, folded and bent, was another letter; a response from Jen.]

Hay,

I miss you too. I've told your family what you said I was allowed to tell them. They seem to understand. They'd like to here from you, though. They want to know you're all right just as much as I do. When do you think you'll be able to come home?

Everything seems to be going well with the baby, which we are not naming Hayden Jr., by the way. We'll discuss that later, when you come home. The doctor said everything looks good and he doesn't foresee any problems at this time so keep your fingers crossed. There's still five months to go. I really hope nothing goes wrong. I also hope you will be here to help me through some of this. When will I get to see you again?

All My Love,
Jen

February 10, 11:00 am

Finally, the wait is over. After two incredibly long weeks, we finally have a new assignment. As of this moment, I have no idea what the assignment entails. I won't know until the briefing. I don't think this assignment could be any more bizarre than the last one. We'll have to wait and see.

February 11, 8:00 pm

I was wrong. I have seen some amazing, unexplainable events in my tenure as a paranormal psychologist, but this has to be, without a doubt, one of the worst assignments I have ever been forced to investigate.

Jakes and I arrived at the XXXXXXX, in XXXXXX, XXXXXXX around 4:00 for the briefing. The same man who briefed us on the XXXXXXX house, briefed us here. How does he know so much? I can only assume this man will be our briefing man from now until I get out of this God-forsaken job. This room is remarkably similar to the last briefing room: a skinny podium, gray walls, two silver-colored folding chairs. We sat down and awaited our briefing. The man fumbled around with a cordless remote for a moment then pulled down a white screen mounted to the wall.

"As always, gentlemen, this assignment is strictly need-to-know. Should anything happen to either of you, the Agency will deny any and all knowledge. William, we chose you for this assignment specifically for your background in abnormal psychology."

The man flicked the light switch. Darkness filled the room. A projector, somewhere in the back of the room, blinked quick pulses of light on the wall in front of us and settled as an unclear, blurry, discolored image on the screen. The picture was completely out of focus and impossible to distinguish, with any degree of certainty, what might be imprinted on it. The man pointed his remote toward the back of the room and the picture quickly came into focus.

The picture was appalling. I averted my eyes momentarily then looked again. Curiosity killed the cat. It's like that car wreck analogy: you pass by a car that's all but burned to a crisp on the side of the road and you have no idea if anyone is trapped inside so you look. But, here's the catch: you don't look to make sure there isn't somebody in there, you look to make sure there is somebody in there and that you'll be fortunate enough to catch even a quick glimpse of something so horrific you won't sleep for weeks. Bodies, burned and charred, body parts in the road, anything. The human mind is funny that way. Your superego tells your ego that it's not socially acceptable to want to look but all the while, your id is yelling and screaming like a child in a tantrum to see this hideous, gruesome reality. Your mind tells you to look away, just look away and drive but that other side of your mind, the insatiably curious side, takes control of your body and yells, "Look, goddamn you!"

So you look.

And feel guilty later because you saw something you weren't supposed to be privy to. I've seen a plethora of images the human eye was never intended to be subjected to and the haunting images plague me daily.

But nothing I have seen to this date was even comparable to the image displayed on the projection screen in front of me. I wasn't prepared for it. I don't think Jakes was, either. He also looked away, ashamed.

"This, gentlemen, is your next assignment."

The quiet clicking of the projector sounded as loud as a bat hitting a metal pole in my ears. I couldn't even blink. Even when I did, the image was still there, scorched into the backs of my eyelids: a young girl, maybe 18 or 19. If you were to just look at her face, she would appear almost peaceful: eyes shut and head tilted slightly to the side. She looked cherubic. If you were to only look at her face. The rest of her was a bloody mess. Her throat had been slit from ear to ear. She had been stripped naked, bound by some type of cloth, and left pinned to the wall in the shape of a crucifix. Her head was tilted to the right, her arms were outstretched and nailed to the wall with 12-inch galvanized nails pounded through her wrists. Her feet were placed on the floor as if she were standing at normal posture. In the middle of here chest, carved into her skin, was a pentagram.

"We found her two days ago. She was 17-year-old Carol St. Peter. She was 17 years old. The police received an anonymous phone call from an untraceable number. We assume it was the killer. Two weeks before the victim was found, the XXXXXXX state police received a package in the mail. Inside were two pieces of paper." He pointed the remote toward the back of the room again and clicked a button sliding the next picture into the projector. "This was the first piece of mail. A simple poem with no return address. It reads:

So many times
our bodies become
useless
to us. Why?
How can we
die without
actually
knowing or understanding
our
true and unrealized
aspirations?

154

"And this was the second piece of mail." He fumbled with the remote again. "It reads:

> Can inverting an entire continent
> allow one to find the answers
> he is looking for?"

He pushed another button on the remote and the projector flickered off, the quiet clicking sputtered for a moment then dissolved away.

"These are your clues, gentlemen," he continued. He switched the lights back on. "William, we're hoping you will be able to use your knowledge in abnormal psychology to help the authorities in the apprehension of the man whom the media is labeling 'The Pentagram Killer.'[91]

"The killer also left another poem at the scene; stapled to her left breast. This poem, we assume, was handwritten by the killer. We're not completely certain at this point. It reads:

> Ask not why
> linear dimension
> always
> brings us back to
> a place in time when all that
> matters is saving
> a life.

---

[91] Read Arthur Richard's *The Evils of Psychotic Rage* and *The Manifestation of Evil: A Complete History of the Pentagram Killer*. The books were published by Clatter Publishing. *The Evils of Psychotic Rage* mentions the Pentagram Killer in Chapter 11 (pgs. 189-225). *The Manifestation of Evil: The Complete History of the Pentagram Killer* chronicles the life of this savage killer. I will supply you with enough information to suffice the ego, but to really satisfy your id, I strongly recommend you read both these books. Warning: the graphic nature of these novels is not suggested for young children or the faint of heart. The bloody accounts of the Pentagram Killer from his first attack to his last are detailed vividly in these novels. In depth interviews with friends and family members of the victims and others involved in this matter are also included in *The Manifestation of Evil.* See for yourself what evil really lurks in the hearts of men.

"I have no idea what in the hell either of these poems mean. I do know that they are clues. Some kind of hint. William, what do yo think?"

"Most serial killers want everyone to know what they are doing. They want everybody, especially those in authority, to know exactly what they are capable of. It's all due to a massive inferiority complex. These individuals feel inferior to us, for whatever reason, and so they feel they must manifest their inadequacies by showing the world that they are not inferior at all. In fact, most of these killers are the smartest people on the planet. Dahmer, Bundy; all intelligence testing indicated that these men tested well into the 140s. Which is considered genius. These men want you to know what they are doing. They want to give you every opportunity to stop them, but they're going to make you work for it. I have no doubt that these are clues. All of them. The hard part is getting into their minds to unlock the riddle."

"Can you do it?"

"I won't know until I try."

"Get on it."

He left the room. Jakes and I left behind him.

I've been sitting here ever since, racking my brain trying to unlock these damned riddles. I can't do it. I'm mentally and physically exhausted and I don't think I am prepared to tackle this assignment. It could be weeks before the killer claims his next victim. I can't squeeze enough information from these two clues to solve the case. Unfortunately, another young girl is going to have to become a sacrificial lamb. When we get the next clue, we'll have a better, clearer understanding of exactly what this guy's intentions are.

This guy is different, though. Most serial killers do what they do to satisfy a grotesque need to overcome their own inferiority. This guy seems to have more purpose. What's special about this guy? What's his gimmick? Why a pentagram and why a name like St. Peter? Is it just a fantastic coincidence or is there a connection? Again, answers we won't know until the next poor victim is found nailed to a wall with a pentagram carved into her chest. I wish it didn't have to be that way but bad things happen to good people all the time. As unfortunate as that sounds, it's the truth. So, I raise my glass and toast you, Awful Truth. You spiteful, remorseless son of a bitch.

February 15, 1984

Jen,

I think I've done it now. This is the strangest thing I've ever seen. There's a serial killer on the loose. They found a body in XXXXXX, XXXXXX; a young female. She was crucified and a pentagram was carved into her chest. I ask you, what the hell is this world coming to? What the hell is going on? The killer left us taunting clues that I can't figure out and the Agency is depending on me to figure them out. If I don't succeed here, who knows how many other young girls will die at the hands of this maniacal monster. Why does stress carry with it such a heavy burden?

I wish I could offer you some estimated time when I will be able to return but the way this case is going, I could be gone for quite some time. I can't even begin to comprehend how long it will last. It could be over next week or next year. I'm really hoping for the former rather than the latter.

How's Hay Jr.? I know how much you love that name. Just let me enjoy this for now. We don't have to name him Hay Jr. I'll let you pick the name. Just nothing off the wall, okay? How's everything going with the pregnancy? What are the doctors saying?

I wish I could write more but time is limited. I hope this letter finds you in good health and good spirits. I'll see you as soon as possible. Know that I am always with you because I carry you with me always.

All My Love,

Hay[92]

---

[92] A very interesting side note: when I interviewed Jen, I showed her the drafts Walker had written in his diaries and they did not match the letters Walker

February 17, 1984

Hay,

I wish you would show a little more concern. I realize how hard everything must be for you. I forgive you for that. I don't expect you to write because you think I'll be angry if you don't. Write when you have something to say. I love you and I understand your situation. Just don't patronize me with three line letters. I look forward to receiving any kind of communication from you but when I get my hopes up and all you've written is a three line letter, it's discouraging. Everything is still fine with the baby. Stop worrying. I'll be fine. I hope you will be here when he's born. Do you think you will be?

Jen

February 20, 8:00 pm

She didn't even write, "I love you." And what the hell is she talking about anyway? If she doesn't want me to write, I won't. I'm

---

sent to her. It appears that the Agency was forging the letters Walker wrote to Jen and his family. You'll see more as we progress but it seems incredibly evident that the Agency was manipulating Walker's letters to a certain format. The letter Jen received simply read:

Jen, I wish I had more time to write but time is limited. How is everything going with the pregnancy? What are the doctors saying? I hope this letter finds you in good health and good spirits. All my love, Hay.

Jen told me how short and impersonal Walker's letters were.

"I just thought he didn't have time to write or he couldn't concern himself with me because everything was going so strangely on his assignment. I always thought he was losing touch with me. His letters seemed so distant and stoic. I feel horrible reading his real letters. There very personal and heart-warming. I should have believed him but I couldn't. I couldn't. He was gone for so long and missed so much of our lives. It was like he had abandoned us. I couldn't believe him after that. I couldn't trust him. And now that I know it was the Agency manipulating him, me, everybody, it tears me apart: to not know until now, years after everything went wrong, that he loved me all along and I turned him—no, forced him—away from me. I hope he can forgive me. I hope, wherever he is, that he can find it in his heart to forgive me."

only concerned for her health and the baby's health. I didn't think the letter was that short. She was obviously over-exaggerating. But why the tirade? What's going on? I don't understand her some times. I hope she isn't angry with me. I'll write her back in a few days. Give her time to cool down. We'll see what happens then.

February 20, 1984

Dear Mom and Dad,

I apologize that it has been so long since I have made any attempt to contact you. The boys here are a little stingy when it comes to contact with the outside world. Jen tells me that she has explained to you my situation. I hope you can forgive me. I am not ignoring you. I just have such limited time. How is everything going? Is Dad still feeling well? I hope so. I love you both.

Maybe you can tell me something: what's wrong with Jen? I wrote her a letter last week but when she responded to my letter, she seemed bitter and a little hateful. Did I say something to irritate her? Did she mention anything to you? Please, help me out. I fear the worst may be yet to come, for me that is, and I need all the support I can get. Anything you can find out would be greatly appreciated.

I'll be on the road for the next several weeks. I have a bit of a strange assignment. I'm not allowed to talk about it, though. But trust me, it's bizarre. You'll probably be reading about it in the papers soon enough; if things get as ugly as I think they will. Every day I fear for my life. I never know which day in the field might be my last, not just in my professional career but as an inhabitant of this planet. I've worked some strange assignments but this is, hands down, without a doubt, the strangest assignment I have ever been unfortunate enough to investigate. I'm terrified. I lay awake nights cursing the day I joined the Agency. Not like I had a choice though, right? It's my lot in life: whenever I feel like I'm one step ahead, I suddenly realize that I have one foot in the grave. Which step will I fall into? That's the eternal question. That's the question that keeps me up nights.

Things would be better if I knew what was wrong with Jen. Whatever you can find out, Mom.

Otherwise, write to the address on the envelope and your letter will get to me eventually. I don't know when and I cannot guarantee a quick reply but I will guarantee a reply none the less. I look forward to hearing from you.

All My Love,

Hay

[Folded into the same page of the diary]

Dear Hay,

Things are going well here. Your father is feeling almost 100% better. He's getting stronger every day. He's not running marathons yet but I have my hopes. So does your father. He wanted me to express his regards. He wants to know what they're paying you at the Agency. He says he can get you a job here that will match whatever you're making now. But if I know you as well as I should, you're not doing this job for the money. You're doing it for the thrill of the hunt, the subtle mystery of it all, and the opportunity to answer all the questions men have been pondering since the dawn of time. We're so proud of you, son. We miss you like crazy. But, we understand what you're doing. We wish you the best of luck on this assignment. You be careful. I don't want to read in the paper that you've been killed by some deranged psychopath. But, I guess, that's not really paranormal, is it? And, from what I gather from you, you shouldn't be in harms way too often. Good luck, honey.

I spoke with Jen the other day. She's just frustrated, Hay. She needs someone to support her. I'm not trying to tell you how to be a husband or anything. I am very proud of what you do but what Jen needs now is someone to reassure her that everything's going to be fine. I know you want to be there with her but your occupation doesn't allow you the time. Which is unfortunate, I know. Just keep in contact with her. She'd love you to call. She was telling me how much she missed hearing your voice. She said it always comforts her. I'll keep talking to her. I'll take your place for now but sooner or later she is going to need you. She only has about four months left until she's due. She's scared and frustrated and she needs someone to talk to. I didn't get the impression that she was angry with you. I don't know if she was hiding it or if you read too much into her letter. I hope it's the latter rather than the former. She doesn't seem angry at all. She was telling me how proud she was of you. I think she just misses you, like the rest of us. Come back to us safe, and soon.

All Our Love,

Mom and Dad

February 24, 8:00 pm

I think the letters from home are the only things that keep me sane. This assignment is going to give me an aneurysm. They found another victim today. Same scene, different girl, different state. We're in Alabama now. The second victim's name is Stephanie St. Matthew. I know that the names have special interest. Both victims have names that represent some sort of saint. The inverted pentagrams indicate that there are religious implications here. What and why aren't important. Perhaps the killer is committing these murders in the name of God for some reason or other. I'll never understand all the killing that ensues in the name of God. Some of the bloodiest, most murderous wars were all fought in the name of God. Psychotic killers kill in the name of God. Why? Are they really doing God's work? Would God allow any of this to transpire? Why would he do that? What implications does this have on the case? Unfortunately, the names of the victims only serves as a small purpose. We still don't have any clue why this guy is doing this or who is next. We can't detain every woman, 17-21, with the last name St. Something. There are far too many of them. So what can we do?

There has to be some kind of connection. Something in these clues has to help us understand what is going on.

Jakes stopped in. He handed me a Ziploc bag with the word EVIDENCE written in black ink on the front. Inside was a folded piece of paper. There were several drops of blood on the outside portion of the paper.

"What's this?" I asked.

"Our next clue."

"Another poem?"

He nodded.

"What does this one say?"

"It says, 'No one can tell how everyone else views them. Amid darkness and dankness, all are dead in my eyes.'"

"Very romantic."

"Isn't it? What do you think it means?"

"I don't know. I'll see what I can come up with."

I've been looking at this thing for almost two hours now. I can't make heads or tails out of it. There has to be one big, giant clue here and we're obviously–I'm obviously–too stupid to pick up on it. A good night's sleep and I'll get back to it tomorrow.

February 25, 12:00 pm

"Is there anything to indicate cyclical patterns?"

"Not 100%. Not yet, anyway. There was a two-week span between the killings, exactly two weeks. The killer sent the letters two weeks ahead of the day they found the first victim. We can assume that we have two weeks before he kills again. But his pattern is different. Normally, if there is a cyclical pattern, it is based on moon rotation; every full moon or new moon, the killer will strike. This guy's different. He strikes every two weeks, while the iron's still hot. Why doesn't he wait?"

"Premature ejaculation?" Jakes asked.

I had to laugh. "Christ, this case is going to be the death of me."

"I know what you mean. I haven't been able to understand this assignment at all. Why are we even on it? Why not let detectives handle it?"[93]

"I don't know. Maybe they wanted my expertise in abnormal psychology. But none of that matters anymore because the killer has crossed another state border. This case goes to the FBI in a few days. Maybe the Agency wants to show us off. Prove to somebody that screwing with the Agency is the wrong move, even for the FBI."

"You're a dreamer, Bill."

"That I am, Jakes. That I am."

February 26, 4:00 pm

Stopped by the house of Mr. and Mrs. St. Matthew. The brooding presence of loss and grief loomed over the house like one of those giant thunderclouds you see in the sky on days where inclement weather is imminent. Mrs. Stevens opened the door. She had obviously been crying: puffing bags sagging heavily beneath her bloodshot eyes. She dabbed at her face with a tissue that was visibly soaked through with tears and stained black from running mascara. Over her shoulder, I could see a crowd of relatives, neighbors and friends, a convened council for comfort, huddled closely together. None of them looked in our direction, even after we told Mrs. Stevens who we were. Sniffles and gasps of air, forgotten breaths, were the only sources of sound emitted by the circle.

---

[93] This question always bothered me because it was never answered in the diary. After extensive digging, I came upon a lead that seems to be the best possible explanation: the first victim was the St. Peter girl, daughter of Philip St. Peter, who was mentioned in one of Walker's earlier diary entries but omitted by me due to lack of importance to the story. Now, I'm not so sure this section was not important. However, what I ascertain from Walker's diary is that St. Peter was one of the head advisors for the Agency. Again, Walker never states this in the diary, it is merely implied because Walker seems to be using this man's real name. Also, how else can we justify the Agency taking over this case. Any other murder case, the South Dakota police would have handled the investigation; same situation with the Alabama killing. So why did the Agency stick their big egos into this assignment? The only plausible answer, to me, is that the daughter of St. Peter, a member of the Agency, was the first victim.

"Mrs. St. Matthews," I said in a calm, soothing voice. "I understand the hardship you and your family are undergoing and, believe me, the last thing we want to do is infringe upon you during this period of mourning." I tried to sound calm and relaxing. I didn't want to send her over the edge. They'd all been through so much in the past 24 hours, the last thing they needed at that moment was some two-bit paparazzi swinging by the house. I wanted to make absolutely certain that they knew we were not there to over-glorify the situation, that we were there, in fact, to help them through this by finding the killer. "I wonder if we may take a look in your daughter's room."

"Sure." Her eyes were watering as she dabbed a Kleenex to them. "Follow me."

We followed her up two flights of stairs and entered the third door on the right. Stephanie's room. "If you'll excuse me, gentlemen, I can't be here right now."

She left without saying another word.

We quickly scanned the room for any sign that might indicate why she might be with the killer on that night. Most probably, the killer researched her. He knew where she lived, which room was hers. He may have even tried to watch her.

"Check the window for any signs of forced entry," I said.

Jakes walked to the window, opened it, and hung himself over the window sill. He examined the outside frame of the window for a moment, then popped his head back in. "Nothing. But that doesn't mean anything. The window was unlocked on the inside, easy enough to open from the outside."

I noticed a dark imprint on the floor beside Stephanie's bed. "The son of a bitch watched her sleeping. Look." I pointed to the soiled stain on the floor. "There isn't much of an imprint here but I'd be willing to bet money it's his imprint. He could have snuck in the window late at night. There's plenty of shade to cover him with those trees blocking the view. He could have climbed in the window and walked right over to her, stood right over her. He could have smelt her breath and touched the naked flesh on her arm; all while she was lost in slumber. That son of a bitch."

"How do you know those aren't Stephanie's prints?"

"Did you notice all the shoes by the door when we came in?"

He nodded.

"And did you notice that none of those poor people down there were wearing shoes?"

He shook his head.

"Look at this house. It's immaculate. I don't even see any shoes in this room so I'm sure they always take their shoes off before entering the house. Now, I seriously doubt that Stephanie's socks were so muddy that they would soil her carpet. And, she couldn't have possibly weighed enough to make this kind of imprint in stocking feet. No. This print was made by some sort of boot or shoe. I can't tell which. But it was definitely him. But did she know he was here?"

"You just said she was sleeping."

"I know, but maybe she secretly had him meet her here. Maybe her parents wouldn't allow her to see boys yet. She was only 17. I've seen stranger things."

"Bill, this guy must have just hopped off a bus or plane. Did Stephanie's profile indicate that she was the type of person who would pick up a stranger and invite him to her house for a late-night rendezvous?"

"No. You're right. She didn't know he was here. But he knew she was here. He definitely studied her before he killed her. He must have followed her for days, memorizing her schedule; exacting measures would have to be taken. He would have to know when she was most alone, most vulnerable to attack. Maybe that's why there's the two weeks between victims: he's studying them. I have to see the crime scene. Let's go."

We left the house without saying goodbye. I don't believe they even knew we were gone.

We drove for almost a half hour before we pulled into the parking lot of the Greenpoint Motel.[94] The place was run down; grass was sprouting up between cracks in the pavement, the paint was chipping

---

[94]   The Greenpoint Motel is just off Route 65 in Montgomery, Alabama.

all over the building and half the bulbs that were supposed to be lighting the parking lot were blown.[95] This place is the perfect place to commit a murder. No cars, no occupants in any other rooms, an old man who couldn't hear a woman screaming if she was standing right next to him and his earpiece was turned on high. The darkness of this place would provide adequate cover in case he was spotted; the darkness would deny any eye witnesses a full, accurate view of him. The killer had done his homework.

Inside the room, the smell of hot, rotting blood was nauseating. I gagged as I ducked under the police tape that cris-crossed the door frame. The moment I looked up, I was staring at a chalk outline in the shape of a crucified martyr; there was blood running down the wall form where the nails had been pounded through her wrists. The holes left behind made the eerie effect of blood actually seeping from the walls. On the floor, directly in front of the chalk outline; the carpet was still soaked through with blood.

Other than that, the room was in excellent condition. The bed was still made. The Bible still nestled in the drawer by the bed. The remote control to the TV was still screwed into the night stand. The only thing that separated this room from the other twelve in the motel was the chalk outline and the red, blood-soaked carpet.

"I've seen enough, Jakes. Let's go."

We drove home in absolute silence; quiet contemplation was what both of us needed. Whether it would prove to be useful or not is yet to be decided.

February 27, 3:30 pm

Where's my killer tonight? He's out there, right now, plotting his next murder and I feel so fucking worthless. I can't help them. Any

---

95 Fifteen years later, the Greenpoint Motel looked exactly the same. When I visited, the pavement had not yet been resealed, the paint was chipped even worse and *all* the light bulbs were blown. They say that time can change a lot of things; not this place. This was like the motel that time forgot; that everyone forgot. The old man behind the counter, Jed Stillson, was clearly incapable of handling the maintenance and upkeep of a motel and judging by the lack of cars in the parking lot, he didn't really have the money for renovations.

of them. How many more have to die before I can understand this guy? How many more young women will be murdered before I can ascertain the intelligence necessary to identify with this guy? Only after I can identify with him, can I truly understand why he is doing this. I hate to wait and let another young girl die but what choice do I have? I can't understand his pattern yet and I can't understand his riddles. He has no communication with us outside of these riddles and clues. Where are you? I'm going to find you, you son of a bitch, and I'm going to carve a pentagram into your rotting carcass. You too will know and understand what pain is before we are finished. You'll screw up somewhere and I'll be there like an anvil, ready to strike. Mark my words, you will not finish this game you've started. You will never finish. You'll rot in a prison cell for the rest of your life wondering how the hell a stupid paranormal psychologist ever got the best of you. You will. And I'll spend the rest of my life wondering why the hell it took me so goddamned long to crack the code of a lunatic. But I will be happy in the knowledge that I did and put you where you belonged. Believe me.

March 8, 8:00 pm

Tomorrow's the big day. I still have no idea where this killing is going to take place. I don't know what city; I don't even know which state. This guy has already crossed two state borders to play this little game; where he is capable of going is unlimited. I just hope he stays in the country. There has to be a hint somewhere in these poems he's leaving us but what? I feel incompetent compared to this guy. He's always one step ahead of us. Tomorrow, another young girl is going to lose her life, horribly, and I can do nothing to help her. Her death will be so we can piece together another clue. Life sure does have a sick sense of humor.

March 9, 12:00 pm

On our way to Nevada. Police found the body of Marie St. Paul after an anonymous tip informed police where to find the body. Same technique so we know it's our killer. He's everywhere. I'm not ruling out the possibility that more than one person is involved in this twisted, macabre game. But, he's leaving himself plenty of time between killings to get to where he needs to be. He knows exactly where he has to go and we don't. That's his advantage: his itinerary is known to him and not to us. Soon enough, though. I just need a little more time. He's smart, though. We ran a check on anybody buying tickets for planes or buses to the past three sights. No matches. Not one name kept popping up. He's either paying with cash instead of credit card or he's traveling cross country on foot. I believe the former to be more reasonable. Paying by cash, he can avoid being tracked and followed. He's one smart son of a bitch. He's covering his tracks very well.

March 9, 9:00 pm

Arrived in Carson City around 3:00. Same scene: a run-down motor inn with bloody carpets and chalk outlines. He's laughing at me. He knows I can't find him. He knows he's smarter than me. And he's loving every minute of it. That's what gives him thrills, perhaps even more so than the killings themselves: he's smarter than us and he knows it. That must bring a smile to his face. This new poem is not very encouraging:

> To each and every
> exciting
> new day, comes a
> new beginning.
> Every day gives me one more chance to
> save these poor, wretched
> souls who wonder this place
> eternally in unrequited
> ecstasy.

I don't think things will be coming to a head anytime soon. This could go on forever. Why can't I figure this out?

March 10, 1984

Jen,

How is everything going? Is everything fine with the baby? How are your grades this semester? Are you doing as well as you had hoped? I hope so. I miss you. Every time I write I find myself wishing I could tell you when I will be home but every time, something new happens that makes it seem like I might never be able to come home. It's so damned frustrating and depressing. I'm on assignment and all I'm really thinking about is wishing I was home with you helping you through this hard time. I promise I will be home as soon as I can. You have my word. As soon as the Agency lets me go, I'm on the next plane. I promise you.

Things are getting worse, here. Another young girl was murdered in Carson City. It's the same guy but I can't figure out what his game is. This guy is different from all the others. Most serial killers don't leave the state they are killing in; most don't even leave a certain city. So why is this guy all over the goddamned country? What's he trying to prove? That he's smarter than me? We already know that. I keep hoping he'll die on his way to scouting out his next victim so I can come home but that would be too simple. Without complication, life is uninteresting. I just wish there wasn't so much complication.

I wrote to Mom and Dad a few weeks ago. They're doing well. Though you probably talk to them more often than I do. I think they need you just as much as you need them. Right now, I need all of you more than you probably need me. I'm losing my grip on sanity, I think. To find a killer you must think like a killer. Sometimes, though, I find that I'm thinking so much like a killer that I think I might actually be a killer. I don't know if that makes sense but that's how it feels and that's the only way I can explain it. I don't know what's going on. Days and nights blur together and before I know it, two months have passed since I've seen or heard from any of you. I can't even get to a damned pay phone to call and hear your voice. And I could really use that right now. I miss you so much, honey. I love you.

Hay

March 22, 9:00 pm

Another two weeks of useless detective work. Tomorrow, another young girl will die for no other reason other than the fact that I wasn't smart enough to save her. Everyone here at the Agency is counting on me to crack these riddles and I can't. I wish I could. These young girls deaths are on my conscience. I lie awake nights and think for hours how much possibility has been wasted and lost due to the death of these young girls. How much hope and goodwill could have been spared by saving their lives? What futures did these girls have and what future did they all lose because of me? It's ripping me apart inside.

March 23, 9:00 pm

Nashville, Tennessee. He seems to be picking these places out of a damned hat. I can't figure out his pattern. Another young lady, found in exactly the same manner as the other three girls. This one was Jennifer St. Mark. 19 years old and dead because I'm incompetent. This guy is smarter than me. I can admit that. If this is some type of hero's trial to make me realize I'm not perfect, I'll accept that. But, for Christ's sake, do all of these innocent young girls need to die in order to teach me that? Do humility and imperfection carry that great a cost? Enough is enough. I've learned a lot about myself and my ability. Let's save a life, here. If there's anybody up there, I have learned a valuable lesson. Can we throw foolish pride and ability out the window and help me out a little?

Another poem, another dead end:

Are we
really
innocent or does our
zeal make us
obtuse to our true
needs and
all that we desire?

What the hell does that mean? These riddles ponder some existential queries but to what point? What is he trying to tell me? Or show me? Maybe looking at all of them together will help.[96]

March 28, 7:00 pm

That son of a bitch thought he'd outsmart me. I'm on to his little game now. We know he's going to kill the next victim in Phoenix. I met with Phoenix police earlier today.

---

[96] On a folded piece of paper, the same five poems that were placed sporadically throughout the diary were all lined up together. I have no idea how long Walker pondered over these riddles or poems but he finally figured it out. He had found the one clue he was looking for. He must have been so excited to finally release the burden from his shoulders. He had cracked the riddles:

So many times
our bodies become
useless
to us. Why?
How can we
die without
actually
knowing or understanding
our
true and unrealized
aspirations?

Ask not why
linear dimension
always
brings us back to
a place in time when all that
matters is saving
a life.

No one can tell how
everyone else
views them.
Amid darkness and
dankness
all are dead in my eyes.

To each and every
exciting
new day comes a
new beginning.
Every day gives me one more chance to
save these poor, wretched
souls who wander this place
eternally in unrequited
ecstasy.

Are we
really
innocent or does our
zeal make us
obtuse to our true
needs and
all that we desire?

The pentagram killer had told them exactly what state he was going to kill in next. And, all the murders were committed in these state's capitols: Pierre, South Dakota, Montgomery, Alabama, Carson City, Nevada, Nashville Tennessee. The last riddle indicated that the next killing would be in Arizona. So, Walker caught the next plane to Phoenix.

"I need you to cross-reference any young females between 17 and 21 with the last name that begins with St.: St. Matthews, St. Paul, anything like that," I said.

"It's going to take a while."

"That's all right. We've still got a little time. We don't expect him to attack again until the 6th. That gives us just over a week. As long as he thinks he's still one step ahead of us, he'll continue as planned."

We've got you, you son of a bitch!

April 1, 1984

Jen,

An amazing breakthrough. I've cracked the riddles. I know where the killer is going to strike next. I'm in Phoenix, Arizona; that's where his next victim is going to be. We don't know who yet but we're getting more and more information in all the time. It's just a matter of time before we nail him. The son of a bitch slipped up this time. And we're going to nail him to the wall.

Enough about me, how about you? Less than two months until the big day. Are you nervous? If things go the way they should, I'll be home sometime next week. If things go the way they are supposed to. Life has a funny way of turning you in the opposite direction you should be going.

Have you talked to Mom and Dad lately? Are they still doing well? I hope so. I wish I could write more often but there's a killer out there and I'm riding his ass. I'm close on this one. I love you very much.

Hay[97]

---

[97] Another note that was written by Walker to Jen that seemed to be altered by the Agency. The note Jen received mentioned nothing of the killer or his assignment. I couldn't believe how much important information about her husband the Agency was hiding from her. She had every right to know exactly what was going on but the Agency kept it from her. Did they not trust her enough with the information? Who was she going to tell? This logic and rationale does not make sense to me. But, then again, is it supposed to?

April 6, 12:00 pm

How did we miss it? We had our opportunity and we fucked up. We had a wide-open window and we missed it. I don't know if I can take much more of this. Another innocent young girl has lost her life. Christine St. Peter, 18, of Phoenix has been confirmed as the fifth victim of the Pentagram Killer. The bad thing, other than the dead body, is that the killer didn't leave a riddle this time. We have no idea where he's going next. All we know is that we have two weeks to figure it out. Back to the drawing board.

April 7, 9:00 pm

What in the riddles he gave us tells us what he's trying to do? He must have some higher purpose. Something to shoot for. The riddle we received in Alabama, about linear dimensionalism, what did that mean? And what was that first riddle about inverting an entire continent? There has to be more to this.[98]

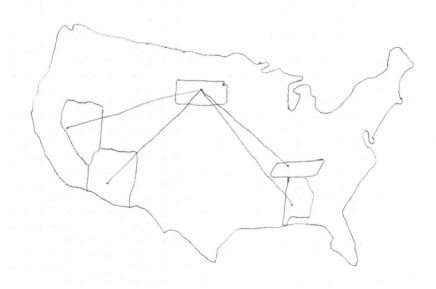

---

[98] The next two pages were occupied by maps of the continental United States. Walker was obviously challenging the linear dimension riddle.

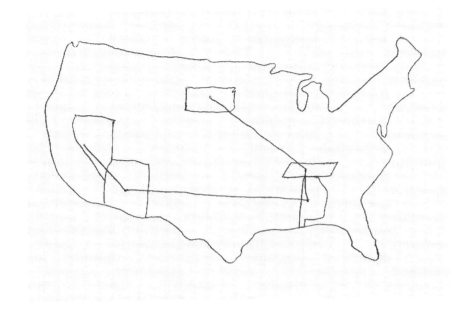

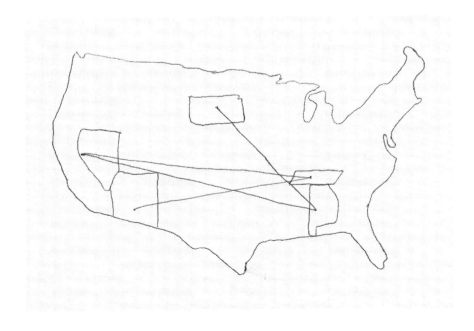

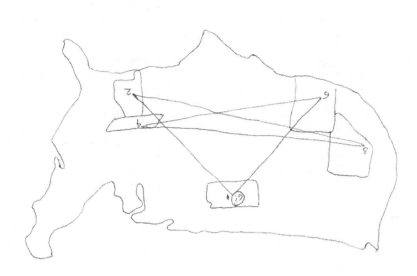

April 8, 2:00 am[99]

"He's going back to South Dakota," I told Jakes. He was still sleeping but this couldn't wait until morning.

"What?"

"I've figured it out. His clues were so blatantly obvious that I was overlooking them the entire time. I feel so stupid. How could I have missed it? Look at the poems by themselves."

---

[99] "Can inverting an entire continent allow one to find the answers he is looking for?" The riddle explained everything. After a few test runs, Walker must have figured out that the lines went from the first victim to the next sequential victim. This is all fascinating stuff. I suggest you read Ivon Kosolov's *Malicious Intent* printed by Cabot Publishing in 1979. The book has no mention of the Pentagram Killer but it spends two chapters discussing and arguing the mathematical and linear dimensionalism that can be associated with killers such as this. Kosolov has many fine points about this subject; one of them being that the "prudence and probability of mathematical and linear facts cannot only be implied in cases like this but insisted. It is unprofessional to dismiss the possibility that the killer is not killing just

He took the poems from me. "Yeah. So?"

"Now, look at this." I showed him the poems all lined up with the code broken.

"We've already established that. Where are you going with this?"

"His clues were right in front of me. I was trying to read too much into the riddles themselves. The poems are riddles but the real riddle was looking me right in the face. He's definitely going back to South Dakota."

"How can you figure that out looking at the riddles?"

"His first words to us. Do you remember?"

Jakes shook his head.

"Look at this." I showed him the map diagram with the star. "He didn't pick these states out of a hat; he was very strategic about it. All the murders took place in the capitols of each state. Each point on the map was the end point of the star. But, the star is incomplete. Only if he goes back to South Dakota and kills again will it be complete. Now, look at this." I flipped the star upside down. "'Can inverting an entire continent allow one to find the answers he is looking for?' He's not the Pentagram Killer because of the pentagrams he carves into the chests of his victims, he's the Pentagram Killer because that's exactly what he wants to be. And, look at the states. What letters do the states he killed in start with?"

"S . . .A . . .N . . .T . . .A. So?"

"Santa. It's almost humorous, right?"

He nodded.

"But an anagram for Santa is 'Satan.' We're dealing with one very disturbed individual here. And if he is who he thinks he is, or if he believes his delusions enough to actually be Satan, I can almost guarantee who his next victim will be."

---

for the sake of killing, but to prove a point or make a statement"(pg 231). Similar killings are cited in Kosolov's book as happening in England, France, Germany and Russia, Kosolov's home country. "You see, then, that these happenings are somewhat of an epidemic. We see them in every civilized country in the world. Mathematic and strategic planning are at the root of all murders that are premeditated"(pg. 248).

April 9, 9:00 pm

Arrived in Pierre, South Dakota. Not wanting to waste any time, we headed straight for the police station.

"How are you doing, today?" I asked the sergeant behind the desk.

"I'm fine, thank you. And you?"

"I'm doing really well, thanks. I wonder if I could speak with one of your detectives."

"I could put you in touch with Detective Harper. He's in today."

"That would be great."

"Who should I tell him is waiting for him?"

"William."

"Just William?"

I nodded.

"Okay." He picked up the receiver and pushed a button on the phone. "Harper, there's a William here to see you." He paused briefly. "I don't know. That's all he said: 'William.'"

He waited a moment with the phone pressed to his ear then said, "All right. I'll send him right in." He placed the receiver back in its cradle. "Follow the hall down to the first T, take a right to the next T, take a left and it's the third door on the left."

"Thank you."

I followed the maze to a door that read DET. HARPER on a glass window. I knocked to announce my presence.

"Come in." I opened the door to see a young man sitting behind the desk. I wasn't expecting to see a detective so young. Usually it takes years to reach that stature. This guy was different. He's young; maybe that's good. It means he must be ambitious to strive for such an achievement so early in life. He had to have promise, determination, and that is exactly what I need right now.

"How are you doing, Detective Harper?"

"I'm good. How are you Mr . . .?"

"Just call me Bill. What we share in this room must stay in this room. Is that understood?"

"Absolutely."

"I work for a government agency that normally deals specifically with paranormal and supernatural phenomenon but we've shifted gears a bit and now we are heading up a major investigation that began here about two months ago; do you remember?"

"Refresh my memory?"

"Young girl, murdered in a motel room, a pentagram carved into her chest."

"Carol St. Peter. Of course I remember. What does that have to do with supernatural phenomenons?"

"Nothing, really. I was surprised when I got called in on this investigation. They needed my background in abnormal psychology. They wanted me to profile this guy and maybe crack his code."

"What are you talking about?"

"This guy has been killing all over the United States. For a while, we thought his pattern was random. That he was killing at random actually classified him as a mass murderer but the ritualistic manner in which he chose to dispose of his victims and then the carving in the chest of the pentagram makes him a serial killer. The only thing we couldn't figure out was his pattern. Now we've discovered his pattern and believe he is going to strike again, in Pierre, on April 20th."

"Why do you think that?"

"I'm not at liberty to discuss the details of this ongoing investigation, Detective Harper. I'm here to ask you for your assistance. I think I have a pretty good idea who the next victim is going to be and I need your help to track her down. Can you do that for me?"

"Whom are you looking for?"

"All the victims have been young women, 17 to 21. They all have a last name of St. Something: St. Peter, St. Matthews. I think his next victim is going to be a young female with the last name of St. Michael. Can you run a scan through the cities residents and see if there might be any young females with those qualities?"

"Sure. Come back tomorrow, we'll have a list for you."

"Thank you, and thank you for your cooperation." I shook his hand and left the station.

"Why St. Michael?" Jakes asked me later.

"Just a feeling."

"St. Michael? Why?"

"Look, I'm not a religious man. Up until this case, I didn't even believe in Heaven or Hell. Now, I'm surrounded by Christian theology. All I know is what I've seen in movies and read in books. You too?"

"Sure."

"You know anything about this?"

He shook his head.

"From what I understand, when God created man, some of the angels were pretty pissed off. God was basically replacing them with a better model, right? So, some of the angels revolted in a fight for Heaven. The angels that revolted obviously lost and were cast out of paradise and into perdition. You following me?"

He nodded.

"What I gather from movies and things is that the archangel Michael was the angel responsible for besting Lucifer leaving him to God's judgement. Something like that, anyway. If this guy really thinks he's Satan, which I don't think he disbelieves, he's going to have a serious grudge against A.) saints, angels and religion, and B.) anyone named Michael. If you put the two together, his biggest grudge would be against anyone named St. Michael. I think he's saving the best for last, so to speak."

"I hope you're right, Bill. If you're not, another young girl is going to die and the killer will have won this little game."

"You don't have to remind me of the stakes, Jakes. I'm well aware of the consequences. Besides, I'm right this time. I know it."

April 10, 7:00 pm

Back at the station.

"We've got a list for you, Bill." He said, emphasizing my name with a hint of sarcasm in his voice. He either wasn't taking me seriously or didn't appreciate that I was hiding something from him. I'd gladly tell him everything if the Agency would let me. Every piece of information he knows about the case would be beneficial for

179

all of us. The more minds brainstorming the better. Unfortunately, the Agency won't allow me to tell him anything. He handed me a piece of paper with a short list of names on it.

"Is this it?" I asked.

"We ran a scan of all the St. Michaels in the city. We came back with six families. Of the six, only two of them have young girls: Michelle St. Michael and Emily St. Michael."

I nodded. "I want someone tracking them at all times. We know our boy won't strike until the 20th, unless he suspects he's getting some heat, then he might bail. We can't afford that. We've got one last chance at this guy and we have to catch him in the act. I need you to put a couple of guys on both of them. If either of these girls goes into a restroom, I want somebody outside making sure she comes out. But I don't want you to be obvious. Our boy is in town. He'll be doing his homework. If he notices an entourage of men in suits walking around his next victim, he'll get suspicious. We need to be invisible. Understood?"

"Sure."

"We've got ten days. Let's not screw this up."

Later, Jakes and I got together to discuss the matter.

"Should we have someone walking with her?" he asked.

"No. We have to be out of sight. We have to trail her but stay far enough behind so the killer doesn't feel like he's being watched."

"We have to let him take her?"

"Yes, we have to let him grab her and take her to whatever motel he's going to take her to."

"Don't you think that's a little dangerous?"

"It's incredibly dangerous. We'll only get one shot at this. If we fuck up, Ms. St. Michael is as good as dead."

"Can we try putting a decoy out there, maybe an undercover agent?"

"No. He knows whom he wants to kill. An agent is not a St. Michael. If it isn't a St. Michael, it won't be good enough. Besides, he's too smart for that. He knows what his victim looks like, every inch of her. Her body is imprinted in his mind. The second he grabbed the decoy, he'd know. Then, he'd know that we're on to him and he'll bail. That won't work. It has to be the girl he's been tracking for the last two weeks."

"You do realize we're putting an innocent girl in harm's way?"

"She's already in harm's way, Jakes. I didn't pick it that way; it wasn't my choice. You don't think I'd rather have any number of undercover agents out there? Hell, I'd do it myself if I thought our boy was stupid enough to fall for a decoy. But he's not. We have to respect that."

"Okay, I'll respect that. But if this girl dies, I'm not taking the fall for it."

"She's not going to die, Jakes. I promise. We've got this guy by the short and curlies. All we have to do is pull and he'll topple to his knees. We've got this son of a bitch."

April 15, 6:00 am

I just had a horrible nightmare. Jen was crying and clutching at her stomach, doubled over in pain, and screaming. Doctors came out of nowhere and, all of a sudden, all I could see was her face as she screamed, surrounded by dozens of blue-hatted heads moving and bobbing in unison like balloons blowing in the wind. A montage of voices shouting back and forth, instruments being passed back and forth. A crying baby drowned out the confusion of the doctors. I bolted upright in bed. I have to call her. I'm sure it's just nerves. She's not due for another few weeks. I've had so much on my mind. As soon as I get a chance, I'll sneak to a pay phone and call.

April 15, 8:00 pm

I called Jen but no one answered. Now that I know why, I almost wish I hadn't called Mom to see if she knew where Jen might be.

"She's in the hospital, Hay."

"Is she in labor?"

"No, honey. She's sick." I fell to my knees right there at the pay phone. I couldn't stand, my legs wouldn't support the weight.

"What's wrong with her?"

"She has toxemia."[100]

"Is she okay?"

"I think you should go home, Hay."

"I will. I'm on the next plane out of here."

"I hope everything's all right, Hay. Give us a call as soon as you get in and let us know what's going on."

[New Entry, no date, no time]

After I got off the phone with Mom, I called Dunnett to tell him I was going home.

"No one leaves the Agency, Mr. Walker."

"Sir, my wife is very sick and in the hospital. She's pregnant and I don't know what might happen to the baby. I have to be there."

"No one leaves, Mr. Walker."

"I've solved this case for you. You know who the next victim is going to be and where it's going to be. Let Jakes stay behind and

---

100 Toxemia is a medical condition in which the body, instead of discarding the bacteria and toxins in the system, through urine or perspiration, redistributes the toxins into the blood stream. Without proper medical treatment, toxemia can be lethal. Toxemia is somewhat common in pregnant women; their bodies cannot adjust to the fluctuation of hormone levels and the body doesn't know what to do with all those extra hormones and toxins. If a woman is pregnant, toxemia is not only lethal to the mother but to the unborn child as well. Jen Walker was admitted to St. John's Medical Center at 5:45 am, probably about the same time Hayden was waking up from his nightmare. The doctors diagnosed her immediately and put her under medical surveillance. She called Carl and Norma Walker around 8:00 am to tell them what was going on and asked if they might be able to contact Hayden. Of course, with Walker on assignment, they had no idea how to get in touch with him. It was blind luck that Hayden called them and was able to ascertain the information about his wife. Unfortunately, there is no real technique for handling toxemia. In the case of pregnant women, the baby must be delivered before the toxemia kills the mother and, in turn, kills the baby. At 10:43 am, Jen Walker gave birth to a three pound, two ounce baby boy. The baby was almost two months premature and was dangerously close to being a still-born. Doctors resuscitated the baby and placed him in an incubator on the NICU wing of the hospital. Jen was placed in ICU until her vital signs were stable and no trace of the toxemia could be found. Two days after she gave birth, she was placed in a regular room at the hospital and spent countless hours praying for the health of her sick son.

supervise. You don't need me here. Just let me go home for a few days. I may even be back by the 20ᵗʰ."

"You know the rules, Mr. Walker: while you are on assignment, you do not leave until the assignment is finished."

"It is finished, goddammit! All you have to do is arrest the guy. How fucking hard can that be? Please, I am begging you to let me go. I have to see my wife."

"Calm down, Mr. Walker. When we chose you for the Agency, we chose you for your ability to remain calm and poised in situations that most people would buckle under. You were different. You were special. Don't ruin that image, Mr. Walker. The rules were put into effect long ago to ensure absolute control, regardless of personal problems. My answer to you, as it has been to individuals who have found themselves in situations similar to your own, is no. Nobody leaves the Agency while on assignment."

I slammed the phone down and ran. I needed to get to the airport. I didn't have time to stop and tell Jakes what was going on. It didn't matter. There would probably be Agency men there waiting for me anyway. I hopped into a cab.

"Get me to the airport."

I don't really remember the drive. It didn't matter; there was no way it could have possibly seemed as fast as it needed to be. Every second ticked by like an hour.

At the airport, the line at the ticket counter seemed endless. There was probably only three or four people in front of me but it seemed like I was in line for an eternity. When I finally got up to the counter, I was so distraught, I could barely talk.

"I need a ticket."

"Where to?"

"California."

"Where in California, sir?"

"Where?"

"Yes, where?"

"Uh . . .Los Angeles."

The lady typed something into her computer.

"The next available flight is in five hours."

"Five hours? I can't wait that long. Is there anything else?"

"No, sir. And that flight is the last one to Los Angeles today. Would you like to book a seat?"

"Yes."

Five hours of excruciating torment. How would I survive? I had to talk to Jen. I had to know she was all right.

I called Mom again.

"What's the number at the hospital?"

"She doesn't have a phone in her room. She's in ICU so you won't be able to call until she's well enough to be in a regular room."

"The next flight out of here doesn't leave for another five hours. What am I going to do?"

"There's nothing you can do. I talked with Jen's mom about two hours ago and she said that Jen was doing all right. She was still a little groggy but she was going to be fine."

"What about the baby?"

"It's a boy, Hay. We don't know how he is yet. He's in an incubator right now. The next few days or weeks will be critical."

"Why couldn't I have lived a normal life like everyone else?"

"Worry about that later, honey. Right now, you need to be calm. Everything's going to be fine. Just fine."

I couldn't stay at the airport. I purchased the ticket with my own credit card so they would be able to track it.

I walked around the city for the next four hours. The Agency would know what time my flight was taking off and they would be waiting for me at the airport. I would have to be invisible when I returned. But, I couldn't go back too early; that would increase the probability of one of the agents spotting and detaining me. I would have to arrive just in time to board the plane and fly away. Luckily, nightfall provided the secrecy and cover I needed. I wandered around for four hours wondering what was going on in California. Was my wife all right? Was the baby? God, please, if You're up there, help me out. Don't let anything happen to them. I beg you. I spent four hours praying to a God I didn't know for sure existed.

When the waiting was over, I went back to the airport. As I suspected, several guys in black suits were standing at the door. I approached with my head down hoping they wouldn't notice me. I slipped by them easier than I had expected. Or, were they setting a trap, a place with no exit, a room with no doors? I walked past more men in suits who didn't so much as glance up at me. I was getting nervous. I approached the young man at the boarding gate and handed him my ticket.

He looked at it. "Mr. Walker?"

"Yeah. Why do you need to know?"

"We all do, Mr. Walker."

"What are you talking about?"

"You know the rules, Mr. Walker: nobody leaves."

A trap. A goddamned trap. I couldn't get on the plane unless I could get passed the guy at the boarding gate but I didn't think I would make it back through the terminal. I didn't know what to do so I ran. I don't know where I thought I was going but I couldn't give up without a fight. Agency men were everywhere. I was running from everybody with nowhere to go. I was trapped. I did the only thing I could think of: I ran for the boarding gate hoping I could tackle the guy guarding it and board the plane anyway. I dodged a few agents and ran as fast as I could. I wanted to get some power behind this tackle. I wanted them to know they shouldn't fuck with me. The man was in my sight. He was big, too. It didn't matter, though. Sometimes size cannot match the desperation of wild rage. I must have looked like a wild bull charging him. He remained unflinching as I ran toward him.

I dove at him, knocking us both back into the loading dock, and kneed him in the groin. He grabbed at his crotch and I planted a closed fist into his forehead. An explosion of blood gushed up as he shouted in agony. When I got to my feet, I looked back and saw more of them coming at me so I ran down the hallway to the plane, boarded it and closed the door behind me.

"Sir?" The flight attendant asked.

"Mind your own business. Get this plane in the air."

"Sir!"

"Don't fucking 'sir' me. Get this goddamn plane in the air."

"Mr. Walker." I froze. The voice was coming from behind me and was very familiar.

I sighed deeply and laughed. "You guys are persistent."

"Don't you think you've carried this on long enough, Mr. Walker?"

I turned around. I had been so hellbent on boarding the plane that I never stopped to think that they might already be on the plane waiting for me. Obviously, intelligence cannot match the desperation of wild rage, either.

"Take Mr. Walker into custody," Dunnett said.

"No one leaves, right, Dunnett?"

"That's right, Mr. Walker. No one."

"Okay. You got me." I turned to let them think I would go quietly with them. Two men approached me from either side, each taking me by an arm.

"Let's go," one of them said.

Before we even took one step, I turned on my heals ripping myself from their grasp and punched the guy on my left. I turned and tackled the second man into the first class section and punched him twice before someone lifted me from the ground. A man charged at me from the front while one held me from behind. The man charging at me drew back to punch me but I kicked him in the groin; he toppled to the floor, grabbing at his crotch, pathetically whimpering. I rammed the back of my head into the face of the guy holding me. The effort was exhausting but I was running on pure rage and adrenaline.

A man tackled me from behind and knocked me to the floor. A second man jumped on top of him. In a matter of seconds, I was pinned to the floor underneath a pile of agents. I tried to buck and kick my way out but there were too many of them.

"That's enough, Mr. Walker," Dunnett said. His voice never cracked or wavered. He remained calm and stoic the entire time. I felt a prick in the crook of my arm and I woke up here. I don't know where I am or how I got here, but I'm here. I don't know what day it is let alone what time of day it is. The only light I am afforded is a mere 40 watts from the lightbulb that dangles overhead. There's no windows, either. Where the fuck am I?

Nobody's come in to check on me or to see if I'm still alive. I assume they don't really care at this point. Somebody will eventually check on me.

Some day, Some time

Dunnett came in today. Why haven't they taken my diary? Maybe they will. I don't know.

"Mr. Walker, we feel we have been too lenient with all who work for the Agency. We feel your little 'incident' the other day may put some ideas into people's heads. We cannot tolerate insubordinate actions or behaviors, Mr. Walker. Therefore, we are incarcerating you."

"For how long?"

"Until we feel you have been rehabilitated to meet the demands of the Agency."

"My wife is very sick!"

"I understand, Mr. Walker, but you're missing the point."

"Fuck the point, Dunnett. This is my life."

"Wrong. This is your life. And that's the point. The Agency should be the only life you know. I know you have problems at home and we can appreciate your concern, we can tolerate your concern. What we cannot tolerate are members of this agency running amok. If we do not maintain a sense of order, we cannot maintain the appearance of authority and superiority. We cannot have members running around like lunatics. You must remain in control at all times. Do you understand?"

"Yes."

"Good. You'll start your sentence tomorrow. When we feel you have learned a valuable lesson, we will release you.[101]

---

[101] Evidently, the Agency did take Walker's diary from him. This entry was the last entry for the next two months. We can assume from how the diary entries start back up, that the Agency detained him for the entire two months. Walker missed a lot of important events while incarcerated. On April 20th, the Pentagram Killer attacked and assaulted Michelle St. Michael. She was abducted on Forest Ave. while walking home from school. Detectives Harper and Shields were following her. They had talked with Michelle prior to the attack and told her what was going on. She had agreed to do what they asked: walk home like she didn't know what was going to happen. Imagine the courage that must take; to walk home alone, even with people following you, knowing the entire time that some deranged serial killer is going to jump out of the bushes at you. And what happens if the police lose track of the killer on his way to wherever he decided to kill her. She is a braver,

better person than I'll ever be. She put herself in harm's way, to stop a killer and serve justice. And all the while, she had no idea if the killer would actually get a chance to kill her. An absolutely amazing test or courage. The killer took Michelle to the Oak Lodge Motel, the same motel he had chosen to murder Carol St. Peter in. The killer must have rented the room earlier in the day because he had a key. He dragged Michelle in through the front door and slammed it behind him. She tried to scream but the killer had his hand over her mouth. While the killer was inside, outside a cadre of police cars pulled in to the all-but-abandoned parking lot. A team of twenty officers huddled outside the door bashed it in with a mini-battering ram, stormed the room and tackled the killer to the floor. Michelle was slightly shaken up but other than that she was in good shape. The killer, Leon Schilling Grant, a thirty-five year old male with a wife and three kids in Charlotte, North Carolina, was arrested immediately and taken into custody by an armed SWAT team. Leon: Caucasian, brown hair, brown eyes, 6'3" tall, 240 pounds, was literally a monster; not just in mind-set but in physical stature. This guy was mammoth. If you ever saw him, and many of you probably remember seeing him in all the newspapers, you'd cringe. His eyes were empty and vacant. He looked like he didn't care about anything. I'm still in shock that he was married; not just married but somebody stayed with this crazy son of a bitch long enough to have three children with him. Most of you probably remember all of this. It was all over the news and in all the papers from California to Maine. There was actually a mini-series on one of the big network channels starring Holly Stevens as Michelle St. Michael, Jackson Dempsey as Detective Harper and Gage Smith as Leon "the Pentagram Killer" Grant. It ran for two nights but the ratings were quite poor so it never saw a second showing. If you're interested, a cheesy b-flick was also made from this real-life tragedy called *Satan's Messenger* starring people you've never heard of; I've never heard of them and I watch a lot of movies, so what does that tell you? The interesting twist on this movie is that it is told from the point of view of the killer. Most made-for-TV-movies, and regular movies for that matter, would normally have taken the POV of the detective or the helpless victim. This one didn't. I wish I could find the writer; I'd love to ask him why he chose to write the screenplay in the POV of the killer. Of course, in both the mini-series and the made-for-TV-movie, no mention was ever made about any Agency members. Nobody knew. How can you write a part for someone who doesn't really exist? Anyway, if you're interested, I suggest you check it out; if for no other reason than to satisfy some morbid, twisted need for carnage.

The next big thing Walker missed while incarcerated was the birth of his son. He must have spent two torturous months in solitude. Sometimes I can drive myself crazy just thinking to myself, but Walker had all of this juggling around in his mind; it must take its toll on the sanity. Walker's son, Steven, spent three weeks in intensive care before he was released to Jen with a clean bill of health. The baby seemed to be fine; no repercussions from the toxemia or the three weeks in NICU. Jen spent two days in the hospital before she was released. She spent the next three week's evenings at the hospital praying for her son. Her grades slipped at school and she ended up dropping out. She slumped into a deep depression. Her life consisted of nothing but sitting at the hospital waiting for the doctors to tell her, one way or the other, good or about, about her son. Her mother tried to console her but she just wouldn't listen. She was inconsolable. Carl and Norma flew in from Maine to try to help her through the hard time. She seemed to feel a little better two weeks after the birth when doctors told her Steven's vital signs were looking good. A week later, Steven Walker went home with his mother and her entourage of parents. None of them had heard from Hayden. The last communication anybody had with him was his mother when he called her from the airport in South Dakota. At that moment, no one was too worried about him. They were too happy with Steven. Hayden almost slipped their minds, I guess. Until a very unexpected turn of events occurred.

On June 2nd, Carl Walker was admitted back into Eastern Maine Medical Center in Bangor, Maine. His cancer had returned. The doctors told Norma that there was nothing they could do for him and that things would progress extremely fast. They told her to encourage him with love and affection. They told her to get the whole family together; something he could find pleasure in. They told her to make the next two weeks the best she could for him; surround him with family and friends and love. Two weeks later, Carl Walker died due to complications caused by his cancer.

Still no sign of Hayden. All this time, he's still stuck in solitary confinement. He has no idea what's going on on the outside. He has no contact, that I can find, with the outside world. He can't write to his family or call; he is completely cut off. The funeral for Carl Walker was held at the Second United Congregational Church in Bangor. The pews were filled with friends and family members who gathered not to mourn a death but to celebrate a life; a good life.

"I remember thinking how disappointed I was that Hayden never came home," Norma recollected. "I hadn't heard from him in almost a month. The last thing I knew, he was supposed to be with Jen about six hours after I talked with him. Things were never the same after that."

When I uncovered all of this information, I remember thinking how sorry I felt for the Walker family. They thought that their son/husband was neglecting them or ignoring them when, in reality, the entire time he was confined to a tiny, dimly-lit room; probably thinking of nothing other than how much he wished he was with them. It always makes me sad to think back to the days I was going over the material with Norma and Jen; they cried for hours after they discovered the truth about what happened. At times, I am glad that they finally knew the truth but at times I feel responsible for

June 18, 9:00 pm

What the hell is going on? Why won't they listen to me? I finally got out of that fucking hole three days ago. They're kind enough to give me a plane ticket back to California but when I get here, I'm not welcome.

I pulled up to the house around noon. I thought she'd be happy to see me. I knew she'd be pissed about me being gone for so long without so much as a phone call but I thought when I explained everything, she'd understand.

"What do you mean, 'I'm lying'?"

"The Agency called me, Hay. Two weeks ago. I picked up the phone, a man says, 'Do you have any idea where your husband may be?' I said, 'no, why?' You know what he said, Hay? He said, 'He went AWOL about two months ago and we haven't seen or heard from him since.' Two months, Hay. Where the hell have you been?"

"Jen, you have to believe me. I have been in solitary confinement for two months. They wouldn't let me call or write. I have been in agony wondering if you were all right, if you were still alive, even. Not to mention the baby. Is he all right?"

"Yeah. He's fine."

"Where is? I want to see him."

"That's not a good idea, Hay."

"Why not?"

"I think you should leave."

"What?"

"You've done nothing but lie to me, Hay."

"They are lying, Jen! Please, believe me."

"I can't, Hay. I can't. You've lied for too long. You have ignored and neglected me and your family for too long. Do you even know that your father passed away last week?"

---

supplying more pain and misery that they didn't really need. They had gone through enough when they thought Hayden had abandoned them, now they knew that he didn't and the fact that they turned him away weighed heavily on their consciences.

After two months, the Agency must have released Walker from his "prison sentence." The diary entries started back up but they started up suddenly and abruptly.

I felt like vomiting. "What?"

"Cancer, Hayden. Your family tried to find you. But, guess what? They got a call too: 'Have you seen your son? He ran away two months ago.' You've been lying to me. You've been lying to your family."

"He's dead?"

"Don't play stupid, Hayden. Maybe if you didn't lie to them like you lied to me, you'd know. I want you to leave."

I didn't have the strength to argue. What the fuck did the Agency do to me? I realize I was insubordinate but isn't this lesson a little severe? My father is dead. I missed his fucking funeral and I was oblivious to the whole damned thing. I couldn't imagine how my mother would react to seeing me.

I called from BIA first. "Mom, I know the last thing you want right now is to hear my voice, but I need to talk to somebody. Can I come over?"

CLICK. She hung up on me.

I made the twenty minute drive in ten. I pounded on the door until she let me in.

"Where have you been, Hay?"

"Remember when I called you from the airport in South Dakota?"

"Yes."

"I tried to run from the Agency. They wouldn't let me fly in to see Jen so I ran. They found me, tackled me to the ground, drugged me, and placed me in solitary confinement for the past two months. I went to see Jen but she kicked me out. I didn't even get a chance to see my son. How does he look?"

"He's got your eyes."

"Mom, please forgive me. I know I missed Dad's funeral and I can never, ever, forgive myself for that. I'll live the rest of my life knowing I never got to say goodbye to my own father. He meant the world to me and he's gone. Don't you leave me, too. I love you, Mom. Do you believe that?"

"Yes, honey. Of course I do. And I love you. I always will. But I can't believe your story. I can't. You've abandoned us too many times before. I'll forgive you one day. I know I will. But right now, I can't. I just can't. Not right now."

I've been sitting here in this lonely hotel room ever since trying to figure out what happened. And I can't. I'm losing my fucking mind. Maybe I am crazy and I'm the only one who doesn't know it.

I'm

Losing

Grip.

I'm

Losing

Me.

Why can't I ever

Catch a fucking break?

Am I asking

too much

of

life?

I don't fucking think so!!!!!!!
ALL I WANT

IS FOR THINGS TO BE
NORMAL again!!!!

I tried to talk to God today, but he wasn't home or he didn't answer. Maybe he wasn't there. The ice cream was good though. I think she likes strawberries but I can't remember. Sometimes I can't remember things very well. Sometimes

I just try to tell myself that it's not worth it:

Remembering shit is for the elephants and birds down in Africa.

What was I saying?

I forgot.

Shane Layman

I'm

going

slightly

MAD![102]

---

[102] Is this real insanity or a ploy? I can't tell. The unique format I have written in is exactly the way it was written in the diary. It seems incredibly bizarre. Normally, Walker's train of thought is very straight-forward and very convincing; but here, he babbles incoherently and changes his thought pattern almost mid-sentence. Walker underwent enough stress to suffer a temporary schism with sanity. I would argue that Walker had a complete mental breakdown. That would answer a lot of questions. However, the one question it won't answer, is why this is the last entry in this diary even though the entries date only in to June. What happened to him after this entry? Where did he go for the next year? More importantly, why didn't anybody hear from him again until early in 1992? Eight years went by from this diary entry to the next. And, it's not as though he just stopped writing in his diary; he completely disappeared. His family didn't hear from him, Jen didn't hear from him. Perhaps he felt they were too angry to try to reason with. Walker vanished off the face of the planet for a period of eight years. My ultimate goal in life is to find another diary. There has to be at least one diary out there somewhere that explains the gap between 1984 and 1992. He didn't die because he does pop back up in 1992. So, why the gap? There has to be a reason. But, until that diary surfaces, if it ever surfaces, the eight year gap will remain a mystery

Diary 5

June 18, 7:00 pm[103]

Life sure does have a sick sense of humor. After all I've been through, all the darkness and discomfort, the pain and suffering, I'm still here and still investigating paranormal activity. Strange.

This case I'm working on now dwarfs all my previous cases in comparison to strangeness. Five bodies have turned up in a small town in Nebraska. All the bodies have been found in the same corn field. Their bodies strewn to the side like discarded chicken carcasses. The strangeness comes in the fact that all the bodies have been eviscerated, split from sternum to groin, the contents not only removed but taken. There are no traces of blood in the surrounding area. Nobody can explain it. I read about it in the paper and thought I'd take a look. I wish I hadn't gotten involved now. In this particular case, I fear for my life more than I ever have before. I don't think

---

[103] I have no idea who sent this fifth, and final, diary to me. We know it belonged to Hayden Walker because his name is printed on the inside cover, just like the other diaries. I've spent months trying to unearth more information about this period of Walker's life. The date on the inside cover reads 1992. I know Jen filed for divorce in 1987, even though by that time, Walker had been missing long enough to be declared legally dead. She never saw him during this period of his life. Nobody in Walker's family has seen him since 1984 either. He just pops back up into existence. Was he in hiding? If so, he did a pretty good job of it. I couldn't find one iota of evidence that would suggest he was alive and well and living anywhere on this planet. For all intents and purposes, Hayden Walker was dead; until 1992. He materializes back into existence and he's working again. He makes mention of bad times, as you'll read. I'm wondering if he may have admitted himself into a mental hospital or something of that nature. How else can you explain the long gap between diaries? Perhaps, at some obscure mental hospital, somewhere in the United States, there are several leather-bound diaries, with a piece of thin-sliced leather tied in a knot around them. The life he knew before 1984 was over. His wife and family had long since figured him for dead or that he just ran away without looking back; like he had so many times before. Maybe that's the case. We may never know. The one question weighing on my mind is why, all of a sudden, in June of 1992, does Walker pop back into the world? Not only pop back into the world but working again as a paranormal investigator. Who was he working for? Was he free-lance or hire-by-contract or was he working for some company? If he was, I can't find any connections. He simply disappeared and reappeared like nothing happened. Why?

I'm going up against anything human here. That thought scares me more than anything. A human can usually be reasoned with because of our ability to rationalize. Something that is not human does not have the ability to rationalize; therefore, cannot be reasoned with. Something without rationale cannot comprehend the idea of consequences and responsibility.

I have ruled out the possibility of these victims being attacked by wild animals. If the bodies had been victims of animal attacks, some type of wolf or something of that nature, there would be very distinct claw and tooth marks on the flesh and rib cages of the victims. There is nothing. The incisions are as clean as though they were cut with surgical equipment, that much precision. But I don't think we have a demented surgeon on our hands either because the amount of blood that would be surrounding the area would have to be phenomenal. And what about the organs? Where are they? I can't understand what is going on here and for the first time in my life I am completely and utterly terrified. What can I expect? What does fate have in store for me? We'll have to wait and see.[104]

---

[104] Once again, Walker vanishes. No more diaries have surfaced and no more leads have been left to investigate. I have exhausted all of my resources in trying to find the truth about what happened to Hayden Walker. Thirteen years have passed since the last diary entry and nobody has seen or heard from the man who was Hayden Walker. Did he just take off again? Move to some obscure country living out the rest of his days on some secluded beach with Margaritas and Strawberry Daiquiris to keep him company? If so, why has he made no attempt to contact his ex-wife? Why would a man, who expressed so much interest in having a family, abandon his wife and child? Why would he make no attempt to even see his child? Walker never once saw his son. Steven is now twenty years old. He has never seen his real father in person. So what happened to him? Did whatever he was investigating catch him off-guard and eviscerate him like it did its other victims? Nobody knows. Until further truth surfaces, Hayden Walker will be considered legally dead, for the second time

The following interviews have been conducted to recollect a life; the funeral, if you will, of Hayden Walker: a man who was misunderstood in death just as much as he was in life by those he loved and by those in authority to him. I am hoping these interviews will bring some sense of closure to those who knew Hayden Walker well enough to call him Hay.

The first interview was conducted with Eugene Carter, Walker's psychology teacher in high school.

Shane Layman: What do you remember most about Hayden?

Eugene Carter: I remember Hay being an exceptional student. He received the only 100% grade I ever gave out in that class. And he earned it. Hay was a good kid. I think he was interested in the subject matter and really enjoyed the material we were covering in class. He was always very outspoken, and well-spoken. He was a smart kid.

SL: Did you ever think he would go on to become a paranormal investigator?

EC: I always knew he'd end up in psychology, I just didn't think paranormal psychology would be his interest. He was always most interested in abnormal psychology, the workings of the brain and how it affects different people in different ways. Of course, at the time, parapsychology was relatively new, at least it wasn't being taught seriously at schools yet so he was never introduced to it. He always liked new challenges, so it doesn't surprise me that he would take the leap from abnormal to paranormal psychology.

SL: Did you ever follow his career as a paranormal investigator?

EC: I never did. I always liked Hay but, like all of my students, I rarely get a chance to see how they are doing career-wise unless I see them at the reunions, which he never attended.

SL: There's a lot of speculation surrounding the death of Hayden Walker. Some suggest he was killed on assignment by some strange, inhuman creature that he was investigating. Others believe he turned tail and ran. What do you believe?

EC: The Hayden Walker I knew would never back down from a challenge. I don't think he would run away from anything, personal or professional.

205

SL: So you think he was killed?

EC: I couldn't give you an honest answer to that. Being a man of reason, I cannot completely accept or grasp the idea of some intestine-sucking creature being out there feeding on innocent human beings. I wish I had a better answer for you, but I don't. I really have no idea what actually happened to Hayden Walker.

The next interview was conducted with Dean Starking, Hayden's mentor in the field of paranormal psychology.

Shane Layman: Dean, you and Hayden go back a long time.

Dean Starking: (smiles) A very long time.

SL: The two of you worked together for about three years, correct?

DS: That's correct. Hay came to Stanford in 1980 and I recruited him shortly after that from the abnormal psychology department. We worked together until around Christmas of 1983. That's when he handed in his resignation.

SL: Do you remember that day?

DS: Absolutely.

SL: What was your reaction to him handing in his resignation?

DS: I was shocked. I couldn't understand why he would resign. Everything was finally going well for us. The department heads were impressed with our research, business was really starting to pick up and, out of the blue, he hands in his resignation.

SL: What was his reason?

DS: He never really said. He just said personal reasons. What could I tell him? No, you can't resign. I refuse to let you. No. I had no choice. Of course, I let him go. I hated every second of it, but I let him go. Hay was one of the best and brightest students I ever taught and it was my honor and pleasure to have had the opportunity to work with him; even if it was just for a short while.

SL: Do you ever think about him?

DS: Occasionally, yeah. I always wondered what actually happened to him. Now that I know what I know, it blows my mind. I can't believe something like that would happen to Hay. It was a tragedy. The world of parapsychology lost a good investigator and the world lost one hell of a great man that day.

SL: So you think he was murdered on assignment?

DS: I didn't say that. [smiles awkwardly]

SL: What *do* you think happened, then?

DS: I don't know. I'd hate to think something tragic happened to him. Maybe that's why I can't believe that stupid rumor about the intestine-sucking creature from Mars. [laughs] He was too smart to be killed. Unless he really let his guard down, there was nothing that could outsmart him.

SL: Do you think he ran away?

DS: No. Hayden would never run from anything. That's why there's such a mystery. I can't believe that he would turn his back on his family and Jen and their son. He cared so much about all of them, for him to just abandon them would be incomprehensible to me.

SL: Did you ever have contact with him after he joined the Agency?

DS: That goddamned Agency was what did it. Sometimes, I kick myself for asking Hay to come out of his sabbatical for that case in New Mexico. If he'd never gone there to investigate, he may still be working for me, he may still be happily married to Jen with a good son and he'd never have had that split with his family. Sometimes, I think it's all my fault. I knew Hayden was the only member of the staff qualified to handle such a case. I needed him and, as my good friend, he didn't refuse me. Now, looking back, I wish he had. I feel like I have ruined the life of a good man and the future of what could have been a great family.

SL: Why do you think that whoever sent me the diaries would edit some of the more interesting and pertinent information, such as the case in New Mexico?

DS: Who the hell knows. Those government boys are funny that way. They want to be this exclusive group of individuals that has all the answers to all the questions we've ever pondered. Unfortunately, for them, there are people like me out there pondering the same questions and searching for the same answers. Hay was one of those people, too. He was a good man and a great friend. Wherever he is, I hope he has managed to finally find some peace. He's earned it. If he's still alive, I'd really love to hear from him. Even if he just wants to tell me to go to hell for forcing him into such a rotten position.[he smiles]

The next interview was conducted with Norma Walker in her home in Newport, Maine. She was very emotional during the entire interview and, although we had talked many times before, she asked me to keep most of the interview out of the book. To honor her request, the interview is quite short and to-the-point. I owe her that much.

Shane Layman: What happened between you and your son when he came back after your husband passed away?

Norma Walker: Things were never the same. I only saw him the one time after that, when he came to me with the story about the Agency imprisoning him and whatnot.

SL: You didn't believe him then, did you?

NW: I couldn't. He had abandoned us so many times before that what he was saying seemed outrageous to me. I couldn't bring myself to believe that the Agency would detain him while his wife was in intensive care along with his son and while his father was dying of cancer. I was so hurt that he never called during those months where nobody heard from him that when he finally came back I was furious. I don't think, at the time, I wanted to listen to any stories. But, at the time, I also figured that he would come back in a few days, after tensions had swelled and quelled. As it turned out, I never saw him again. [begins to cry]

SL: What was your reaction when I showed you the diary and you realized that he *was* telling you the truth?

NW: I cried. I cried for days. I couldn't believe what I was reading. I thought he was lying all the time and it was me who wasn't willing to believe him. I just didn't think anyone would be capable of holding someone against their will while their entire world was falling down around him, and all the while, he had no idea that everything was crumbling apart.

SL: Were you happy or sad to discover the truth?

NW: Both. I was relieved to know that he wasn't ignoring us all while everything bad that could happen did happen. I was relieved to discover he wanted to be with us and help us all out. But, on the other hand, I was so sad to find out he was telling the truth and we accused him of lying. I was more angry with myself for not trusting my own son [cries again] when he begged me to believe and forgive him.

[I waited several moments to allow Norma to collect her bearings. She dabbed a Kleenex to her eyes]

NW: I'm sorry.

SL: It's perfectly understandable, Mrs. Walker. Would you like to stop the interview?

NW: No, we can continue. Until I start to cry again. [lets out a nervous chuckle]

SL: If Hayden were here today, what would you say to him?

NW: I would grab hold of him and hug him as tight as I could and beg him to forgive me; like he begged me to forgive him twenty years ago. I would tell him I know that he was telling the truth. And that I could never apologize enough for not believing him. But, again, I figured I would have the rest of our lives to reconcile what happened. I was hurt and angry and bitter and I couldn't find the love in my heart that he needed. I was still mourning Carl's death. I just didn't have any extra love to express. I wish I did now, though. I wish I did. Because now, I have to live with the fact that I turned him away twenty years ago and I haven't seen him since. I have to live with that.

SL: Mrs. Walker, do you believe your son may still be alive?

NW: He better not be. [another nervous chuckle] I wish he was so I could tell him all of this but I don't think so. I think he would have come back to reconcile our differences by now. And, he has so much family up here, he would have tried to call one of them to talk to me about what happened. I don't think he's alive. And if he is, he'd better get his butt home. He's been gone far too long.

The final interview was conducted with Jennifer Wilkins, Hayden's estranged wife. After Walker disappeared, Jen couldn't handle the stress of being a single parent and juggling schoolwork. She dropped out of Stanford in 1984 with only one semester left before graduation. She moved back to Sacramento with her mother for a while until she met Jeff Wilkins. The two married two years after they met and moved to Nebraska with Jen's son, Steven.

Shane Layman: Jen, you and I have spoken on many occasions. Do you mind if I ask a few more personal questions about your ex-husband?

Jennifer Wilkins: Not at all. You know just about every personal detail anyway. [she smiles]

SL: When did you first notice a change in Hayden?

JW: A few months after we got married. He got a call from Dean saying he needed him for one job. 'One job is all I need you for. You'll be back home in four days.' He disappeared for *two weeks*. Things were never the same after he returned. He was distant. He wasn't the Hay I knew and he definitely wasn't the Hay I fell in love with.

SL: What was your reaction when he came back after those two weeks and was different? How did you react when he told you about the Agency?

JW: I was a little nervous. He never told me 100-percent what the Agency was. He was very secretive about the whole thing. I didn't know if he was lying or if he was telling me what I needed to hear. I think I wanted to believe him so badly that I did. Even if he was lying

SL: And then when you found out what really happened, when you realized that the truth was exactly what Hayden was telling you, what happened?

JW: I cried. I couldn't believe that I didn't trust my own husband, the father of my child. At the time, I couldn't believe him. The Agency was very convincing when they were calling the house looking for him. All the time, they were lying and he was telling the truth and I believed the lies rather than the truth. I figured, why would the Agency lie? What did they have to lose? They had no reason to lie. All they were losing was an investigator. They could replace him. Why did they have to ruin his life?

SL: What was going through your mind the day he came back and you asked him to leave?

JW: I was absolutely furious. I figured he was lying to me all along. I figured he made up the story about the incarceration to pad the fact that he was free to come home whenever he wanted to and didn't. I thought he was out there, on his own, doing God knows what, and not giving a damn about me or his son. Sure, I was angry. But when I discovered the truth, I realized that the lies were easier to buy. I figured, we were angry and things would blow over. He'd come to his senses and come back and tell me the truth. That's all I wanted was the truth. And he was telling me the truth all along. Anyway, I never saw him again after that day. I feel horrible. The one chance he had to see his son and I deprived him of it. He never even got a chance to see him.

SL: Do you think he is still alive?

JW: No. He would have tried to see his son by now, if he was. If he is, he's done a damn fine job of convincing the world he doesn't exist. Sure, I'd like to think that some day he'll stumble up to our doorstep with some soap opera amnesia or something. Or he's finally come out of some coma and returned to find the love that slipped away. I'd love to think that. But I don't think he's in a hospital room, unconscious, hooked up to machines. I don't think his skeleton is rotting in a corn field somewhere out here. I don't believe he's living the good life on some tiny island.

SL: What do you believe?

JW: That I was stupid not to believe him. That every day I wish I could turn back time and instead of turning him away, I could embrace him and tell him that everything is going to be all right. I believe I drove him away for no other reason other than the fact that I was too stupid to distinguish the truth from the lies. [begins to cry.] That's what I believe. And I'm none the better for it . . .[crying harder]

SL: Are you all right?

JW: I'm sorry, Hay.[uncontrollable sobbing] . . . I'm so sorry.

Dear Reader,

Whether you choose to believe or not, the diaries and interviews you have just read are absolutely real. I realize that there are skeptics and critics out there who will jump at the chance to label me a charlatan, a fraud, a phony, even, yes, a liar. I can accept that. I never promised you that what you were about to read would be easy to swallow or digest; I simply promised you it would be the truth. I feel I have kept my end of the bargain to the best of my ability.

I also realize that there are many of you who will not accept this story as fact, rather the over-zealous imagination of a man who has seen one too many horror movies. I can accept that as well. All I ask, in return for the absolute truth is that you never dismiss that which cannot be explained as fiction. Or, at least, give it some thought before you cast it aside. You should never doubt something you cannot explain; rather, you should explore the possibilities that lie before you.

Fear of the unknown *is* rational paralysis. I understand that now. I too used to be a non-believer. However, I have seen and heard too much in my life that not only suggests but insists that there is another level of existence living among us. These diaries further that belief for me. For those of you who don't believe, who choose to continue on with your drab lives where things that cannot be explained do not exist, those same things that cannot be explained will continue to exist whether you want them to or not. Why are people afraid of the unknown? Because there are no rational explanations. What people like Walker and Starking and myself have tried to do, in providing these accounts to the public, is open the doors of knowledge and understanding and bring to light questions that we have been pondering for countless centuries. Jim Morrison once said, "There are things known and things unknown and in between are the doors." Of course, on one level, he was talking about his highly successful rock n' roll band but, on a totally different level, he was talking about the doors in our minds and imaginations, the doors that separate that which is known from that which is unknown. Sometimes, all you have to do is crack that door just an inch to discover the difference between known and unknown is non-existent.

For those of you whose perspectives have not been altered by this experience, give it time. You'll come around some day. For those of you who *have* been changed by this experience, the doors are always open. Come in anytime.

Shane Layman

Definition of Terms

abnormal not normal; not average; esp. to a noticeable degree.

Abnormal Psychology the study of the behavior of abnormal people.

apparition 1. anything that appears unexpectedly; esp. a strange figure appearing suddenly. **2.** the act of appearing or becoming visible.

EMIC (Electro-Magnetic Ionic Charge) hand-held instrument used by paranormal investigators to indicate any change in the electro-magnetic ionic field.

ethereal plain not earthly; heavenly, celestial. A level of existence that coincides with ours but is not visible in ours.

free-floating apparition a strange figure appearing suddenly which has the ability to be seen hovering in certain areas.

> **level I free floating apparition** the weakest of all free-floaters. Has the ability to be seen for a very few moments and cannot make contact with the terrestrial world.
> **level II free-floating apparition** stronger energy level than a level one. Can be seen for a longer period of time but cannot make contact with the terrestrial world.
> **level III free-floating apparition** Much stronger energy level. Can be seen for as long as ten minutes and can make minor contact with the terrestrial world.
> **level IV free-floating apparition** strongest energy level of all free-floaters. Can be seen for as long as thirty minutes and is capable of inflicting harm upon members of the terrestrial world.

free-roaming apparition a strange figure that appears suddenly which has the ability to move around from one area to another and can move for an unspecified amount of time.

level I free-roaming apparition the weakest of all free-roamers. Has the ability to roam around the confines of one specific room. Does not have the ability to harm the terrestrial world.

level II free-roaming apparition stronger energy level than level one. Has the ability to roam freely around certain rooms and hallways. Does not have the ability to contact the terrestrial world.

level III free-roaming apparition much stronger energy level. Has the ability to roam around entire houses with little difficulty. Has the ability to inflict minor harm on members of the terrestrial world.

level IV free-roaming apparition the strongest and most dangerous of all free-roamers. These apparitions have the ability to roam from house to house and move around in unspecified amounts of area. Capable of inflicting major damage and harm to members of the terrestrial world; even lethal damage.(see also *poltergeist)*

full-torso apparition a strange figure that appears suddenly and can be observed from the waste to the top of the head. .

ghost (see apparition)

macabre ghastly and horrible.

medium a person who is used to communicate with spirits from the other side through deep, meditative, trance-like states.

Negative Ionic Energy determined by the EMIC; field of energy that is saturated with negatively charged ions.

paranormal psychic or mental occurrences outside the designated field of normal

paranormal psychology study of psychic or mental occurrences outside the designated field of normal.

PDC100x(Paranormal Density Change) hand-held instrument used by paranormal investigators to determine any change in air density.

PDC450c(Paranormal Density Change) prodigy of the PDC100x; has the same basic features but tends to be more reliable. A special filter at the end of the PDC450c allows the instrument to pick up density change from twenty feet away where the PDC100x can only determine air-density change from a distance of five feet.

poltergeist an entity that has an extreme amount of negative energy build-up caused by telekinetic and potential energy and can cause physical harm to the terrestrial world.

Positive Ionic Energy a field of energy that is saturated with positively charged ions.

potential energy energy in a system that is dormant or inactive. In paranormal terms, the energy stored by the physical body after the physical body has passed on.

psychology field of science dealing with the emotional, chemical and mental processes of the brain and its effects.

supernatural of, or pertaining to, a level of existence that is not natural; that which cannot be explained by rational procedures.

telekinetic energy the initiation of movement that has no possible means of physical progress; movement of objects without the assistance of human or mechanical processes.

TIS50c(Thermal Imaging Scanner) hand-held instrument used by paranormal investigators to determine any change in thermal activity.

Bibliography

1. Dan Crockett's "What's Super About the Supernatural?" *The Undead* v. 5430 November 1985

2. George K. Peterson's "The House That Jack Built" *True Hauntings* v. 240 July 1982

3. Keith Peter's "That Old, Familiar Haunt" *Ghosts* v. 89 January 1978

4. Jennifer McPherson's "Cause and Effect of Violent Behavior in Minority Youth" *Sociology Weekly* v. 3479 May 1982 and *Youth Violence Manifesto* v. 109 October 1982

5. *Encounters With the Beyond* v. 8 Chapter 5 (pages 52-57)

6. Arthur Richard's *The Evils of Psychotic Rage* and *The Manifestation of Evil Acts: The Complete History of the Pentagram Killer* copyright 1987 Cabot Publishing.

7. Ivon Kosolov's *Malicious Intent* copyright 1979 Clatter Publishing

Further Reference

1. Steven Clark's "Investigative Reports From the Paranormal" *The Realm of the Supernatural* v. 7451 June 1995

2. William Blair's "Haunting My House" *Real Ghosts* v. 381 August 1998

3. Ken Stock's "The Haunting! The Haunting!" *World of Ghosts* v. 8998 September 1982

4. Stephanie Willis' "What's Up On Elm Street?" *True Hauntings* v. 69 February 1981

5. Gene Schilling's "Bumps in the Night" *Hauntings Weekly* v. 695 December 2001

6. Walter King's "Where Are They Now?" *Another Realm, Another World* v. 101 March 2004

About the Author

Shane Layman resides in Bangor, Maine and has lived his entire life in the greater Bangor Area. He graduated from the University of Maine, Orono in 2001 with a BA in English. This is his first novel.

4142539

Made in the USA
Lexington, KY
31 December 2009